P9-DEW-172

HUMAN ERROR

ST. MARTIN'S PRESS ⚏ NEW YORK

TOM CASEY

HUMAN ERROR

A Thomas Dunne Book.
An imprint of St. Martin's Press.

HUMAN ERROR. Copyright © 1996 by Tom Casey. All rights reserved.
Printed in the United States of America. No part of this book may be
used or reproduced in any manner whatsoever without written per-
mission except in the case of brief quotations embodied in critical arti-
cles or reviews. For information, address St. Martin's Press, 175 Fifth
Avenue, New York, N.Y. 10010.

Book design by Scott Levine

Library of Congress Cataloging-in-Publication Data

Casey, Tom.
      Human error / by Tom Casey.
            p.   cm.
      "A Thomas Dunne book."
      ISBN 0-312-14622-1 (hardcover)
      I. Title.
   PS3553.A79363H86   1996
   813'.54—dc20   96-20775
                                        .   CIP

First Edition: December 1996

10   9   8   7   6   5   4   3   2   1

For Sue Casey
and
Gloria Yates O'Connell
and for
Lindsey and Drew

NOVEMBER 20, 1996

CYNTHIA & JIM —

WE GO BACK
SO FAR, AND YOU
KNOW ME SO WELL,
THAT NOTHING I SAY
HERE WOULD SURPRISE
YOU. BUT I HOPE

THE BOOK WILL —
PLEASANTLY.
LOVE,

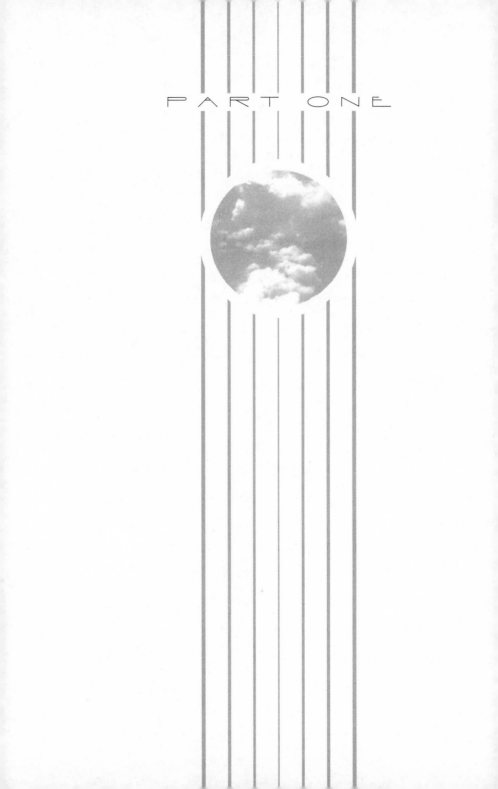

PART ONE

When the wind is easterly, final descent into New York's Kennedy Airport curves off the south shore of Long Island in a gentle descending bank that runs south and then turns north. Airliners arriving from Europe, South America, and the Far East are funneled into a track that circles up the New Jersey coast to the entrance of New York Harbor. One after another they sail across Sheepshead Bay, making landfall a mile east of Coney Island. From there they descend to a mere fifteen hundred feet, following flashing lights that guide them over a more exact flight path. The sight from the cockpit is panoramic. An automobile, a pedestrian passes under the wing. These solitary images register in the eye of the pilot even as, in the near distance, Manhattan and ten million acts of life are also in his range of view. At touchdown, the dream of flight ends in a roar of thrust reversers.

* * *

Hugo Price awakened to a blur of flashing lights and howling sirens. Frightened faces illuminated by flames watched him from a safer distance. The fire's greed for oxygen made a rushing wind above him. It was cool close to the ground, and the palms of his hands were cool. He lay with his face in the soft mud, but through the high grasses he could see a wing burning. Mist fell from arcing jets of water that poured from fire trucks onto the fuselage. The tail rose above the wreck at a disjointed angle like an immense monument to misjudgment. He could breathe if he concentrated but he couldn't move.

"Here! Over here!" Above the din, her exclamation. She was safe; happiness, then a weary indifference overcame him all at once.

A confusion of legs surrounded his head, then an ambulance appeared and he felt himself lifted and heard his own voice protesting in screams. The doors swung open and it swallowed him, and the siren went on and they began to move. A blue light flashed in his face and he felt nauseated. Someone gave him an injection, then it was dark.

He was lying on a table. Faces hovered over him. He asked for water but they wouldn't give him any. Instead, they gave him another injection. The light made him squint. They cut away his clothes. He wanted to get an idea of what was happening but he couldn't move. He tried to speak, but the effort failed. After a while there was only brightness and pain, and then he forgot all of it.

MARCH 15, 1995

Captain Hugo Price, removed to the hospital and barely coherent, repeated Sarah's name.

"Who's Sarah?" The voice belonged to a doctor at work on his leg.

"Sarah McClure. The copilot," said the nurse. "They just brought her in. She's all right."

"Sarah's all right," parroted the doctor, lifting his head momentarily to address Hugo. That was enough to know. Hugo went to sleep after that.

When he woke he could not move; he tried to look at the IV bottle but the effort made him dizzy. Pain was gone for the time being. He faded in and out, remembering where he was, forgetting again, remembering. His fingers tugged at the sheets.

The visions he had were of a remarkable clarity and color. Tall flowers on a hillside marked a path through fragrant yards to cottages where women waved him welcome. The sound of somebody crying nearby—and then the flowers were heads of cheering people, but they fled in panic, and he could see it, feel it, hear it all over again. Going down! Going in! The furious truth, and he was on the ground being helped onto a stretcher. A nurse came into the room and checked the IV. She hovered over him, appeared gigantic. He went to sleep again, dreaming of his mother. He slept fitfully throughout the first night and day. When he was lucid they moved him to a private room.

"How do you feel this morning?" The doctor read the chart quickly and made a notation to eliminate morphine. Without waiting for Hugo to respond, he put the chart down and spoke candidly. "Your right leg is broken in three places, with a compound fracture. Your left arm is broken above the elbow." He was a short balding man, about Hugo's age. He seemed harried. "There is no internal damage. We're going to keep you in traction for six weeks. It won't be pleasant, but you'll heal." He paused a moment. "All things considered, you were lucky."

"I don't feel lucky."

"Tell me if you feel this." The doctor tickled the bottom of Hugo's right leg.

"Yes."

"And this?"

"Yes."

Finished with his examination, the doctor made a notation on Hugo's chart.

"I want to talk to Sarah McClure. May I call her?"

"The first officer?" The doctor momentarily smiled.

"Yes."

"She's downstairs now. She's been waiting. I'll send her up."

"Thank you." He closed his eyes, relieved.

The doctor wrote quickly on a small pad and tore off the page. "Take these pills. I've prescribed them for pain, the nurse will give them to you." He turned to leave but paused at the door. "Captain?" said the doctor, almost as an afterthought. Hugo looked over. "You will fly again. That should be of some relief to you." It was no relief at all, and then the door closed.

Alone, Hugo stared out at the bright morning sky. Now it was a broken world. His leg throbbed. One day at a time, he thought.

An older nurse came into the room. "Sarah McClure is here to see you," she said. Her voice carried a hint of cheerful conspiracy that somehow depressed him. "I'll leave you alone for a while."

Sarah appeared in the doorway looking tired and drawn. Her face carried a new depth, not of sudden age, but rather of youthful features written over abruptly with experience.

"Hugo! Are you all right?"

"I'm okay."

His right leg hung suspended from two cables above the bed and his left arm was braced in a cast that kept it perpendicular. His right arm was free and his left leg was unhurt, but he looked pained and drugged. The sight of him upset her, but she concealed it. She went quickly over to the bed and kissed him gently then held his face in her hands. Her eyes were luminous, her throaty voice was soft as a whisper.

"We were falling, and you tried . . ."

"I remember the impact," he said. "And running. I can see the people, and the passengers, and then it seemed that all at once everything was different and I was outside and the ground was on fire."

"You pulled me out," she said. "Do you remember that? I was in shock."

"I remember being hit with, with something from behind—"

"I couldn't move. You got me out of the seat. We jumped."

"How many?" he said. He watched her eyes. She brushed his hair back with the side of her hand and stroked his cheek. Then she looked away.

"Forty-five at last count."

"Forty-five." There was wonder in his inflection, amazed disbelief. He wanted to say something appropriate but words failed him. Forty-five dead. His mind could not undertake it.

"We survived," Sarah said.

Hugo looked up at the ceiling's blank whiteness.

"And we'll be together from now on." She stroked his hair. "I'll be with you."

"Yes," he said, taking her hand. This was the single coherent fact in the confused moment, beyond which, as he groped for understanding, was nothing.

MARCH 16, 1995

aptain Dan Danielson, Chief Pilot of the International Division, leaned back in his swivel chair and rubbed his eyes. In his mid-fifties, peppered gray hair and athletic leanness gave his taut profile a presence of command. His desk was a litter of reports. Copies of letters of investigation issued by the Federal Aviation Administration and the National Transportation Safety Board lay in front of him, and two personnel files. He studied the first.

Captain Hugo Price was forty-three years old at the time of the accident. Records showed a bachelor of arts degree from Indiana University. He'd been an Air Force pilot during the late Vietnam War era; military undergraduate pilot-training records indicated high scores. He graduated with distinction. Airline training records indicated no anomalies. Photocopies of his airman certificate described him as six feet two inches tall, 180 pounds, command-qualified in several transport aircraft types. Total flight time: 12,303 hours.

He opened the second file. First Officer Sarah McClure was thirty-two years old at the time of the accident. She had come to Nation Air from a rare kind of civilian flying background: she had flown solo night cargo for eight years. Long hours aloft and alone in the dark had made her a seasoned pilot. Her records indicated a total flight time of 5,644 hours—no training anomalies. Copies of her airman certificate described her as five feet ten inches tall, weight 140 pounds. Bachelor of arts degree from Bennington College. Her photograph complimented strong good looks, dark avid eyes under the shadow of her uniform cap, and an ambiguous smile.

Captain Danielson had been at his desk all afternoon assembling records, transcripts, and reports related to the crash of Nation Air Lines flight 555. The pilots' attorney, Edgar Latimer, had called from union headquarters suggesting a meeting prior to the informal hearing to review all information assembled to date. An FAA Air Carrier Inspector assigned to the investigation had requested yet another meeting.

"Transcripts just arrived."

Danielson looked up. His assistant was standing in the door holding a Federal Express envelope. He opened it, leafed quickly through pages loosely bound with red ribbon. "Make five copies of this, would you please? And could you get Latimer on the phone again?"

Danielson sat back in his chair. He turned toward his window, and, hands fingertip to fingertip, gazed at his sweeping view of the jet ramp. Typically investigations uncovered an intricate interplay of malfunction and human error. New transport aircraft were remarkable for their technical refinements, but they operated in a dynamic environment. The atmosphere was a sea of invisible quakes and eruptions. Eventually, inevitably, infinite variables overcame a defense of technology and training. An accident of this kind was especially frustrating.

Danielson was proud of the caliber of flight crewmember manning the cockpits of America's largest airline fleet, and Nation Air Lines hired the best flying talent in the country. Each pilot applicant was screened exhaustively in three phases. Interviews probed the candidate's sense of himself, or herself, then the applicant was put in a simulator and told to fly a simple instrument flight profile. A career was riding on that one performance, and so evaluators could readily observe an applicant perform in the cockpit under stress.

Danielson closed the personnel files. He eyed a model of the airliner on the shelf across the room, the newest addition to the Nation Air Lines fleet. Powerful, graceful, fuel-efficient, with an internal network of interfacing computers that monitored every system, it was, Dan Danielson supposed, perhaps the safest aircraft in the world.

The charred wreckage of Nation flight 555 was removed from its point of impact and reassembled in a hangar at Kennedy Airport. Under direction of the National Transportation Safety Board, or NTSB, the voice and flight data recorders, "black boxes," had already been retrieved, removed, and analyzed. An independent FAA investigation was initiated, headed by airworthiness and operations inspectors. The engines would be taken to the General Technologies plant in Union, Nevada, for a complete teardown and inspection. Transcripts had been made, graphs would follow. Accident investigators would begin immediately to reconstruct the flight. Following established procedures, variations in altitude, airspeed, and vertical velocity during the approach would be plotted. Engine thrust readings and instrument indications would be entered into a computer; satellite weather data and photographic radar records of flight 555's last minutes assembled. Investigators would discover the attitude of the aircraft and the velocity of impact. They'd try to determine why the fuselage broke up in the way it did, allowing survivors, who certainly would have perished otherwise, to scramble to safety before the final explosion. All this data would be entered into a computer program that could extrapolate the profile of flight Triple-Five, and identify what many already suspected was a major contributing factor, an invisible specter called microburst.

An accident Board of Inquiry was to be convened under the auspices of the NTSB. The board would be comprised of engineers, design consultants, performance supervisors from the Gantry Airplane Company, specialists from General Technologies, the power-plant manufacturers, pilot instructors, airline management representatives, and safety investigators from the Association of Air Line Pilots, the Federal Aviation Agency, and Nation Air Lines. In addition, meteorologists from the National Center for Atmospheric Research would analyze the weather conditions on the night of the crash. Finally, an aviation psychologist whose specialty was "cockpit resource management," or how crewmembers respond in the unique airborne environment, would analyze the psychological profiles of the captain and first officer, examine their professional, and even their personal relationships. The inquiry was a search for explanations, for a logic of acceptable risk against titanic forces of nature and human error.

SEPTEMBER 30, 1994

ugo Price checked the clock: precisely eight hours and forty-seven minutes since their departure from Munich. In the warp of east-west travel, three hours had passed in nine. After they docked at the jetbridge, the hands of both pilots moved quickly to accomplish shutdown procedures. When checklists were completed, Hugo extended his hand across the center console. "Thanks, Ray," he said. "Pleasure working with you."

"Likewise."

A retiring captain once observed that you make a lot of acquaintances at the airline but few friends. Ray Ellis, the first officer, had found this to be true. Ray always enjoyed working with Hugo Price. He liked his easy humor and relaxed manner, but he didn't know him at all. Ray closed his flight case. "Who are you flying with next month?" he asked.

"Sarah McClure."

Ray smiled coyly, willfully withholding a grin. Hugo probed his expression. "Is there something I should know?"

Ray pursed his lips and shook his head. "She's an excellent pilot, from what I hear."

"And?"

"Well, she's—" Ray scanned the heavens for inspiration, found none, and said simply, "She's—well formed."

"Well informed. That's what you meant say."

"Yes. Hugely. Well informed."

Hugo laughed. He was looking forward to flying with Sarah Mc-Clure. They had never formally met, but he knew who she was. Women were famously few in the cockpit, but those Hugo knew were smart, and solid, excellent aviators. He folded his charts and closed his flight case.

The Van Wyck Expressway was bumper-to-bumper northbound. Hugo's Jaguar was quiet and cool. A child's sullen, bored eyes watched him steadily from the back of a brown sedan packed with bags and people. A cab cut in front of him and sped into the right lane, its driver in a pink turban. Home, Hugo thought, is a refuge from the terror of contemplating other people's lives. Traffic ahead began breaking up, and the Whitestone Bridge appeared ahead of him, connecting two land masses and two states of mind. He tossed a token into the basket. Cars were moving swiftly again.

When he pulled into his driveway it was nearly four P.M. An autumn sun shined in hues noticeably less golden than summer, and brought to every sunlit surface hints of fading days to come. Sailboats at their moorings dotted the harbor, and their halyards chimed in the gentle wind. The channel bell sounded at unregulated intervals, its lonely note striking and failing out to sea, and amidst these man-made sounds the unmodulated wash of waves against the breakwater. In mists, the groaning timbre of the foghorn finished this moody music of the waterfront, sonorous, provocative, poetic, and magically harmonious with feelings.

The mail had come, and Hugo picked it up on his way into the house. He dropped his bag by the stairs. The living room faced the water and when he opened the double doors, a sea breeze blew through. He stood in the sun and lingered at the familiar sight, wondering if people on the sailboats were as happy as they seemed. Perhaps human beings only imagine togetherness, he thought vaguely, and then he became conscious of the thought and put it down.

Lydia was late.

After sunset the wind came up, thunderstorms moved overhead and Hugo heard their rumbling approach, and then the rains came. He liked heavy rain, the sound of it pounding on the roof consoled him. He sat in the living room, in his chair by the fire, with a glass of port. A note from Dan Danielson lay on the table with two first-class tickets to Europe.

Subject: Equal Time Point

Dear Hugo,

I did some calculations on your seniority last week and made a discovery. This month marks the midpoint in your career. Congratulations on this milestone. I will tell you this, however; in the Tao Te Ching, it is mentioned that a journey of a thousand miles must reckon the halfway point as nine hundred. Nevertheless, I am proud of the job you have done. I hope that the second half of your career will be twice as rewarding as the first.

Sincere regards,
Dan Danielson, Chief Pilot

Hugo had penned a reply:

Subject: The Point of No Return.

Dear Dan,

Your quotation from the Tao te Ching is wonderfully sly, I've grown fond of your new depth. In one sense, observing a career mid-point is a meditation on death—a look forward or backward has separate but equal anxieties. However, I feel fit to soldier on with wisdom of the great Yogi taken to heart: "It ain't over till it's over."

Hugo Price

He had been dozing when he heard a car outside, Lydia's voice talking to someone, then laughter. He glanced at a small gold clock on the bookcase. Nearly eleven. The car drove away. He heard her heels as she approached. The door opened suddenly. "I'm home," said Lydia, standing at the threshold, mink coat on her shoulders like a cape. He pretended to read. Seven hours of waiting had fueled his anger.

She tossed her fur on the floor. It lay in a heap like a dead dog. He'd never liked that coat—it was pretentious, and never mind the gruesome arrogance of wearing another creature's skin. First she was silent, then she began to attack volubly, staggering a bit.

"Mr. Perfect," she said. "Where do you get off?"

"I am off," he told her, sitting up. "This is my stop. I live here, Lydia."

"We were the Brambles of Salt Lake City. Mormons! What would you know about anything? My grandfather was an Elder."

That again. She'd been drinking. He looked into her eyes—eyes once clear and blue, not red and glassy, and focused on his, not drifting in different directions.

"God appeared to your Elders recently, didn't He? To tell them that black people could belong to your church."

"That was years ago," she snapped, leveling a glare at him. "My brothers went to Princeton, where did you go? They all have IQs above a hundred and fifty. What's yours?"

"A hundred and nine," he said, inwardly amused, even in this sour moment.

She looked down at him, astonished.

"What!" She went slack-jawed to exaggerate incredulity. "A hundred and what? Nine?"

"But it's above average, Lydia. Isn't the average one hundred? Does it make a difference?"

"Yessss," she hissed. "You're at the low end of the cog, goglative—"

"Cognitive distribution?"

"Under the dumbbell curve!" She laughed, then muttered, "I've been living with a moron!"

"You're projecting, Lydia."

She tilted her head, squinting her eyes, and he could see the wreckage of a sarcasm that once had been part of her charm. "How did I end up with you?" she said with genuine puzzled curiosity.

"You made me ask you to marry me. Don't you remember? It's your fault." Hugo tossed his book to the floor. Lydia began to pace.

"Oh, really? And where would you be without me? When we met you had no furniture. You were living like a rat." Hugo knew that when she got like this she would not let up. Any pretext would escalate the argument to a flash point and insidiously he would play his part.

"Mr. Perfect, the pilot," she said.

"Have you been having an affair, Lydia?"

"Mr. Perfect," she said again, ignoring his question. "Well, you're not Mr. Perfect." She wheeled and leaned down uncertainly like a marionette taking a bow. "A bus driver," she growled. "That's what you are. That's all you are."

What were these cruel ghosts she tricked up? He wasn't fooled by her excursions with Helen Linden, and he felt that something between them was behind this retreat further and further into herself, or at least away from him. She went on and on, making him furious, yet always there was a modifying factor that forgave, made from memories of better times, and hope that their marriage could be salvaged.

"You're a faggot," she said finally.

"You're confusing me with your brother," said Hugo, alluding to her oldest brother's recent divorce, and a dubious relationship with an office boy, a part-time student at Brigham Young who had a remarkable feline aspect and a quality of lurking passivity that in certain youthful homosexuals is nearly radiant.

"How dare you insult my brother, you—you uniform. Face the facts," she said. "I married beneath myself. No one I know approves of you."

"Shall we face facts, Lydia?" Recent frustrations began to bubble. "In the last three years you have made life hell for both of us. What do you want? Do you want a divorce? Say the words."

Lydia seemed slightly taken aback at the word "divorce," and it broke her invective. She stood glaring silently at her husband with that alcoholic scrutiny that tries to understand why everyone is a stranger. Then she looked up, as though formulating a thought, and at last said, "You are the most selfish individual I have ever met."

"Selfish?"

"Yes."

"How am I selfish? I have been sitting in this chair waiting for you to come home, looking forward to seeing you as a matter of fact, eager to share my day, but you're late, and you've been drinking, and you're looking for a fight."

"*I'm* looking for a fight? Who just mentioned divorce? I have a speech to make tomorrow, and you're asking for a divorce. That's great. Just wonderful. Every time I have an important day, you do something to upset me. How can I concentrate? Why do you do it?"

"I *haven't* asked you for a divorce. I *don't know* what you're doing tomorrow. You're using me for an excuse."

"Stop it right now, Hugo."

"Wait a minute—"

"Stop it! You're doing this to me on purpose!"

"I'm doing nothing. Lydia, you're doing this to yourself. Listen to what you're saying."

"All right, Hugo, *you* listen to what I'm saying. Are you listening? FUCK YOU." She said the words slowly.

"I can't believe I'm hearing this. It's too much."

"Is that so? Let me clarify: FUCK YOU."

Hugo was about to respond but he paused. He sat stone-still.

"Lydia, go to bed."

"Oh, really?"

"Please. I'll be in in a minute."

"WHO ARE YOU TO TELL ME TO DO ANYTHING?"

She took a book from the shelf at the fireplace and threw it at him. He didn't see it coming and it hit him squarely in the face. His eyes teared and his nose began to bleed, and for several seconds he was stunned.

When he recovered, he restrained his movements, gathering in the strange rapture of rage. He looked into Lydia's angry face and saw an image of his own blind fury. Rising from the chair he went slowly into the kitchen, and with measured deliberation picked up a quart of scotch and held it out calmly while he scrutinized the label. He threw it with all his strength at a small spot on the wall. The bottle hit with tremendous velocity. Plaster dropped to the floor and exposed the wood lathing beneath, making a Rorschach of marital stress: to Hugo, it was a woman with a drinking problem and not much longer to live.

It was a mistake to indulge for a second in the pleasure of that throw. Lydia came at him from behind and tackled him with a bloodthirsty growl. Suddenly they were struggling, they spilled onto the floor in queer postures like lovers and Hugo felt sharp pain as a sliver of glass went into his hand. He held her in a bear hug, but Lydia kicked and clawed violently, trying to reach his eyes with her fingers. Wrestling savagely, they moved across the floor in spasms. Hugo struggled to get free, and he nearly disengaged from her, but she lunged and sank her teeth into his arm. The bleeding was instantaneous, the pain enormous, and he howled like a stricken boar.

He hit her with the heel of his hand and threw her off, then somehow they were standing, and he got away from her into the tiny hall between the basement stairs and the bathroom. She hurled herself at him again and he lost his balance. His head crashed against the corner of a bookcase and her fingers closed around his face and raked down hard. A skullgrin of berserk joy came over her as he began to bleed again. Skin on his arm hung from him like a flap.

Hugo stood and took hold of her at the edge of the stairs and looked down the stairwell. A wave of pure violence passed through him, and Lydia could see it, feel it, and she was ready to submit to it with a giddy, conquering exaltation. But suddenly they both realized what was happening to them, and the violent moment passed away, followed by a remarkable poignance that lasted for quite some time as they scrutinized each other closely like intelligent strangers. He released his grip suddenly and went into the bedroom. Lydia called the police.

OCTOBER, 1, 1994, TWO A.M.

I 'VE CALLED THE POLICE. I'VE CALLED THE POLICE.
I'M GOING TO TELL THEM EVERYTHING! EVERY-
THING!"

What everything?

Lying on the bed and still breathing hard, Hugo stared at the ceiling. Every breath was a question. He dabbed his face and held up his
bleeding arm. The room began to throb as he lay contemplating the
end of his marriage, for surely this fight was the end. His years with
Lydia were a hazy calendar of overlapping arguments. First love, then
affection, and finally therapy, had failed, leaving them stranded on
exhausted soil, creatures of disappointment.

Lydia had grown fond of phoning the police. A little more than a
year before, she had called them screaming abuse, but when the squad
car drove up, she got belligerent with the officer and assaulted his
headlight with her foot, shattering credibility on the spot. The

stunned man arrested her immediately. Hugo appeared at her side in night court before a harried judge. The judge was unclear as to who had done what to whom. He mandated marriage counseling for both as an alternative to jail for Lydia, thus Hugo felt unfairly drawn into squalid officialdom. But he had had no choice. He and Lydia hadn't yet calculated the zero sum in their long emotional descent from affection through hatred to violence and indifference. They felt the need to make an effort to fix things, so they went to see a psychiatrist who specialized in broken relationships.

"What's this?" said Lydia, peering into a terrarium, part of the spare decoration of the therapist's waiting room. Under the fluorescent light, several small living cacti stood amid artificial flowers. She turned to Hugo with an irritated look, then walked around the room closely examining the few paintings hanging on the walls—the dark head of a dog, a small lonely house on a broad plain, an impressionist portrait of Sigmund Freud.

"The man's an eccentric," she muttered indignantly.

The door opened and the doctor appeared.

"Please come in," he said.

Hearing his words, Lydia turned from a small framed scroll of the Desiderata that she had been reading (alas, without comprehension, thought Hugo), and smiled at the therapist with a floodlight of considerable charm. It was her way with the world.

A tall man of indeterminate middle age, he wore a sweater buttoned professorially, and he appeared to smile. But it wasn't really a smile, Hugo thought, more a neutral facial salutation. Later, trying to recall his image, Hugo couldn't.

They were invited to sit together on a couch opposite the analyst, who took notes and tape-recorded all they said. Lydia spoke:

"He's always leaving, always saying good-bye. I work at a real job in the city. He goes away for three days and comes back with a tan."

"Is my life a vacation? Is that what you think?"

"You call that work?"

"You know nothing about what I do," said Hugo, irritated.

"I know enough to know that you don't work more than twelve days a month."

"You manage to spend the paycheck well enough." The clock ticked audibly. How long has she been a stranger to me? he thought. The therapist watched and listened, then intervened. "Lydia, you seem rather irritated that Hugo—"

"Save it. I know what you're getting at. I hate my job." She clutched the armrest and stiffened in her seat. "What do you expect?"

The therapist sat silently.

"Last month there was a reorganization and now I report to—to a man who made me autograph his football! This is supposed to make me feel like part of his team."

The therapist chuckled.

"The football is his phallic symbol, Lydia," Hugo offered.

Lydia cocked her head wrathfully. "Then why don't *you* play catch with him and put me on the next plane to Barbados?" She turned to the therapist. "Do you see why I'm angry? Am I going to be in a cubicle for the rest of my life? This wasn't what I planned."

"I thought women wanted to work." Hugo shrugged.

"I want to do something fun."

"Work is different from that."

"Then I want to retire and take up golf."

Hugo threw out his hands. "Do you see? Golf is a game for people who need disappointment. Disappointment is her security."

The therapist remained impassive, shifted in his seat, and addressed himself to Hugo. "I think I see the current difficulties. But let's go back. Why don't you begin by telling me how you and Lydia met?"

"How we met?"

"Yes. Were you introduced by a friend? Did you meet on a bus?"

Though the therapist was a paid listener, he was a stranger; why tell him anything? Yet Hugo felt an eagerness to speak that shamed his pride and threw up resistance. How desperate we are to be validated and approved, how lonely life is, how fabulously real illusions can seem. He began to reckon how much of the ongoing present is spent reinventing the past and imagining the future.

"It seems impossible to explain frankly that our relationship seemed doomed from the start."

"Then why did you enter into it?"

"I saw in Lydia what I thought I needed. She made me laugh, we enjoyed similar things, the same books, the theater. It felt good to be together. Then I could feel a change. She didn't understand my life away from her, flying, whatever. Suddenly she seemed to be a different person, frustrated, resentful. After a while I thought we had made a mistake. But it's hard to face something like that. You become entrenched, and the whole idea of leaving the life you have, even if it's awful, seems impossible."

Even as he spoke, Hugo was amazed at the extent to which, since the beginning, he had created, from the raw clays of Lydia, a woman she had never been, never could be, knowing that for her the marriage had been first a refuge, then a cage, as time exposed the truth of things. Those vacations with her friend Helen Linden, their self-conscious secrets, their absurd baby-talk—did he have to be hit over the head with it? Her drinking, moderate at first, had over the years become severe.

"When did you meet?"

Hugo thought. When had they met? Was it really ten Septembers ago? It was. Back then, thirty-two years old, recently separated from the Air Force, out of the culture of weaponry at last, he was living near New York once more.

"We met ten years ago. At a museum."

The sky had been threatening all day, but not a drop had fallen. Once it broke, however, rain came down hard in sheets, and you could hear it sweep across the side of the building, and see it teeming against the slate roof if you stood by the door. Water cascaded from gutters that were overflowing; traffic disappeared into a curtain of rainfall. Hugo watched for a while with the satisfied fascination of one who was warm and dry.

The sky darkened on the avenue outside the museum. Traffic slowed and the headlights of cars came on. Gusty winds made umbrellas unmanageable. Hugo went to get a cup of coffee at the museum cafe. His first sight of Lydia was from behind. Frazzled, she was in line ahead of him, tearing through her purse looking for change. He handed a dollar to the cashier. "For both of us," he said.

"Thank you." She turned to examine him; irritation changed to a smile, then changed back. Her eyes furrowed. "Look at me, I'm drenched. Would you mind holding this?" She handed him her coffee. She ran her fingers across a wet strand of hair, drops falling to the floor. They moved away from the cashier. Hugo searched for a place to sit.

"A couple is just getting up," he said. He ushered her over to the corner and held her chair.

He took her wet jacket and hung it on the chair. They sat at a table under narrow Romanesque windows built into limestone blocks. Seated, Lydia continued to ferret through her purse, preoccupied, distracted. Makeup ran down her face.

"Here it is," she said, shoulders collapsing in relief.

"What?"

"The key to my apartment." She held it up, and dropped it back into her purse. "I thought I'd lost it. I'm always losing keys and pens."

Lydia's entire body moved when she spoke. Her voice was broken and had an edge of sultry weariness in it. Nordic, blond, blue-eyed, and square-featured, broad athletic shoulders made her big figure robust. Her blouse was wet and transparent. She pulled at her wet hair, squeezing water from it. She looked from side to side, watching people in the room while she spoke to Hugo without meeting his eyes. She gave him an encouraging smile. "I'm Lydia Bramble," she told him.

"Hugo Price."

"Are you here for the Caravaggio exhibition?" Lydia said. She seemed to snuggle into her seat.

"Yes."

"It got a good write-up last Sunday. That's why I came."

"I saw the same article," Hugo said.

She leaned forward. "Most artists today are crap." She took a sip of her coffee, watching him over the lip of her cup for reaction. He gave none. Her eyes wandered the room, returning finally to him. Then Lydia's personality broke through all at once like sudden sunshine. "You're a handsome man. The best I've seen in months," she said.

"Thank you," said Hugo, surprised, flattered, and slightly abashed. "You're welcome."

Rain continued in a heavy downpour and they could hear it from where they sat. "I'm from Utah," she told him, religiously and geographically the moon in his imagination.

"Is that the 'Show Me' state?" His gaze drifted to her blouse where it was wet.

"No, that's Missouri."

"I've never met anyone from there."

"Missouri?"

"Either place."

"Once I was a serious cellist."

"Really?"

But she had had a kind of breakdown. "I practiced too much. Maybe it was an awakening. It wasn't that I didn't have talent."

"Do you still play?" asked Hugo.

Dry vagueness overcame her expression as she fingered the sugar spoon. "I kept at it for a while," she said. The words seemed to fade as her interest had. She took a sip of coffee and looked off to the side, squinting at someone or something over Hugo's shoulder. Then she opened her purse and took out lipstick and a small mirror. She put the lipstick on with two or three quick swipes and snapped the mirror shut. "I look like hell," she announced, and dropped her purse to the floor beside her feet. Hugo looked into her eyes and tried to imagine her music, but her eyes evaded him.

There was a presence of some unusual precocity that set her apart; she was self-absorbed, but in a curious way that was both interesting and annoying, the way a small child with an adult vocabulary can be at the same time charming and grotesque.

"What do you do?" Hugo asked. She raised her eyebrows, questioning. "For a living, I mean."

"Public relations," she said. "Press releases, speeches, that sort of thing. I write a lot." This last disclosure was her point of pride and vulnerability, he could tell. She cocked her head and narrowed her eyes. "You look like a lawyer. Are you a lawyer?"

Hugo smiled. "No."

"A dentist? No, a chiropractor!"

Hugo shook his head.

"No, not that. Wait. I'm good at this. . . ."

Hugo waited.

"You could be a doctor, but I don't think so." She watched him closely.

"A doctor?" he said, and then paused. "No."

"An unemployed actor?"

"No."

"Employed actor?"

"No."

"All right, what?" By now she wasn't interested.

"I'm an airline pilot."

Lydia dropped her shoulders and laughed. "You don't look like a pilot."

"What does a pilot look like?" Hugo said, slightly offended.

She made a stern face. "Like someone else's father. You look like a kid."

"Thanks."

"How old are you?"

"It's the crew-neck sweater and the blue jeans," he said, throwing out his hands. "I'm thirty-two."

She rolled her eyes. "I'm thirty-nine. You *are* a kid." Older women intrigued him. All at once her aspect softened, her eyes took his measure and she leaned forward over her coffee cup. "Actually, you're not a kid at all."

Hugo began to like her mercurial way with him. Something vaguely threatening in her appealed to his love of challenge, yet she seemed vulnerable underneath.

Hugo was about to make a comment when Lydia's aspect froze. "Oh my God!" she said, looking over his shoulder. He turned in his chair.

"What?" he said.

"That man! His sports jacket. What do you think?"

Hugo turned. "Pretty dreadful."

"A druggist, I bet. And his wife. She's fat as a pear. Look at that coif, holy Toledo." She began to laugh, making Hugo slightly uncomfortable. "People are fun to figure. I love to play guessing games."

Which, like conspiracy theory, thought Hugo unkindly, is conceit not accountable to validation. Ordinarily, Hugo's critical faculties were stern. He did not believe that she was insightful, but it didn't matter. If his perceptions remained keen, sensing discontinuity, their message was overruled by Lydia's blue eyes, which were catlike, and by her foot, which had begun to seek his under the table.

"Are you a good judge of character?" Hugo asked.

"Oh, absolutely." Lydia's attention seemed to dart over, under, and around him, then her eyes ceased scanning the room and lingered on his. She smiled magnificently and took his hand across the table. "Shall we see what we came to see?"

The museum swarmed. They were caught in a swamp of the curious, the bored, the homeless, the vacationing, and those with nothing better to do.

The paintings of Caravaggio made perhaps a less than ideal background for romance. The artist's disturbing biblical figures caught in murky degradations spoke of something raw in God and sadistic in human nature. Light always fell from the left in Caravaggio. The exhibition had created a sensation, and Hugo had been eager to study the work of this strange genius whose short life ended violently.

Hugo and Lydia stood in front of *Salome*. The figures appear uncomfortable with the murder, and Salome looks away as the executioner holds the severed head at arm's length.

"It's beautiful," said Hugo, "I mean to say, terrifying."

Lydia continued to study it in silence.

Drifting with the tide of visitors, Hugo and Lydia were together in their perceptions of the paintings, which existed at the edge of spirit where God, sex, and death converged.

The Flagellation, on the wall opposite, caught Hugo's particular attention. Intrigued by the larger work, he stepped across the room to its vast canvas. Grim and intense, the Christ figure, bathed in light, squirms under a savage scourging. The intimidating scale of the painting, its dungeon-light scheme, and, as Hugo saw it, an erotic immediacy about the tormentors, gave the painting a fierce brutality.

"Cheerful, isn't it," Lydia said.

"I've counted five 'Ninas.' "

"Look at that," said Lydia, missing or ignoring his joke, and turned to *David with the Head of Goliath*. They moved closer to it.

"That's the self-portrait," Hugo said.

"Which?"

"Goliath's head."

Lydia studied the painting closely. A sorrowing David holds the head of the vanquished giant, bruised, bloodied, disembodied, yet with a gruesome glimmer of life shining in the left eye.

After passing through the last exhibition room they went down-stairs.

"Well," Lydia said. "It was wonderful." She extended her hand. Hugo took it, although the gesture seemed oddly formal.

"I feel like we've been through something together, although I'm not sure what." He let go of her hand. There was a long pause.

"Actually," she agreed, "I'm feeling rather excited."

Good, he thought. They walked to the exit.

"Thank you for the coffee."

"You're welcome." Hugo held the door for her. They both looked at the sky. She said, "The rain's stopped." Another long pause sought for words.

"Well?" she said, looking directly into his eyes. "Shall I say, 'Have a nice life'? Or would you like to come home with me?"

Hugo put his arm around her fondly; she fell against his shoulder, smiling.

They took a cab to Lydia's West Side apartment and walked up three flights of stairs. Hugo absorbed her surroundings. The apartment was small, but neatly arranged and comfortable. A large bookcase gave the room a settled character. A trio of framed oil paintings were curious, he thought; a landscape of bones: femurs, vertebrae, and bird skulls entangled in various ways, stuck in bedsprings or coiled in vines, disembodied, bleached, mired. They made a contrast to lace curtains and a blue gingham tablecloth that countrified the kitchen area, where tiny vases held minute dry flower arrangements on a false windowsill. There was a large mirror over a working fireplace in the middle of the room, but only one window in front had a view of the street. Heavy overcast had darkened the sky prematurely. Lydia lit a candle.

Hugo sat at the tiny kitchen table while Lydia got a bottle of red wine from the cupboard and took two glasses from above the sink. She put the glasses down and poured the wine and Hugo watched her do this with expectant silent pleasure. Sexual tension seemed magically caught in the candle flame that danced inside the curved glass as Hugo raised it to make a toast.

"Are you comfortable?"

"Yes. Quite comfortable"

"Good."

Hugo studied her face. Smooth curvatures of youth were echoed in pronounced definitions of a woman past thirty. Her eyes were restless, and from time to time an expression of tense impatience overcame her, but it vanished quickly, lost in the sudden sparkle of a remarkable smile.

"How did you happen to have a Thursday off?" Hugo asked.

She laughed. "I didn't. I took a mental-health holiday."

"Do you have that kind of flexibility?"

"Sometimes." She sipped her wine. "Do you go to the museum much?"

"Once in a while."

"Where do you live?"

"Connecticut."

"Why?"

"I like being near the water. Why do you live in the city?"

Her fingers encircled the stem of the glass, and leaning forward, she whispered, "I like to be near excitement." She took his hand and led him into the living room, also the bedroom as it turned out. The apartment was a modified studio. Hugo helped open a sofa bed. She tossed him pillows from the closet, then went into the bathroom. "I'll be right back," she said.

Hugo undressed, got into the bed, crawled under the covers, and made a place for Lydia beside him. The candle, now at bedside, threw out a pale light.

He waited for her. Then the bathroom door opened, and in a moment before she turned off the light, he saw Lydia's naked figure emerge in slanted light as though floating, and then she was in bed with him and they were alive to the flesh, discovering in the course of the next few hours certain excruciating pleasures and a few unexpected thrills.

"And so after that night we began to see each other, and after a few months we moved in together and a year after that we were married."

"Well." The psychiatrist leaned forward and pressed the Stop button on the tape recorder. "We'll take this up next week." He opened his hands and spoke candidly. "I'd like to recommend a course of therapy for you to practice at home."

"For us to practice at home?" repeated Lydia with comic reluctance.

The therapist smiled. "Yes. It's nothing too difficult. But I would like you to do it at least three times a week. Three times a week, minimum. I'd like you to massage each other. Go to the pharmacy and buy a lotion, a skin cream. Rub the cream into your partner's back, and arms, and legs gently, with no other intention than to have your partner relax. Can you do that?"

"We can do that," said Hugo, nevertheless repulsed by the idea. He felt in his bones that Lydia experienced the same revulsion. How far their enjoyment of each other had strayed!

"Finally," said the doctor, "I urge that you each see me separately. In addition, I ask that you not discuss the individual therapy with your partner. Can you agree to these terms?"

Later at home, Hugo felt that some progress had been made, but his confidence in the process was fragile. Recalling Lydia as he remembered her when they met made him feel estranged from the unhappy creature she had become.

"His furniture is dreadful," Lydia said. "I think this is all unnecessary. Make me a scotch."

Always scotch, Hugo thought, the drink of choice among friends of his parents who were alcoholics.

"How about a massage?" he said.

"Hugo, please, give it a rest."

After three weeks of individual therapy, Lydia became suspicious of clinical conspiracy.

"What did you tell him?" she asked.

"He said not to confide what we spoke about," said Hugo. "It's a rule."

"He didn't mean about everything." Her eyes avoided his.

"Lydia, he meant what he said. The therapy won't work if you don't play by the rules. The man is a physician. He knows more than we do about these things."

"He doesn't know anything about anything!" Her face reddened and her eyes contorted like a wrathful cartoon. "I told him that you're perverted. He agreed with me that there's something very wrong with you."

Hugo winced. Lydia was a puzzle. She could be sweet as a sunny afternoon and full of fun but she had the tenacity of a toothache when it came to ruining a day. She was sporadic. That was the problem, it wasn't a case of which side of her was real, they were both who she was. The drama of Lydia was that one side denied expressly the existence of the other. Denial was the signature of her personality, the foundation of her untenable character.

And yet, there had been wonderful moments. A week spent aboard a sailboat cruising the Virgin Islands; yes, Hugo recalled the sun on Lydia's face at dusk, the splendid menus she concocted, the delight she took in making tiny quarters work to best advantage. In their ten years together they had explored deserted beaches and made love on nameless islands, climbed volcanic hills, lain naked in the sun, and for a while, been happy. These were the moments he had believed in.

"And furthermore," she said, "he says I don't need therapy anymore. I'm normal. There's nothing wrong with me."

"Really?" Hugo said. "And what did he say, exactly?"

"I'm not supposed to tell you anything. Those are the rules, remember?" she sneered, like a nasty little girl of forty-five.

"What did he tell you?" Hugo repeated. "Exactly."

"He said that continued therapy was unnecessary for me," she said. "He shook my hand and wished me well. He's a very knowledgeable person."

"I'm sure he is."

But Hugo was exasperated. Could it be true that she had fooled the therapist? Or was it that he saw she was incapable of therapy? What, he wondered, was all of this meant to accomplish, anyway? Then he thought suddenly: Perhaps it's meant merely to point out the daily misery that togetherness has come to mean. It seemed that for years they had lived back-to-back. With such precarious support every forward step created tension until they only moved in circles talking to the walls. Still, anxiety spoke for compromise; there must be a way to avoid losing everything.

The police arrived like a carnival at two o'clock in the morning. All at once the neighborhood was alive with five-thousand-watt strobe lights, blue-and-red rotating beacons, sirens blasting on the narrow, peaceful, uncongested street where they lived.

Shrewdly, Lydia had let herself bleed. Her clothes gave a greater appearance of gore. Two squad cars and an ambulance, four policemen and a total arsenal of six guns, a blackjack, two nightsticks, and forty rounds of ammunition advanced on the house. Astonished faces appeared in windows up and down the block.

Before their arrival Lydia had gone out into the rain to get wet so that she might present an even more abused aspect. She opened the front door. They were the liberation army; she welcomed them like a raped farmgirl. "Look what he did to me," she said as their faces approached in the dark. She collapsed into the arms of the younger rookie cop.

His seasoned partner held a flashlight on her. She turned from her savior's embrace and squinted into it.

"Where is he, ma'am?" he asked.

She made to say something but only managed to gesture toward the bedroom, so overcome with gratitude was she, so saved amid flashing lights and sirens. Medics brought her smelling salts and insisted that she sit down at the kitchen table, a kitchen that smelled woefully of scotch.

Hugo woke to the sound of voices in the hall. He felt for the light switch and the room went harshly bright around him. Softly, politely, came a knock on the bedroom door.

"May I come in?" A policeman opened the door slowly, holding a flashlight. His gun was holstered. Hugo stepped back. Each man took instant measure of the other.

The policeman scanned the room. "She said you beat her."

"And what else did she say?"

"She said you locked her out of the bedroom and refused to take her to the hospital or call for help."

Hugo paused. "I locked her out to keep her away from me." His tone was calm, ruminative. "She wanted to kill me. She has ugly moods. Perhaps she wanted me to kill her."

"She says you wanted to kill her. Which one of you is telling the truth?"

"Neither one of us. It's an impossible situation."

The policeman raised a skeptical eyebrow and returned his flashlight to a hitch on his utility belt.

"Are you all right?" he asked.

"I put a Band-Aid on this." He pointed out his wound. "She's descended from cannibals, a recessive gene I didn't know about."

The policeman's expression did not change.

Lydia was taken to the hospital in a motorcade worthy of the governor. When the police left it was near dawn, and once again, at last, the house was quiet. Hugo went into the living room and built up the fire. In darkness and silence the events of this night did not seem real. The extremeness of discord and discontent had not seemed as great as it now appeared in the aftermath of their brawl. Hugo sighed. Flames danced like playful spirits. He wept. The flames danced and multiplied as he watched them appear and disappear between the logs until he fell asleep again.

OCTOBER 1, 1994, EIGHT A.M.

He woke chilled in the late morning, and Lydia had not returned from the hospital. Hugo paced his living room. He squinted through the window where the cold sun shined on the water in silver animations. Taking his cold cup of coffee he went over to the narrow table where a number of bottles stood in a regiment of spirits. He poured out a shot of bourbon, thinking, What the hell, though it irritated his sense of right that he should drink in the morning. As he warmed the spiked coffee in a microwave, something nagged at him, some unborn thought.

Over the years it had become essential to his serenity of spirit to live near the shore, a facetious conceit because his domestic life had not been serene—rather, it had been insane. Since leaving college, even in the military, he had lived by the shore. Perhaps, Hugo reflected, he only thought that the sea was a peaceful inspiration, when in fact it was a cause of calamity. All of his life he had tried to do the right thing but, with best intentions, always he had done exactly the wrong thing. Hugo finished his coffee and felt the fine warmth of bourbon spread in him like sunshine, but heavy melancholy settled in his mood. He resolved firmly not to have another drink, and in slow deliberate steps, he went into his study.

He picked at books on the shelves, opening this one, reading a paragraph here, and then that one and a paragraph there, closing each in turn and putting it back in its place. He sat down again near a stack of old *National Geographic* magazines and leafed through them. Here were Portuguese fishermen on the Algarve; how he envied them their fishing dories and their simple, toothless mirth. There was farm life in Nebraska: rugged brothers mending fences, husky sisters feeding swine. Hard work absorbed their animal energies and made them malleable to their Luthernicity. Hugo sighed: I will never be a fisherman or a farmer, he thought, with genuine sadness under the spell of depression's impossible regret.

Hugo's mind was reeling from the night before.

He left the house at lunchtime and went to a small restaurant nearby. He ate thoughtfully and sat alone. Normally he drank wine in the evening, but today he wanted something strong, and he continued his early start with bourbon. After finishing his meal he went to the bar and lingered, remaining until late afternoon. Hours passed, and he greeted a succession of regulars with flushed amiability. There was much talk, and he discovered himself suddenly filled with perspectives on life, and a desire to share them.

"You know what I hate," Hugo said to a real-estate agent, "I hate speed bumps—you know where I'm talking about, over at that condominium complex near Hillside Avenue."

The real-estate agent, a large man with a shiny bald head and a jaw that jutted thoughtfully as he pared his fingernails, put down the nail clipper and cleaned his thumbnail with a toothpick, examining its harvest briefly before placing it in an ashtray. "I know exactly where you mean. I scrape my muffler on those damn things every time I have to show a unit."

"That happened to me, too, and I thought, Where is all this hostility coming from, what's it all about? Then I thought: It's disappointment. It's an automotive way for residents to say 'Fuck you' for a kind of failure they feel for living there."

The real-estate agent folded his nail clipper and put it into his pocket. "Utopia disappoints," he said, rather pleased with himself for that comment.

"But our culture is founded on disappointment, that's exactly the point," said Hugo. "We are conditioned to be unsatisfied. Satisfaction undermines the economic premise of capitalism and cannot be allowed, except as an advertiser's promise as in, 'Smoking satisfies,' or 'One-hundred-percent satisfaction guaranteed.' Happiness is subversive, we're not *supposed* to be happy. That's why ugliness has become an absolutely essential part of our style. It disappoints."

Wisdom was alight in him. He spent the rest of the afternoon in conversation with strangers on such topics as ugly automobiles, unimaginative space exploration, and the decline of the American empire reflected in popular music, bad architecture, and gridlock politics. Afterwards, when he went to other bars, the conversation miraculously resumed where it had left off, only with different people, as the night dissolved in a blur of lights and laughter and smoke and talk. There were many hands shaken, cards received, and numbers exchanged in a world suddenly populated with soul mates.

He blinked in painful awakening. His thoughts hurt, even his blood ached, it throbbed, and blood was everywhere in him, poisoned from alcohol. Broken images coagulated into incomplete memories, and he felt his own frontal lobe for signs of regression. A cold sweat broke out on his forehead and his stomach began to churn. Breathing was labored. Wicked spasms radiated through him.

Later, Hugo stood in his living room and looked at the cold fireplace, and at the books on shelves on either side of the mantle, thinking, This is my home and I will have to leave it. For a long while he tried to understand what had gone wrong in his marriage. His true spirit had gone to sleep like a leg or an arm does, still attached but heavy and lifeless. He felt like a guest in someone else's life, but it was his own; worst of all, Hugo did not have a clear understanding of how it had come to this.

OCTOBER 5, 1994

"Why don't you just leave?" said Lydia.

"Really? Why don't you?"

"Because it's my house."

"Your house? When was the deed transferred? How is it your house and not mine?"

"Because my lawyer says so. What does yours say?"

Hugo put on his epaulets and tie and ignored her last comment, deciding that to begin a long night's journey to Europe with an untenable argument was a bad idea. He picked up his kit bag and put on his hat. "Good-bye, sweetheart," he said in his best impression of a happy husband.

He stood eating a cookie by the union bulletin board at Kennedy Flight Operations. The first officer had not arrived, and as he checked his watch for the third time he heard a distinctive voice behind him.

"I got stuck at the toll."

He turned.

"The bridge?"

She nodded.

A puzzled expression crossed his features. "In New Jersey they have real human beings who collect dimes for the state," he brushed cookie crumbs from his jacket with the back of his hand, then he looked up. "How do you explain that to your children?"

She laughed, and extended her hand. "I'm Sarah McClure."

"Hugo Price," he said.

She was a woman of legible good looks, taller than average, with high cheekbones and a lapidary nose, dark avid eyes and a sonorous, slightly broken voice with that hint of morning-after which, in a woman, gives strong impressions of erotic misdemeanor. Her uniform, he also noticed with some surprise, did not undermine her feminine profile, but rather finished it with equestrian airs.

For her part, she liked his looks, his folded arms and how he slouched against the bulletin board, tall, darkly handsome, his face unlined and youthful, an easy unintimidating manner. He had longish hair, clear green eyes, and a watchful personality. His alligator shoes, she noted, countered two pilot stereotypes: sartorial ineptitude and stinginess. She wondered if he smoked.

"Do you have the paperwork?" he asked.

She handed him a large yellow envelope. They moved over to the planning table. He opened the envelope and spread the flight plan, Notices to Airmen or NOTAMS, weather and airport data, weight and balance forms, the plotting chart, dispatch release, and departure plan, across the broad area of the planning desk.

"How long have you been flying in the International Division?" Hugo asked.

"Four months." Sarah checked the printout of their North Atlantic, or NAT track, coordinates against the coordinates on their master flight plan.

Hugo checked planned fuel against minimum fuel required for dispatch release. "You don't mind late departures?" he said.

"I flew night freight for years." She traced their course on the plotting chart. "Darkness appeals to the romantic in me."

Hugo moved through the paperwork slowly and methodically. He noted destination weather and flight conditions along their intended route of fight. Together, they confirmed their coast-out coordinates.

"What sort of freight did you fly?"

"Canceled checks. Videotape, when we could beat satellite rates. Corpses, occasionally."

"Corpses?"

"Never heard a complaint."

"What kind of aircraft did you use?"

"Old Beech 18s for most jobs. Beech Barons otherwise. A couple of Piper Navajos."

"Beech 18?"

"Piston-poundin'. A Harley-Davidson of the air."

"Absolutely." Hugo smiled. Sarah was a purist.

Hugo signed the departure release, then collected the remaining flight documents and handed them to Sarah. She put the paperwork into her flight case. "I'll start the preflight and meet you in the cockpit," she told him.

When she was gone, Hugo went into the technical library to look up a minor item for clarification. In the quiet there, he opened a manual. A few minutes passed before he realized he'd been staring at the page without reading a word.

Sarah walked through the terminal. A giant mural depicting aviation history from Icarus to the space age spanned the broad reception area. Docked aircraft were visible on the ramp beyond the wall of windows, and small blue maintenance trucks, catering vehicles, and baggage conveyers darted back and forth underneath them. Sarah passed through security and went out to the gate, unlocked it, and walked through the jet bridge.

Outside, the airliner shone brightly in the late sun. Even at rest, it seemed alive, pampered, a thoroughbred beast. Predeparture crews swarmed around it: fuelers pumped a hundred thousand pounds of kerosene into the wing, conveyer belts moved cargo into the belly, and catering trucks delivered food and linen to the cabin.

Sarah got her flashlight and went down steep stairs to the ramp. She stepped carefully over the external power cable, ducked under the baggage conveyer, then began her walk-around inspection in a methodical clockwise pattern starting at the nose gear, carefully checking cowling latches, door panels, and access plates in various positions. She went under the gear well to inspect the tires and brake lines, and then stopped at the pumping station under the right wing to collect the fuel slip. When she returned to the cabin, Hugo had already stowed her bags and was programming the flight management computer.

"How does the outside look?" He turned to Sarah.

"I think we'll make it."

Sarah hung her jacket in the narrow closet behind the circuit-breaker panel and climbed into the right seat. Once settled, she performed the cockpit readiness inspection as Hugo continued programming their course. In a systematic sweep of the overhead panel, she moved switches to their proper preflight positions. Finished with that, she tested her oxygen unit, copied down current airport weather, and requested departure clearance through the ACARS communications computer.

"Ouch!" Hugo flinched and began to rub his arm gently.

"Tennis elbow?" Sarah had a touch of it herself.

"Ever have a dogbite?"

"Once when I was a girl."

"It hurts like hell."

"A dog bit your arm?"

"No. My wife."

A ground crewman signaled from outside. Their clearance came across the cockpit printer. Sarah tore it off, reviewed it for changes, and attached it to the master flight plan. "Kennedy Three departure, Canarsie transition, radar vectors East Hampton, five thousand feet. Squawk four-three-five-one. It's set."

Hugo nodded.

They were ready for a final check of coordinates. Hugo scrolled the flight plan and verbally read the latitude and longitude of each waypoint while Sarah checked him. Sarah checked her navigation display for continuity. Their course to Rome appeared as a continuous white line on the CRT. Coordinates re-verified, he signaled to the ground supervisor standing by outside and ordered ground power disconnected. Abruptly the flurry of preparation was over. Hugo reached up and turned on the Fasten Seat Belt sign. "Before Starting Engines checklist," he said.

A short while later, they were stopped on taxiway Double Kilo near runway 31L at Kennedy, waiting in line for takeoff clearance. "You fly it over tonight, I'll take it back on Thursday."

Sarah nodded.

"Let's brief the departure." Hugo set the altitude alert. "Any engine failure or systems malfunction recognized prior to V1, call it out, I'll make the decision to abort, take control, and execute a rejected takeoff. After V1, all emergencies will be considered in-flight emergencies. If we lose an engine we'll use eight hundred feet for cleanup, begin emergency actions at that time, keep it in the pattern, and bring it back here. I'll start the APU right away to get you backup hydraulics and electrics. Otherwise, left turn Canarsie, five thousand feet, radar vectors on course. Any questions?"

"No questions," Sarah said.

Nation Air 547, cleared for takeoff.

Hugo maneuvered the airliner into position on centerline. Sarah took over the controls. City lights shimmered in the distance against a background of red dusk. Sarah advanced the throttles; Hugo made the velocity callouts:

"—eighty knots, thrust locked—V1—VR—"

Sarah applied back pressure on the yoke, the nose lifted, and they were airborne for Rome.

"—V2—V2 plus 10—"

"Positive rate, gear up," she commanded.

"Landing gear up," Hugo confirmed. He reached across the center console and raised the landing-gear lever. The gear retracted with a thump. Sarah eased the pitch to a deck angle of twenty degrees, and at eight hundred feet she called, "Check speed, rate change, climb power, flaps up." The jet banked gently left as she established the departure heading.

"Slats retract."

Hugo moved the flaps/slats lever to full retract. Sarah retrimmed as their airspeed increased.

"Clean machine," he said. "Let's go to Rome."

They climbed out eastward along the south shore of Long Island toward Nantucket. Daylight retreated rapidly behind them and most of the dark clouds seemed to be due north. Hugo watched the lights of Block Island pass under the wing, and he could make out the cliffs of Gay Head on Martha's Vineyard in the distance. They continued climbing smoothly through high, thin layers of stratus cloud. Sarah hand-flew through twenty thousand feet, then engaged the autopilot while Hugo, on the PA, gave the passengers particulars about their route of flight, weather, and time of arrival in Rome. Departure duties were completed by Nantucket. Farther on, the coasts of Maine and Newfoundland appeared. Hugo watched the shoreline lights silently.

"It's magical, isn't it?" he said.

Sarah leaned forward and looked out. Star clusters above shone vividly. Her face seemed dreamlike in the pale cockpit illumination. "I never get tired of it. It's like an experience that exists only in the mind."

Hugo turned in his seat to face Sarah directly. "For me, there's Zen involved with flying, I go inward. The tighter the approach, the further in I go. The further in I go, the freer I feel." Hugo faced forward again. "If it's really tight, if there's a problem of some sort, low fuel, shitty weather, no room for error, you break through a barrier. That's when the true Zen kicks in and it all comes together, you become the situation and the solution all at once. I think Lindbergh described it as the sublime moment when life is infinitely precious and valueless in the same instant."

"The purest feeling." Sarah paused pleasurably on the thought. "I understand."

"Yes." Hugo scanned the instruments. "I think you do." Her eyes remained on him, luminous in the semi-light. They had flown from dusk into night darkness, and now they settled in for the crossing. The ocean lay ahead like a vast future, and they sped into it headlong, miles passing into dawn.

OCTOBER 6, 1994

Rome

After an ocean crossing, time had a different feel. Morning or evening mattered less than feeling tired or being hungry. They had agreed to meet at six for dinner. Hugo slept deeply through the day, woke at five-fifteen, showered, put on blue jeans and a white cotton shirt, and went downstairs. Sarah was waiting for him in the lobby. She was casually dressed in black slacks and a purple pullover. As he walked across the lobby, he plucked a rose from an elaborate arrangement beside the elevator bay.

Sarah stood. "I saw that."

Her eyes followed his hand as he fixed the rose in her hair, an astonishingly bold gesture, but he carried it off. She turned to see it in the mirror, readjusted it slightly, and smiled at his reflection.

"Let's walk down by the Forum." Hugo held the door for her.

They walked along the via Fori Imperiali near the ruins. A pale rim of blue light lingered on the horizon with coal-red clouds above it. Construction crews had erected scaffolding for a rally and ruined the view, so Hugo pointed north. "Let's go this way," he said. They went up toward the via Del Corso, then turned into an area of narrow *vicoli* where there was less traffic. There they strolled in softer light that seemed to shine, as it does in Rome, from no place in particular.

"I want to see St. Peter's. And Moses. And the Sistine Chapel." Sarah had never been to Italy.

"Did you know that Moses was conceived as a tombstone?"

Sarah turned, surprised. "A tombstone?"

"For Pope Julius II. One of forty statues commissioned for his grave."

"For the grave of a pope?" Sarah said. Her surprise made Hugo laugh richly.

The air was humid. Stars began to appear in the night sky. "Do we know where we are?" Sarah asked.

"Not a clue," Hugo said.

"I thought you were leading." That was a futile hope; he was merely walking, but it didn't matter because Sarah was in the same frame of mind, happy to wander. They passed through a pedestrian tunnel to an exclusive neighborhood on the other side where cars were parked along a tree-lined curb in front of a row of Italian town houses. Sarah pointed to a comically tiny automobile under a street-lamp across the street. Hugo went over to it, knelt on his shoes, leaned on the car at a jaunty angle, and waved like a dwarf.

"Perfect." Sarah took a picture.

They turned down another, wider *vicoli* that serpentined to a piazza a short distance away. Four tables, set with linen and candles, were arranged outside a small restaurant.

"What do you think?" Sarah asked.

Hugo shrugged assent. "It seems pleasant enough," he said.

A waiter standing at the entrance saw them coming, waved at

their approach and greeted them with exaggerated hospitality. *"Buona sera,* good evening," he said, and held a chair for Sarah. Hugo sat down and turned to face the piazza. The waiter handed them each a menu. "Something to drink?" he said.

"You choose," said Hugo. The waiter handed the wine list to Sarah.

"It's a good list," she said. "Do you know wines?"

"Not really."

She opened the list so that he could see it, then pointed out some of the selections. "The Tignanello '85 is a tight wine. The Barbaresco '82 is elegant. Italian reds are distinctive. What are you in the mood for?"

"Something local?"

"Here's a good one. A nineteen seventy-seven Taurasi 'Reserva.' "

"Describe it."

"Earthy."

"Earthy? As in dirt?"

"You'll see." Sarah pointed out the Taurasi to the waiter.

Hugo began to feel the influence of the Italian night as he settled back in the chair, absorbing the geometries of buildings, their windows and rooflines, their smell of cool damp stone. The piazza appeared defined by the backs of buildings that formed its perimeter, including a church. Stars shone like pinpoints above the lighted atmosphere of the street.

"You like to travel, don't you?" Sarah said.

Hugo smiled. "I like having adventures. Tomorrow we can stroll the villa Borghese."

Their waiter returned with the Taurasi and two glasses. Tourists strolled past, talking in English about Trevi Fountain, apparently nearby. Hugo moved his chair slightly to give the waiter room at the small table, to display the bottle. "Reserva," he said. Sarah nodded. He corked the bottle with swift ceremony. Sarah performed the scenting ritual. The wine poured red and rich. She tasted, approved.

When the waiter left, Hugo stretched his legs out on the cobblestones. He held up his own glass, examined its color briefly, and had a taste.

"How do you like it?" she asked.

"Very good. Different. What *is* that taste?"

She laughed, leaned forward, and said, "Barnyard."

A sudden sense of freedom rose in Hugo with the moon, its white light reflected on rooftops and on the cobblestones, and higher up made a silvery outline of the bell tower. His full attention fell on Sarah, who turned her face a little from his gaze, an abashed gesture that gave him cause to smile.

"How long have you been married?" she asked.

"Ten years."

"Happily?"

"No."

"I was married once for two years."

"Only two?"

"He wanted me to stay home and keep house for him."

Hugo chuckled. "And?"

"I didn't."

A flutter of pigeons rose in a flock up to the belfry. Their movement startled a shaggy dog who had been playing on the side of the square; he bolted down the church steps and ran full-speed up the street. Sarah turned her head to watch the dog, and Hugo's imagination followed the curve of her profile. A heightened sense of life awakened in him, intelligible and close at hand, some mysterious combination of thought and sensation that gathered momentum. He let this pleasurable wave swell and move through him until a dissonant image of Lydia intruded suddenly. Hugo turned his gaze from Sarah and peered at his wineglass where distorted images of himself were trapped.

"Did you ever love your wife?" Sarah asked.

"I admired her when we met"—an honest answer, but its coldness shocked him. Sarah's curiosity about his marriage complicated the moment. Even as he welcomed her interest, all at once he mistrusted all feelings and resolved not to allow attraction for Sarah any gain. He tore at the corner of the cocktail napkin with his fingernail, making little bits of paper which he arranged in a variety of patterns on the table.

"My marriage is a painful topic at the moment."

He picked up the bottle and refilled their glasses. "I enjoy your company," he said, but it sounded desperate and he was sorry he'd told her.

"I'm glad you do."

"Cheers."

"Cheers."

The wine was exceptionally good. Hugo held his glass to the candle to study its color. He felt quite apart from the present misery in his marriage, as though suddenly he'd stepped into a different skin. He felt—well, he felt free. A motorbike wheeled around the corner. The sound of it seemed to hover in the night air and then fade slowly. Inside, the waiter put their dinner on a tray. Hugo poured another glass of wine for each of them.

OCTOBER 18, 1994

Hugo awakened bewildered when the phone rang. The room was stuffy, his face was wet, his skin damp. Sarah had been asleep in his arms. He left the bed and went into the bathroom to give her privacy, but he could clearly hear.

"You shouldn't call, Michael.... Really, it's not necessary.... Besides, it's expensive. Yes...

"That's ridiculous, Michael. Really, you shouldn't worry about me—

"It's sweet of you, Michael, but. . ."

Who was Michael, anyway, calling her on layovers? Hugo faced his tousled reflection. His sleepy mind registered pique. "He wants to marry me," she had told him, but she had seemed rather too matter-of-fact. Hugo felt the onset of proprietary annoyance like the first vague symptoms of flu. He turned off the bathroom light and went back inside.

Dusk had faded, the room was dark, and the tall window shutters opposite the bed were thrown open to the balcony. Evening sounds invaded from the street, the frantic whine of a motorbike, an automobile screeching to a stop. Hugo stood naked in front of Sarah mouthing endearments. She waved him away dismissively. A group of boisterous tourists speaking French went by on the sidewalk below. Sarah scissored her fingers and pulled the bedsheets above her breasts. Hugo lit a cigarette and handed it to her.

"Tomorrow, late. . . . Call me on Wednesday. . . ."

Hugo went to the balcony and leaned into the night air. Lights shined on the ruins of ancient Rome, resurrecting them. He could see the Roman Forum.

"I will, I do. . . . Me, too."

Hugo turned his head to look at Sarah and laughed. "Me, too," the most equivocal expression of affection. Lydia had begun to use that phrase one or two years after they were married. Or had he begun to use it first? He tried to remember how he'd felt with Lydia at the beginning. No clear memory came.

"Good-bye, Michael. . . . I will. . . . All right—I will. 'Bye."

Sarah hung up the phone and exhaled heavily, a sigh of relief. Her eyes stared at objects of imaginary interest across the room. Hugo returned to the bed. He sat against the pillows, on top of the sheets, hands folded.

"I don't like it when he calls me on layovers. It makes me feel under suspicion."

"Well?" Hugo lit a cigarette. He saw her eyes clearly in the faint light. They were coldly thoughtful. Sarah handed him the ashtray and he put it on the bed by his side.

She grew petulant. "What am I doing with you? And we're smoking cigarettes. I don't approve of any of this."

Nevertheless, she made a place for him on her shoulder. Hugo lay with her in the pale light, his head above her breast, in her good womanly heat. A Roman breeze blew through the curtains and undulant shadows moved on the walls while Sarah stroked his hair.

"How long have I known you?" she said softly.

"Fifteen days."

Her finger traced along his arm. "Most of me didn't want this to happen."

"Less virtuous parts of you did."

"Is that so?" She shoved him playfully. Hugo wrestled over her and dragged her diagonally across the bed. He threw the sheets off, held her arms down, straddled her breasts. Her eyes watched him, a playful light shining in them; his head hovered above her, disembodied in the dark.

"What about Saturday?" he asked.

"I don't know." She looked away.

"We'll stay at the lake."

"Let me give it more thought." She bit her lip.

"We'll take the Luscombe for a spin."

"I'd have to lie to Michael." She turned her eyes to look at Hugo squarely. "I hate lying."

"Tell him you have to fly, and leave it at that."

"I'll think about it."

"It wouldn't be lying."

"We'll see."

APRIL 1, 1995

The hospital bed was his penance. Further facts had come to light and the same scene repeated itself in daydreams and in nightmares. He brought the crippled engine to maximum thrust, his hand an executioner's: a carbon steel compressor blade sheared as the left engine disintegrated, the blade pierced the cabin and cut down a couple who, only by cruelest chance, were in the wrong place at the wrong time.

At impact luggage careened through the cabin at killing velocity. The disintegrating fuselage threw off a seat pod, three passengers tumbled together and landed upright in a swamp beside the burning wreckage; dazed but unharmed, they unbuckled and stood up, astonished. Infants flew from the arms of their mothers, some to be saved by vigilant evacuating survivors. A man with a briefcase stepped out of the flames holding the son of a grief-stricken woman. He gave her the child and walked away without a word. An uninjured man stepped through body parts of his traveling companions and, in hysteria of denial, would catch the next flight to Paris. "It felt like a dream," one survivor told the press. "Only you couldn't wake up from it." It was a scene of no larger logic than that some had survived and some hadn't.

"It's the same guy!" FAA manager of flight standards William T. Cunningham slapped his desk. "Send Simmons in," he instructed his secretary. A binder of the Federal Aviation Regulations lay open in front of him, and also a page of notes he had taken from information gathered on the background of Hugo Price. The door opened and Inspector Gary Simmons entered. He sat on a black vinyl couch against the wall opposite Cunningham's desk.

"What's up?"

"What do you have on Price, the captain of Triple-Five?"

"Nothing. Clean record as far as I'm aware."

"Do you know him personally?"

"I don't think so. I've never flown with him, if that's what you mean."

Cunningham raised his arms, put his hands behind his head, and sat back expansively in his chair under a picture of earth rising on the moon and autographed photos of astronauts. "We had a call on a pilot a few weeks ago. Ex-wife or girlfriend claimed he went to work drunk. Do you remember that?"

"On the snitch line?"

Cunningham's expression darkened. "I don't like that term." He brought his arms down to the desk and sat forward in his chair, leaning on his elbows. "Wasn't that Price?"

"I don't remember, Bill." Simmons paused. "Wait a minute, I do. I talked to Danielson about it."

"And?"

"Nothing. We had the number of the caller, it was his own phone. He's had marital problems. Danielson dismissed it as malicious. The first officer also vouched for him. It *was* Price, come to think of it."

"The first officer was Sarah McClure, wasn't it? This is the same crew we're dealing with on Triple-Five. What if the allegation was true?"

"It wasn't. Most of those calls are cranks, you know that. These are professionals."

"Well, take a look at this." Cunningham threw a police report to Simmons.

"Six months ago the police nearly arrested this guy. They responded to a call at his home. They took his wife to the hospital with contusions."

"Why didn't they take him in?"

"I don't know. You find out. Also, there may be court records of other incidents. Usually a judge mandates some kind of therapy or educational program, and that's something a pilot has to disclose on his medical under the new law."

Simmons frowned. "You're pressing pretty hard here, Bill."

Cunningham leaned forward and opened his hands abruptly, "I've got a fatal accident in my jurisdiction. When a plane goes down there's a reason for it, damn it. This guy better be squeaky-clean because I'm going to follow up on anything out of the ordinary, and if I find something, I'll hang the bastard."

"What do you want me to do?"

"Get in touch with his wife. Find out if she's willing to give testimony. Find out where Price and the female lived, and how long he'd been with her."

"Why?" Simmons asked.

"A pilot certificate is invalid thirty days after the holder moves if he doesn't submit a change-of-address form."

Simmons understood that his boss, who had been a fighter pilot, harbored a certain amount of resentment against airline pilots, but he did not share that view and felt that it was unjustified. Cunningham, in his mid-fifties, believed his war record carried an entitlement. The seniority system was an airline pilot's sacred rule, but in Cunningham's view it ignored the rightful claim of war veterans who, he believed, should be hired directly into the left seat from military life. Gary Simmons stood to leave.

The last thing in the world Inspector Gary Simmons wanted to do was play private detective in deference to the exasperations of his superior. "He's the kind of a guy who deeply resents any other way of having lived but his own." So Simmons described Cunningham to his wife. "He's never got over his time as a Marine. In the phone book it says, Cunningham, William T., Lieutenant Colonel, USMC, Retired."

Traction immobilized Hugo in an awkward crucifixion while he waited for the union counselor. It was nearly eleven A.M. Where was Latimer? He began to get impatient. He wanted to learn more facts, find clarification for doubts that plagued him. He'd looked forward to this day. Latimer's visit marked the beginning of his own involvement in the accident's aftermath.

The floor nurse opened his door. "Mr. Latimer is here to see you."

Edgar Latimer came through the door in a jaunty stride, fairly beaming, and stopped abruptly beside Hugo's bed, his whole stance frozen theatrically.

"Are you up to this, Hugo?" he asked. "We can postpone it."

"No, don't do that," Hugo told him. "I'm all right, I'm ready."

"Good," Latimer said. He dropped his briefcase flatly on the side table and pulled a chair close to Hugo's bed. "I'm just going to brief you on a few issues, bring you up to date on the investigation, and give you heads-up on one or two topics."

A shrewd, obese Texan with the florid complexion of a drinker, Latimer was the union's chief attorney. He had the easy confidence of someone who had once been handsome and who still saw his youth in the mirror. His quick blue eyes were watery; his fingers moved constantly in a fidget for cigarettes he no longer smoked. A sharp style of dress contradicted his physical profile, but the contradiction somehow enhanced an impression he gave of cool courtroom competence. Union officials had been eager for Hugo to talk to Latimer.

Latimer opened his briefcase and took out some papers. Among them, Hugo saw a letter from Chief Pilot Dan Danielson. Latimer held the letter up. "This arrived earlier today. Has Danielson called you?"

"I spoke to him yesterday. We talked about the inquiry."

"What did he say?"

"He thinks they'll ask a lot of questions for the record," said Hugo. "Maybe try to second-guess my judgment, scrutinize our actions. He doesn't think pilot error will carry."

Latimer shuffled through the briefcase. "Danielson's letter was attached to a transcript of the voice recordings. Care to see it?" Latimer tossed it onto the bed.

"I'd like a copy," said Hugo.

"Keep that one."

Hugo picked it up with his free hand. Latimer sat back in his chair while Hugo gave the transcript a cursory glance. "Everything by the book," he said. "No extraneous conversation after the sterile period; good briefings, thorough checklist. It's all there."

"I appreciate that, Edgar," said Hugo. He looked at Latimer confidently.

"Well," Latimer said, "I wanted you to know, and Captain Danielson wanted you to know, that the transcript confirms proper procedures were followed. That's an important factor in these investigations. The plane had a problem," Latimer continued. "The engine exploded when you applied power. Why? We don't know yet. But wind shear is what drove you into the ground, and there's going to be a lot of speculation there. That's where they're going to probe for pilot error. I want you knowledgeable when they ask questions."

"They can ask away," said Hugo, angry suddenly. The bureaucracy of aviation found its prey at investigations. "There was storm activity, but the closest cells were nine miles away."

"We're going to check on all of that before the hearing." Latimer leaned his arm on the chrome rail that ran along the side of the bed and looked directly at Hugo. "I think several factors conspired against you," he said, adding, "This windshear, the downburst variety, is deadly stuff."

Latimer took other papers out of his briefcase. Then, using the foot of Hugo's bed for a desk, he went through the pages quickly, putting graphs and a numerical table to the side for reference. In one integrated gesture, he pulled a small pair of glasses from his jacket pocket, and opened them with a flick.

"Let me give you some background here briefly," he said, reading from a faxed report. "Wind shear has been implicated in twenty-four accidents, numerous incidents, and over five hundred deaths in the past two decades. In the summer of nineteen eighty-two, recognizing that a phenomenon existed that was little understood, the National Center for Atmospheric Research in Boulder, Colorado, initiated the Joint Airport Weather Studies project, or JAWS, to study wind shear. Sudden downdrafts from convective cells that hit the ground were discovered to be insidious, and extremely violent. Take a look at the graph on page three."

Hugo turned to it. He had seen photographs of trees flattened by these powerful, isolated winds. The graph expressed time/velocity samplings of shears recorded in the study.

"As you know," Latimer continued, "microburst is like a giant splash of air. Vertical windspeeds in microbursts are sometimes in excess of one hundred miles per hour. They discovered that they tend to form in families; in Denver, up to fifteen were recorded in one two-hour period."

Hugo gave a surprised look.

"That's right, Captain, nasty little fickle fingers," Latimer emphasized. "They are associated with thunderstorms but they can occur as far as thirty-five miles from the nearest convective cell. JAWS research determined an average burst's windspeed at fifty miles per hour, stronger than the burst that brought down Pan American 759 in New Orleans." Latimer paused. "I'm telling you all of this because it's obvious that you ran into some pretty bad shear, most likely a microburst, but we'll know more about that next week." Latimer closed his briefcase and put it on the floor next to where he sat. He moved the chair closer.

"The purpose of our meeting today," he told Hugo, "is to prepare you a little for what you can expect from the board of inquiry. As I said, I want you to be knowledgeable. Now, tell me in your own words what happened when you noticed the low oil-pressure warning."

"As far as I remember," he told Latimer, "everything was routine until the oil-pressure light illuminated and we got the ECAM warning. It took us both by surprise. There were no other initial indications. The temperature stayed in the high green."

"Did you consider that it might have been a faulty pressure indication?"

"Yes. We hoped it was a faulty indication. We accomplished the ECAM abnormals procedure, checked the oil quantity, oil temperature, and the filter/bypass for evidence of contamination. The pressure was holding at thirty-five psi, the temperature was within limits on the high side. The quantity was fine, maybe a quart or two down, it's hard to say. I only remember that it wasn't unusual. So I thought the oil filter was clogged. But we didn't get a bypass indication. I was going to keep it running at cruise and continue to Paris, just monitor the pressure and temperature closely. But all of a sudden the pressure went way down and the temperature started to rise."

Latimer gave him his full, close attention. "How far is 'way down'?"

"Ten to twelve psi," Hugo said. He continued: "But the quantity stayed the same. It didn't make sense, unless the quantity indication was wrong. We had to act with what we knew we had, which was rising oil temperature, and dropping oil pressure. We faced a potential precautionary shutdown in the mid-Atlantic. I didn't want to shut it down unless it became absolutely necessary. I brought the number one throttle to idle, and it stabilized. The pressure was twelve psi, and the temperature was right around a hundred seventy degrees centigrade. High, but by procedure we could keep it running. We were thirty-five minutes from our equal timepoint, so I turned back to Kennedy."

Latimer paused for a moment. And then he said, "I know that airports in Nova Scotia were fogged in. And I know that you deviated east from the original flight plan so that your shortest distance back to a suitable airport made your landfall somewhere between Long Island and Nantucket." He paused, a pregnant interrogative Texas lawyer silence. "Why didn't you land in Boston?"

The question, and the manner of Latimer's asking, touched a nerve in Hugo. Diverting to Boston had been an option. He had discussed it on the radio with flight dispatch. They left the decision up to him, while urging that, if he felt he could bring the aircraft back to New York, passengers would be more expeditiously accommodated on other flights.

"Weather was marginal in Boston," Hugo said. "On a night like that at Logan the visibility can go to zero at any time. New York was clearing up, and we would be handled without delay because we had an engine problem."

Hugo looked directly into Latimer's unmoving eyes. "If the weather had been better, I would have taken it into Boston. I didn't want to miss an approach with an engine out. In our circumstances Kennedy was a better choice, windy but clear." Hugo paused. "I wish I had landed in Boston. But I didn't. I took it to New York."

Hugo stared at the ceiling, suddenly overcome. Since the accident, sometimes he woke from sleeping and forgot for a moment where he was, or why. Then the memory of what had happened, the magnitude of it, dawned on him and he felt a leaden remorse. All of what he once took pride in, his personal ambition, his skill, seemed an unsavory presumption in the aftermath of the accident. Alone, he carried the burden for decisions he had made that could not be undone. Alone, he would be judged.

Latimer softened his aspect. "I'm playing devil's advocate, you understand that."

"Yes," said Hugo. "I understand. But you can't look back from the other side of fate and wonder what might have happened if things had been done differently."

"But that's just what the board will do," Latimer said quietly. After a moment, he continued. "Now, this is going to be a public hearing. What you say becomes a matter of record; it's all, technically, testimony. We have to guard against conflicting statements. The power-plant people will want to know why the oil pressure dropped. They're investigating that now. Their speculation will seek to exonerate themselves. They will wonder publicly that had you shut the engine down, and then restarted it for the approach, perhaps it might not have exploded when you pushed the power up."

"Wait a minute—" Hugo protested.

"I know, I know," said Latimer, throwing up both hands. "It's easy to Monday-morning quarterback. Technology offers no guarantees, I know that as well as you do. But that's not what passengers want to hear. When an airplane crashes it violates an illusion, and people react violently when their fears are betrayed. The average person doesn't know how an airplane flies. The average person also does not know how God rules or when he will die, but sermons and superstition influence our lives as much as anything. I'm just saying that people will continue to fly but their confidence must be restored, at your expense if need be, and I want you to be prepared for it." The counselor's Texan eyes narrowed in admonition as he spoke, but Hugo was unwavering.

In the same tradition as the sea, federal aviation regulations upheld a captain's absolute authority, and Hugo deeply believed that extraneous considerations must be discounted in emergency decision-making. It had been a governing principle throughout his career. Absolute authority, and absolute responsibility. He leveled a direct and fraternal eye at Latimer. "As long as there's some oil pressure, and the temperature is within limits, you can run any turbine engine at idle indefinitely. It's not a relevant speculation." He spoke adamantly, but he knew his sensitivity betrayed misgiving, and he knew that Latimer knew this.

"Hugo, I'm on your side, remember?"

"It's straightforward. The engine came apart when it was needed for emergency thrust." Hugo grew impatient. "Now I don't know why we lost oil pressure out over the Atlantic, but I challenge you or anyone to find me a pilot who would have shut down an engine in mid-ocean that was running within limits."

"Hugo, I agree." Latimer raised an eyebrow. Hugo took a deep breath. He understood Latimer's implication. The facts were these: An airplane had crashed under his command. Passengers in his trust had lost their lives.

"Professional flying is a mystery to most people, Hugo. Mystery stimulates the need for answers. That's what we're up against. All right, then," Latimer said, gathering his documents, closing his briefcase, "we've laid the groundwork today. Before the board convenes, we'll get into the nuts and bolts of it, the flight and voice recorder transcripts. Study your copy closely." Latimer stood, put his hand on Hugo's shoulder. "There'll be debate on contributing factors, of course; as far as I can determine, your decisions were well considered, your briefings were thorough, thank God, procedures by the book." They shook hands. "I'll be in touch," he said. Hugo nodded.

He opened the door to leave, but paused at a second thought. "One more thing," he said. He turned to face Hugo and looked at him intently. "I understand that you and your wife are divorcing." Hugo nodded and turned toward the window. "The police answered a call to your address a few months before the accident. Is that a true statement?"

Hugo looked startled. He had forgotten about the police. "How do you know that?"

Latimer shrugged. "A man has a fight with his wife and then goes to work. It's reasonable to assume it could affect his performance. Nothing destroys the ability to concentrate like divorce. I'm only asking to get a clear picture of your state of mind on the night of the accident."

"Are you trying to tell me something?"

"Maybe." Latimer picked a thread off his lapel. He seemed full of small gestures and facial expressions calculated to absorb the awkwardness of direct questioning. "There is a clear link between stressful life events and symptoms of depression. We know that depression degrades performance. But there's no empirical evidence that correlates life stresses and performance errors. The NTSB rarely cites specific events in a person's life as a contributing factor in accidents."

"The incident you're talking about happened in October. My marriage was at the ragged edge."

Latimer threw the thread to the floor. "Why the police?"

"Lydia'd been drinking. She called the police to get allies, to embarrass or anger me, or maybe just because she's crazy, I don't know.

It was the end between us anyway. I moved out in December."

"Where did you move to?"

"For a while I sublet an apartment in Long Beach. Just to get away. I haven't seen Lydia in two or three months."

Latimer rested the bottom of his briefcase on the chair beside the bed. He weighed his next question. His shrewd eyes watched Hugo closely as he spoke. "It seems to be common knowledge," he said, "that Sarah and you are something more to each other than colleagues."

Hugo wasn't sure how much he wanted to confide.

"It's no secret we have a relationship."

"Are you living together?"

Hugo turned a knowing eye on Latimer. "Lawyers know the answers to questions they ask."

Latimer shrugged.

"We moved into an apartment in Manhattan on the day of the crash." Hugo turned away and looked once again through the window at broken sunshine outside. "She's the best thing that's ever happened to me, Edgar. Best of times, worst of times." He looked back at Latimer and was about to say something but Latimer held up his hand.

"I only worry that some may wonder publicly if a relationship of a particular kind might have been a distraction, or perhaps someone might attempt to draw a moral line through professional judgment and side with what they imagine to be your ex-wife's outrage. Personal problems, any irregularity, may be considered to have influenced your state of mind prior to the night of the accident. These are the nineties, my friend, we live in a litigious, not a rational, society." Latimer gave a brief baleful chuckle.

Hugo smiled thinly.

"All right, Hugo," he said, and once again they shook hands. "You get well, now. We'll talk again when you get out of this place."

He opened the door, turned, and gave Hugo a wide smile. "Adios."

"Thanks for coming, Edgar," Hugo waved.

Sunlight fell across the floor in sharp cuts. Hugo turned his head to look out the window. From his bed he could see the edge of town through treetops. In the silence of the hospital room, he reflected on his situation. Fate was indifferent to the will of Hugo Price or anyone else, and he knew it. Most pilots fly through a thirty-year career without a mishap, which is, objectively, a remarkable achievement. What had he done wrong? How had this happened to him, and why? What *did* it mean that police had come to his home? Suddenly facts of his own life seemed to mobilize against him and he began to see how present is connected to past, and that the verdict on anyone's life carried more than a single interpretation.

Octobᴇʀ 22, 1994

Any problems getting free?"

"Don't ask." Sarah got into the car.

All week the weather had been sullen and cold, but on Friday the mist lifted, clouds broke up, and bright sunshine came through, bringing an end to the first frost of deepening fall. The land was hilly and thickly wooded off the turnpike where trees at higher elevations had turned alive with color. This part of Pennsylvania was at its season's peak. Soon this brilliance would be a memory, birds flown, leaves fallen, limbs abandoned to the howl of winter winds.

They followed a sequence of instructions—left at a stable, right at a mill, then fork right up the side of a ridge and down again into a narrow valley. "There it is," said Hugo. A small wooden sign said AIRPORT, with an arrow pointing up the hill. They made a right turn. Rough asphalt turned into macadam, and dust kicked up a whirlwind behind them in the still morning air.

At the top, on a flat clearing, small airplanes appeared in a row like giant magnificent toys. The airport had the character of a picnic grove, with a row of trees on one side and a sweeping view of the valley on the other. Hugo parked. Sarah took off her sunglasses. Autumn testified with earthy scents and air so clean and full of vivid light that living things seemed to tremble.

They walked together behind the line of airplanes tied down in a row on the grass. Once again Hugo felt what he always did when near an airplane: affinity for its fragile design, wonder at its elegance, its simplicity, its cleverness and beauty. Small Pipers, and Cessnas, and some antiques, including several biplanes stood silently in the sun. They paused a moment to study them. Then Sarah took Hugo's hand, and they followed a pebble path to an old white farmhouse. A sign, in big red letters on the porch, said, Flight School.

"Who is Robert?" Sarah asked.

"Robert Burton," said Hugo. "We were in Air Force pilot training together. He's a roving journalist. I call him a raving journalist. You'll meet him sometime."

"How does he happen to own the plane you learned to fly in?"

"I sold it to him when I quit the military. He doesn't fly it much, he's never around."

The land to the right of the house descended into a grassy swale, and there was a picnic grove among three tall trees in the clearing. To the left was the runway, with wide grassy borders on each side, and beyond that, woods. It was a peaceful, isolated location, and the airplanes made a perfect adornment. The owner of the airport, a man in his seventies, greeted them from the porch of the old house. A summer tan and a full head of longish white hair made him appear fit and younger than his years. His eyes were blue and clear and held no calculation. He introduced himself to Hugo and Sarah.

"How were my directions?" he said.

"You're pretty deep in the country here. But we found it all right.

We're on our way to the lake at Crawfordsville. Robert keeps the key with a woman near there who looks after things for him."

The man laughed. "Louise Lewis. I know Louise." He laughed again, to himself, then he pointed toward the other side of the house. Hugo recognized his old airplane, polished and shining in the sun. "Burton told me you once owned it."

"I made my first solo in that plane."

"That's what he said. He said you fly for Nation Air Lines."

"Both of us," said Hugo.

The old man smiled approval.

"You're a stewardess?" he asked.

"Pilot."

He took a step back to appraise her. "And I bet you're good, too. Funny how that is, you can always tell."

"I take that as a high compliment."

The old man looked up. "It's a beautiful day to go up and poke holes in the sky."

Hugo and Sarah walked along the fringe of grass to the pebble path that ran in a line behind the airplanes. They approached the Luscombe. A rope from each wing secured the aircraft to the ground. After Hugo untied it, Sarah helped to push it forward into the grass. It was light and easy to move. Together they examined it methodically, checking the integrity of control surfaces.

Sarah climbed inside and held the brakes. Hugo chocked the left main wheel and stood in front. He signaled to her. Then he grabbed the top of the propeller, and pulled down hard. The engine caught on the first pull. He ran around the wing, kicked the chock out, and climbed in. They were together, and when the plane began to move, Sarah squeezed his hand. Comparisons were unfair, nevertheless he made them. Lydia had always hated to fly.

Hugo taxied over the grass to the downwind edge of the field. Sarah watched him ready the airplane for takeoff. He held the control stick with his left hand and moved it in a circle as though stirring a pot. This was his final check of the flight controls. Now they were ready.

The grass of the airport was trim and green. Hugo taxied onto the narrow runway and applied full power. They gathered speed until they lifted off. The earth fell away. The plane ascended but its shadow adhered to the ground, skimming along the treetops and chasing after them like a ghost of their bondage to gravity.

As they climbed out over the valley, tiny homes in neighborhoods below gave a serene view of life on earth. Smoke from chimneys seemed painted in the air. The ground below drifted past them, and a thousand lakes flashed in the sun.

Hugo banked left and they flew west, climbing all the while. He flew the plane with a light, unconscious touch, familiar, instinctive. The engine hummed, constant and strong. They were up among birds, the rush of air in the slipstream an agreeable howl.

"In the old days I used to put this plane through its paces," said Hugo. "Do you want to play?"

Sarah grinned. "Sure."

At once the nose of the airplane went up steeply until their heels were high above the horizon. He pushed in the throttle as far as it would go and the engine whined. Then he turned fast, and the horizon twisted until they turned upside down. The left wing began to sweep around and the airplane rolled. Then the engine was silent and the ground came around to right-side-up. The sound of rushing air increased and Sarah was pressed into the seat as Hugo brought the plane to level flight, and the engine power came up again.

"Not too bad," he said.

She nodded. "Pretty good. May I try one?"

"Be my guest," he said. "It's got a big wing with a lot of adverse yaw, so don't be afraid to use the rudder."

"Yes, I noticed you dished out of that roll a bit."

"You noticed that."

"Uh huh."

Sarah took over the throttle and the stick on her side. Hugo looked left and right for other aircraft. Then, suddenly, the nose climbed until the earth was at their back. The engine roared and they went over the top. They came around and were pointed straight at the ground. As they accelerated she reduced power on the throttle. A perfect loop. They both yahooed like cowboys.

"Again?" she asked.

"Let's see a roll," he said.

"Here it comes."

She lowered the nose and added ten knots to what Hugo had used. She pitched up rapidly, and as the wing swept through vertical she hit top rudder to keep the nose high for just a moment longer until they rolled through the horizontal plane inverted. Then she swapped rudders rapidly and the Luscombe turned on the horizon with easy coordinated grace.

"You're amazing," said Hugo. "Not one in ten pilots could have done that on the first try in this plane."

"It's sluggish and underpowered," said Sarah. "Extra airspeed never hurts, and you've got to use top rudder or you'll dish out every time."

"Thanks for sharing that," Hugo looked askance.

"You want to try another?"

"No," he said. "You keep it. I'm learning."

Sarah scanned the air for traffic. Then once again the nose went up and their heels were on the horizon and they were looking straight into the sun. She pulled the throttle back and the engine was silent. He looked at her and they exchanged grins. The sound of rushing air was less as they slowed. Suddenly the wings trembled and they fell out of the sky, tumbling to the left. The earth was spinning once, twice, three times around and around. Then Sarah pushed the stick abruptly forward and stepped on the right rudder pedal hard, and at once the spinning stopped and they were diving. The sound of air was high and shrill across the wing, and he looked over at her and she was grinning as she pulled the plane up and over into a loop. The sun flashed as they went inverted through its zenith. On the way down she made a quarter turn, and then up again and over they went, and down again and another quarter turn, and up, after that two more, in a smoothly executed series of cloverleaf loops. Hugo threw his head back and shook it from side to side in laughter, astonishment, and admiration.

And so they flew along together in the small Luscombe high in the air. The sky had always been a place where dreams could be felt in real life. Climbing, turning, and falling at high speed through snap rolls, spins, and loops, they laughed like finger-painting children at the spontaneity of their own colorful geometries.

"I don't get to do this often enough," Hugo said.

"It's nice to get back to your roots again," Sarah said. "Here, you take it."

Lydia hates to fly, Hugo thought.

Hugo took control and pulled the nose up. He closed the throttle, rolled the Luscombe on its back, and dove out of inverted flight in a split-S. Sarah was the laughing passenger now, caught in the exhilaration of aerial ballet.

Now they were close to the ground. Hugo flew over a rocky ridge and then dropped low over a wide pasture, flying just a few inches above the grass. Cows ran from the noise and rush of them. At the end of the pasture he zoomed into a climbing turn, and the ground dropped away quickly. When they were straight and level again, he pulled the throttle back to cruise power. The relative calm of simply flying straight and level created suspense for more thrills.

"Here," she said, shifting position. The confinement of the cockpit made it difficult but she brought her left leg over his lap, slid over him and hiked herself up. They hurtled through the air above the hills while Hugo performed maneuvers of escalating difficulty until, sensing climax, he pulled up into a loop that took them both over the top, and the silver wing flashed in the sun as Sarah came in great waves of laughter and delight on the weightless earthward downside plunge.

"I watched you," said the old man, waving from the porch as they walked from the plane.

"She showed me a few things I didn't think could be done in a Luscombe."

"I doubt that," Sarah said. She put her arm around Hugo's waist affectionately.

"Nice three-point landing."

"Thanks," Hugo said, "I got lucky." They waved good-bye and walked to the car.

"Come again anytime." The old man waved again. Sarah turned to memorize the scene, the blaze of color on the trees, the grass, and the blue sky where it met the horizon on the lowlands past foothills in the distance. It was warm now, but the brittle scent of autumn warned of chill.

Hugo drove out past the airport perimeter. "You're good," he said. Sarah pulled her dark glasses down below her eyes. "You're pretty acrobatic yourself." Dust trailed their path down the winding road.

The big sign out front said EAT. "Home of the bottomless cup of coffee," proclaimed a sign above the cash register. Shiny stainless-steel stools stood along the counter, and dining booths looked out wide windows across the parking lot. "I don't suppose they're serving Pellegrino." Hugo slid into the first booth. Sarah sat opposite and picked up the menu, tucked between the catsup and the napkin holder.

An elderly waitress in a green gingham dress pulled a pencil from behind her ear. "Where are you all from?" she said, with professional good cheer that Hugo always felt a bit harrowing.

"New York," he replied. "Are we far from Crawfordsville?"

"Crawfordsville is about five miles further down in that direction. Not much in Crawfordsville."

"We're just stopping there briefly." He turned to Sarah. "I want to get to the lake before sunset."

"Mirror Lake?"

"I think so."

"That's the only big lake around here. It's pretty out there this time of year. Too cold for swimming, good fishing though."

By the time they reached the center of Crawfordsville, a hamlet in the foothills that seemed only partially integrated into the twentieth century, it was past four o'clock. Along the main street, houses had a fallen, unrejuvenated aspect. Shades were drawn against the outdoors. A gas station on the corner had once been a livery, it had old cylindrical fuel pumps in front, and a tin red Pegasus nailed above a block and tackle at the hayloft sliding door. They got out of the car.

"Number seventeen and a half." Hugo read the address from a piece of paper. "You wouldn't think they'd need fractions."

"I'll get some gas and groceries while you're gone," Sarah said.

Hugo nodded. "I shouldn't be long."

He walked across the street and approached a house at 17½. A rusted pink sign above the door said Beauty Manicures and Permanents.

Certain Dominican villages gave him the feeling he got here, a disturbing sense of alienation, of unknown lives and unknown ways. Timeworn signposts hung there, too. In Puerta Plata, his walks were explorations that took him past the prison near the fortress on the point, past squatters and their fires on the beach, past the madhouse where withered women smoked pipes in shadows on a dark patio, past the police station where gaffers in broken straw hats loitered on steps, and through the square where pimps and schemers lay in wait for tourists. His mind wandered there too, absorbing cheerless pastel colors on dilapidated buildings, brooding faces staring from windows, motionless from boredom, and animals and automobiles fighting for passage in the narrow thoroughfare. In that harsh sun even stones seemed alive, and there, like here, thought Hugo, somewhere in dogs' sounds, in the poultry cackle of the place, high anxiety lay beneath a slow sullen pace of life.

The porch was packed with attic junk. A woman in pink curlers peered at him from inside. He rang the doorbell and waited. The door opened and she unlatched the screen and ushered him on to the porch.

"Room, I suppose?" she said. She was dressed in a purple bathrobe.

"I was given your address for—"

"The shack at the lake?" she said quickly. "Oh yes," and screwed her eyes up, scrutinizing him. They experienced a long moment facing each other.

"Yes, well . . ." said Hugo, thinking Robert's peculiar sense of humor stood behind this choice for trustee.

"Come." She stepped back abruptly. Inside, the carpet was threadbare. The room smelled of uncharming old age, an odor of dry woodpulp and dust. Her husband sat facing away in a chair with the afternoon paper.

"What's your name?" She seized Hugo's arm. Tattered gold brocade had undone itself on her robe. Her jaw jutted.

"Hugo," he said, "Hugo Price. A friend of Robert Burton's."

"Chauncy," she said to the old man. "This is Hugo Price. He wants a room."

"No, not a room," Hugo said, correcting her. "The key to Burton's place at the lake. He said you'd have it for us here."

"Burton?" she said. "Keys. The place at the lake? You're a friend of his?"

"Yes," said Hugo. "I've known him for many years."

"What's his wife's name?" said the woman, screwing up her eyes again, authenticating Hugo's claim of friendship.

"He doesn't have a wife."

"Will you give him the bloody key!" her husband bellowed from the other end of the room, his hands clutching the edges of his newspaper tensely. He was smoking a cigar.

"I am Mrs. Lewis," the cockeyed woman said, and shook Hugo's hand. "The key is upstairs. Come."

He and Mrs. Lewis went out through the porch and around the side to a narrow enclosed exterior staircase. Hugo followed her as she hobbled up the stairs. Dreadful postcards decorated the dark stairwell walls, gamine sun-beauties waving from their long-ago youth, anthropomorphic cats in human dress. At the top of the stairs, Mrs. Lewis opened a small cabinet under the attic stairwell where a number of keys were kept. She took out the key to the lake shack and held it up, then snapped it into her fist.

"I'll need a deposit until you bring it back," she said.

Hugo pulled a ten-dollar bill from his pocket and handed it to her. She snatched it from him, then handed him the key.

She grasped the handrail and started down the stairs, paused suddenly and turned. Hugo towered over her. "It gets cold at night," she said. "You'll need kerosene." The tone of her voice carried the vaguest echo of maternal concern. Hugo said good-bye to the sun-maddened, aging Mrs. Lewis. They parted on the steps beneath the rusted sign and she disappeared back into her home, dissolving into the shadows there.

Hugo walked across the street as Sarah came out of the market holding a bag of groceries.

"What have you got?"

"Things we'll need."

"Mrs. Lewis said to bring kerosene."

They went together across the intersection to the gas station where a blond boy with long thin hair who had fueled their car stood waiting for them with a vague expression on his face. Hugo kept a quick pace, eager to get under way again. Sarah felt the same impatience and had identical impressions of the town, which seemed subdued by some fixed unbending rule of life to be a place of fallen hope and broken dreams. Sarah put the groceries into the backseat.

"Will we get to the lake before dark?" she asked. There was new intimacy in her tone. She recognized it herself. Hugo looked up. "We can make it by sundown if we leave now."

He said to the boy, "Have you got a can of kerosene?"

The boy nodded, went into the garage, and came out holding a red can. He seemed incapable of initiative, but eager to follow any order. Hugo took the can and put it in the trunk, paid the boy, and said, "Thank you." They drove west out of town, and the boy stood staring after Sarah until they disappeared.

A turn off the main road led to a fork where the pavement ended abruptly. The path curled into a wooded area for some distance, and then they could see the lake. It was just before dusk and late sun splintered through the trees, sharp filaments of light fell as silver circles on the water and made the turning leaves glow on the opposite shore.

The shack stood in a thicket of trees, twenty feet from shore. Across the yard, a rowboat belonging to the property leaned on its side against a tree. Hugo parked the car and they went across the small area of tamped earth to the shore where the beach began at the edge of the property. Hugo examined the boat. Behind him, two rain barrels filled with spring water stood against the narrow porch near firewood split and stacked in neat rows by the chimney. Sarah walked to the edge of the landing where she and Hugo stood together for a few moments.

"This is what we imagine without believing it can be true," she said, visibly moved by the spell of the scene's astonishing stillness and beauty.

A new feeling was alive between them and, granting a certain subtlety, everything around them had resonance of it. Their senses were charged with excitement, which each suppressed reflexively because joy, like grief, is unexpected and requires a period of adjustment.

Sarah went into the shack. A large fireplace dominated the interior, and though the furnishings were spare, just a table and chairs, they seemed cut from the same timbers as the roughly built cabinets in the corner, giving the room a basic coherence. Hugo went out to get their bags, and when he came back he filled two lanterns by the stove fresh with kerosene, lit them, and put them up on wooden pegs. Then he went out again to get wood. The screen door opened with a rusty groan and slammed behind him.

Sarah unpacked their clothes and hung them in the bedroom, then arranged the few homey personal possessions they had brought with them, a few books, some bottles of wine, and finally candles that she put on beams around the room. The door slammed again and Hugo tumbled an armful of wood into the hearth.

"Surprise," Sarah said, holding a bottle of Perrier-Jouet Brut. Hugo's eyes brightened. He took the champagne and went outside and put it under water in the lake to chill, then returned with another armful of wood through the door again, stacked it beside the chimney, and lit the fire. While he did this, Sarah dusted and cleaned the table and chairs. She made up the bed with clean linen then lit the candles. The wood was dry and the fire caught quickly and the room filled with the smell of wood ash as smoke rose through the chimney. Hugo stood at the center of the room while Sarah tended the woodstove and water warmed in a tin teapot.

The sun had set, and the fire brought animation to the room, making the lamplight and candle flames kin to its basic warmth. Sarah prepared a dinner snack of bread and cheese and peppers and sun-dried tomatoes. They ate quietly, with good wine. Afterward, Sarah watched Hugo as he moved to the corner of the room and sat on a stool by the fireplace and unlaced his boots. An easy intimacy with Hugo made Sarah wonder how vitality and warmth of this particular sort was absent from her relationship with Michael.

"What are you laughing at?" said Sarah from the window.

"Myself," Hugo said. "I'm laughing at myself. I was thinking how every life has noble moments and idiocies, and I was wondering how far I've come in twenty years to the ideal I held for myself."

"And?"

"I think I'm lucky I had flying in the early years. It's the only solid connection I have, otherwise I tend to drift."

There was an elusive quality to Hugo that Sarah felt in tune with. Spontaneity was part of it, and native optimism, a sense of adventure about life. Nights in Rome, flying in his old plane, here this night at the lake; it all felt right. With Michael everything was planned, or overplanned. The unexpected bothered him. His needs were strenuous and he bored her. Yet she meant to marry him! As she thought about this inconsistency anxiety grew, and all emotions lost validity for her.

"Do you ever feel frightened?" Sarah said. She peered out the window; it was dark; she seemed fixed on the darkness as if trying to find something there.

"How do you mean?" Hugo, in a sudden restlessness, got up, poked the fire and sat down again on the floor.

"My mother used to say, 'Too much laughter comes to tears.' "

"Don't you think that's a little too cute to be true?"

Sarah smiled, turned to look outside again. The fire was going well. Hugo let himself be drawn into the dancing flames and his mind wandered.

"It's so beautiful on the lake," Sarah said. She turned suddenly, her eyes brightened. "Hugo."

"Hmmm?"

"Let's take the boat out."

"It's too cold."

"We can dress for it."

"I just took my sweater off. I'm comfortable here."

"Come on," she said. "We're having an adventure."

"I'm cozy."

"Bring the lantern."

He rolled over and grabbed his boots. "All right."

Outside, the sky was clear and filled with stars, and the moon, past full, rose just above the tops of the trees. Hugo handed the lantern to Sarah while he rolled the rowboat over on its hull and dragged it the short distance to shore. Sarah fixed the oars in the oarlocks, and when Hugo got into the boat, she handed him the lantern. The boat glided away from shore. Hugo fixed the lantern in the stern and began to row, watching the dark outline of trees against the sky reflected in the glassy surface of the lake. He rowed along the shoreline, guiding their course with a light touch. At some places trees grew out of the water, their visible roots in a thick tangle.

"I'm glad I came with you," she said.

"Are you?"

"Yes."

Hugo moved away from shore toward the center of the lake where moonlight played on the surface. The wash of water on the oars was the only audible sound.

"Turn the lantern down," Hugo said.

Sarah reached forward and dimmed the light. They were bathed in lambent moonlight that outlined the edge of the boat and made silhouettes of their faces. The shoreline had a silvery definition. Hugo stopped rowing and stroked Sarah's back gently. He touched her shoulder and she caught his hand, tilted her head to the side and kissed it. He leaned forward and, holding her hand gently, kissed her. It was a long, lingering kiss, as gentle as the still night, and full of the night's unconscious seduction. When their lips parted, he whispered to her.

"What if I—I mean, what if we—" he was unable to complete the sentence.

"I don't know," she said, her head bowed. She let go of his hand and he began to row again. She felt relieved and disappointed, excited and disturbed. The boat moved slowly and soundlessly and the moon rose higher and now it was above the trees and bright stars were visible in the clear sky. Sarah's arm rested along the gunwale and her dark eyes watched Hugo while Hugo watched the moon.

Later, wrapped deliciously in a quilt, lost amidst pillows and blankets on the floor in front of the fire, Hugo poured some of what was left of their champagne into Sarah's empty glass.

"When I was a girl," she said, "I believed in a storybook world. Every child does, I think."

"I do," said Hugo.

"I know that."

"Tonight has been magical."

She felt his warm skin press against her. She fell back and took his hand under the quilt as flames lit the room with dancing yellow light and shadows leaped across the ceiling. She watched the shadows over his shoulder until he rose up, his face hovering above hers. He began to kiss her with avid tenderness, and each kiss had a separate nuance, and at each pause his eyes met hers and she saw a reflection of her secrets. And when he was inside her, she felt the same exuberant freedom that had earlier expressed itself in flight, a love of sweeping motions and rhythms, probing fascination, and a wonderful unintimidated curiosity about the unknown.

Isolated on a brown slope in the hills east of San Diego, Helen Linden's house looked like a Spanish hacienda. Stone paths wound through thickets of oleander. Bougainvillea, cactus, and hydrangeas lined the perimeter of the property. In back, topiary gardens surrounded a swimming pool built into the irregular rock to resemble a natural pond. Flowers blossomed everywhere.

Lydia went through the foyer. A maid led the way. Her footsteps echoed as her thoughts hovered on Hugo and their failed marriage. At least he had moved out, which was a relief. Now she felt free.

She emerged from the house under a wide green awning. Her blond hair was full and shining. It tumbled from under a straw hat. She carried a small blue bag and the cling of her black cotton dress outlined her legs as she walked into bright sunlight. Arthur Linden, Helen's husband, was having a swim. Bottles of champagne chilled in a silver cooler on the terrace. She put her bag down and kicked off her pumps by the glass table. Arthur waved from the water. Lydia tipped up her dark glasses and smiled broadly.

"Helen's dressing," Arthur said. "Come for a swim."

In his late fifties, Arthur Linden had surprising blue eyes, an engaging smile, and an athlete's physique, thickened slightly with age but not gone to fat. He was masculine according to Lydia's notions of masculinity, which hinged on early impressions of her father. Like her father in old photographs standing beside the Chrysler of her childhood, Arthur Linden had muscular shoulders and powerful legs, the all-around look of virile aging and obstinate vigor. Lydia had no enthusiasm for the lean profiles of modern fitness, which, like small sensible automobiles, seemed anemic and sexless to her.

"I'll have to change," she told him.

"Use the cabana."

The cabana was a separate structure with two private rooms off a small patio. Arthur climbed out of the pool and put on a white robe. He took Lydia's bag and led her to the other side.

"You couldn't have picked a better day to visit," he said. An open area with a wet bar was flanked by two dressing rooms. He opened the door to the room on the right. He reached in and turned on the light for her. She walked past him into the room, turned, and then they faced each other. He handed her the bag, then lingered for a moment in the doorway. Lydia removed her hat. She felt his presence.

"Helen's excited to see you," he said.

She closed the door on Arthur's smile.

She undressed quickly, laid her clothes on a narrow bed, changed into her bathing suit, and got a terrycloth robe from the closet. A fan turned slow circles in the arched ceiling above. A faint flowery scent came through the louvered window. All of the colors in the room were right, bone enamel, and pale blue, and yellow. Everything fresh and clean. Lydia liked order, cleanliness.

Lydia took off her sunglasses and put them beside her hat on the table. She took off her robe and draped it on the chair, aware that her figure had Arthur Linden's full admiring attention. She went to the diving board, performed her jackknife dive, surfaced with her face to the sky, and swam to the shallows.

Arthur stood in waist-deep water by the edge of the pool at the far side.

When she surfaced she said, "I was on the diving team in school." An absurd comment, she realized.

Lydia began to swim laps, a slow breaststroke at first. Arthur swam with her. She changed to a backstroke. They swam together in a loose formation until he tired and went once again to the shallow end. Arthur got out of the pool and sat at the table under the broad green umbrella. He continued to watch her.

Lydia swam for twenty minutes more, luxuriating in exercise, the opulence of the sunny late morning, the grandness of her surroundings, and the promise of a pleasant day in good company. Lydia felt Arthur's eyes on her as she moved through the water. His attention gave her great pleasure. She swam a backstroke while he opened a bottle of Brut. The cork popped audibly and champagne geysered into the pool. Arthur stood over the edge as she swam past. She stopped swimming. Arthur's masculine figure above her was large and faceless against the sun. He handed Lydia a fluted glass and filled it with champagne, then leaned down and they touched glasses. The notion of Hugo out of her life was less daunting to Lydia in California sunshine. At first his leaving had frightened her. She feared living alone. But Helen made her see new opportunities in it. She could travel at will and be herself.

Helen came out of the house. She strolled with happy nonchalance, dark hair and dark glasses dominating her appearance. She carried a large straw hat and waved with it from the portico. Long legs, high heels, and lean looks made her seem taller than she was. Lydia, out of the water, wrapped in a towel, stood under the large umbrella and bounced her head against the heel of her hand to clear her ears. Arthur handed her the robe she had brought from the cabana.

"How are you, sweetheart?" Helen said, embracing her heartily.

"I just love it here," said Lydia, expansively regarding the colorful grounds and the sky. "I needed to get away from New York."

"Did you have a good swim?" asked Helen.

"Wonderful," replied Lydia, glowing and still recovering her breath. "It's the only exercise I can stand."

"You know me, I hate to exercise," said Helen. "A massage is more to my taste. I prefer to have my muscles manipulated for me. It's so much easier." In her late forties, she was trim as a thirty-year-old. She scooped a struggling bug from the rim of her drink with a manicured pinkie nail, disposing of it discreetly with a fillip under the table.

"Would you like a massage later?" Helen asked, looking over her glasses for emphasis. "I'll call for one this afternoon."

"Let's not commit to anything," Lydia replied. "But who knows, it might be just the thing." The thought evolved into indulgent daydream.

Prosperous surroundings made Lydia feel secure, and when she felt secure she was at ease, and when she was at ease she said yes to herself. All of this was different from her life in Connecticut, her days in New York at the office, her disrupted home, Hugo. Hugo. His face came to her mind in broken parts. Well, it was too bad if divorce would cost him dearly. Lydia sat back in her chair, crossed her legs and had another sip of champagne.

"Is anybody hungry?" said Helen.

Taking silence for assent, she picked up the telephone and called her kitchen. In a few moments a parade of trays, an array of pastries, eggs, bacon, and breads began to materialize. More champagne was poured. The sun got brighter in the sky, colors in the yard grew more intensely pronounced. Lydia's mood began to shine. Joy shimmered on the surface of this best of moods.

"You're still in public relations?" asked Arthur.

"Yes," said Lydia. "With the Miller, Coruthers Agency in New York. I'm out here working on a power-plant campaign."

"The nuclear reactor they're building near the San Andreas Fault? It's very controversial," said Helen.

"California is going to need a tremendous amount of power in the next century," said Lydia. "Without the new power plant, they won't have it."

"On the other hand," said Arthur, "as an oil man, I have an interest in questioning the wisdom of nuclear power, especially here. An accident is always possible, probable as an earthquake, which is inevitable, wouldn't you say?"

"Except for Chernobyl there has never been a fatality due to—"

Arthur laughed richly and leaned forward, about to counter her, but Helen intervened abruptly. "That's a beautiful bathing suit, by the way," she said with pointed banality. Arthur retreated.

"I got it in New York last week. It's too revealing for a public beach." Arthur's consistent attention acknowledged as much. Brunch proceeded with conversation on politics, travel, and the cultural distinctions between the East and West Coasts.

"California is where overambition and undereducation meet on the beach," said Arthur.

"Remember the waiter who described a wine as, 'like the flight of a seagull above the waves'?" Helen turned to Lydia. "Eating well is kind of a religion out here, a way of holding off corrupting influences."

"Or denying that they exist," said Arthur, musing.

"Corrupting influences are everywhere," said Lydia vaguely. She brushed a crumb from her leg.

Arthur continued to steal glances at her body, but she didn't mind. Lydia was ambitious to be memorable. She relished a power she knew she had, an ability to project her voluptuous sex ambiguously to get attention. It was body language with a complicated line of nuance that changed from moment to moment.

After brunch they all went for a swim. For a while they tossed a beach ball, but soon tired of that. Helen stood under the umbrella drying herself. "I'm going inside for a book," she said. "Does anyone want anything?"

"I'm fine," said Arthur.

She took her towel and went into the house.

When Helen left, Lydia went to the cabana to comb her hair. Arthur followed her, carrying a towel. She stayed silent while he walked behind her, aware of his presence. Once out of sight of the house, he suddenly took her by the arm, turned her toward him and kissed her on the lips. She resisted, turned away from him, but not entirely, and not convincingly. He took her by the arm and led her into the dressing room.

When the door closed, his hands clutched her. When the top of her suit came down she broke away and went to the other side of the room, facing him without speaking, making no effort to conceal her breasts as he came forward again. She turned but he grabbed her from behind, roughly at first, and then relaxing, caressing her breasts with calming greed. Her protests were unconvincing; she yielded because his attack came in accordance with a certain implicit agreement that found terms in desire. She yielded at crucial moments in complicity that encouraged him. Instincts of lust were active as, by degrees, she submitted, while claiming in her mind that he forced her, and, taking her protest for invitation, he overpowered her resistance, correctly convinced that he answered her call.

When it was over, she didn't move, nor did she speak.

She lay in the shadows while he stood against sunlight that came through the cabana's window. For a prolonged moment they regarded each other in silent evaluation, not with anger or remorse, but something else that stopped short of respect. Slowly, deliberately, he retrieved their things. He put on his robe and tossed her the bathing suit. She gave him a thin smile.

In a short while Helen rejoined them out by the pool.

Bright white clouds drifted above the yard like a fleet of extravagant airships. "Sometimes it rains in the afternoon," said Helen, looking up.

"It won't rain today," said Lydia with conviction.

Arthur Linden took his sunglasses off and stood up. "Ladies," he said, addressing Lydia, "if you'll excuse me, I have to run downtown for a few hours." He turned to Helen. "I'm meeting with Gordon Slaughter. He's up from Texas and I promised to see him."

"I'm sorry you have to go," said Lydia, giving no indication whatever of what had transpired between them.

"It was a pleasure, as always," he said.

"Yes," she said.

After Arthur left, Lydia's good mood was quite intact, fueled with champagne and a proprietary feeling of triumph, not over Helen, but over Arthur.

"We haven't slept together in nearly a year," Helen told Lydia. Lydia sipped her drink. Their marriage was unstable. "He drinks when we're alone, and leaves town on business for weeks at a time." Helen looked up at the clouds again, and then out across the yard at the colorful bougainvillea.

The sun, high and hot, threw sharp shadows across the smooth white cement of the terrace. The umbrella gave shade to afternoon's broiling intensity.

"I'm lonely in the house when he's away." Helen handed Lydia a Bloody Mary. "And when he's home I'm lonely."

"It's hard," said Lydia, fingering the celery stick which she withdrew and licked clean and then bit in two.

"I have a dull existence in a gilded cage," Helen continued in a baleful tone. A slight breeze blew strands of hair across her mouth. She pulled them back with her fingers. A tawny sarong stood well against her deep tan, which she examined repeatedly at frequent intervals. "I don't think I could make a convincing argument to most people that my life is difficult."

"Probably not," agreed Lydia.

"I have things, Lydia, lots of things. But no satisfaction." Her aspect became ruminative. "That was the greatest surprise of growing up."

"What was?"

"Discovering that things, past a certain point, don't matter, that past a certain point, nobody really cares about anybody else." Helen looked away toward the view. "We're misinformed about so much."

Lydia looked out across the yard with lazy pleasure. She plucked a pitted olive from her plate and put it in her mouth. "I suppose we are."

"Why did you marry Hugo in the first place?" asked Helen, suddenly direct.

"I don't know. He was young, very handsome. He had a lot of charm." Lydia shifted in her seat and finished the last of her drink. "Maybe I was afraid of not having another chance with a man." Helen gave her a scrutinizing look over her glasses and smiled ambiguously. Lydia shrugged. "Silly, I know. Men and women are such different creatures."

"Very different."

"There are too many surprises when you grow up as a woman." Lydia put her empty glass down rather too heavily, and leaned forward, closer to Helen. "What girl could guess that regular bloodletting was the signature of womanhood?"

Helen burst into laughter. "That's exactly what I mean." Helen poured another Bloody Mary for Lydia from a crystal pitcher.

"But men," said Lydia, rolling her eyes. "Why does hair—" She became comically emphatic. "Why does hair grow out of their face?" She began to giggle.

"It's awful when you think about it," Helen agreed, and they began to laugh like schoolgirls.

Another low cloud drifted in front of the sun; its shadow swept across the lawn and ran up the oleander hedge on the high border of the property.

"I love your letters," Helen smiled. "Will you always write to me?" Lydia reached over and took her friend's hand.

"Yes. I'll always write. It feels good. I know you care about me."

"I do." She squeezed Lydia's hand, and there was a note of desperation in her manner, but her desperateness excited Lydia. It always had. Alcohol was making Lydia sentimental.

"I come into town next month," Lydia said.

"Stay here with me," said Helen. "Arthur will be gone."

Lydia took her sunglasses off and smiled. "I will."

The sun grew hot. Beads of perspiration formed on the brows of both women.

"I can't say I'm surprised, really," Helen said. Lydia raised her eyebrows. "About your divorce, I mean. Hugo is an okay guy and all that, but you two never seemed together on anything."

"I kept him around longer than I should have. I was bored into cruelty. Is there any champagne left?" Helen got up and poured them each a glass of champagne, and Lydia watched. Now the skies were clear, a very dark blue, and the sun was intensely bright.

"You're very beautiful, Lydia." Feeling Lydia's gaze, Helen's voice was wistful, then nimble and self-consciously clever. "Men are thick about certain things, don't you think?"

"Yes, about most things," said Lydia. She sat up and leaned forward to get the tanning lotion on the table but as she did this she upset her empty Bloody Mary glass. Ice cubes fell on the hot flagstone and melted instantly. She righted her glass and pointed to the lotion. "Would you mind passing that to me?"

Helen passed her the bottle and Lydia rubbed her arms, and then her legs with it. "You need some of this, too, or you'll burn," she said. Lydia got up and moved over to the chaise beside Helen, who had been lying on her stomach. "Here. Come here. Turn over. I'll do it."

She put oil in her hands and rubbed it on Helen's arms, on her legs, squeezing the flesh with her thumbs, rubbing it in deeply. Helen made no move, except to open her legs as Lydia's fingers worked their way to her thighs. She looked down at herself. Lydia moved her hands in a circular motion with a slight pressure. Helen was motionless, then she threw her head back, smiling, and made no protest when Lydia rubbed both breasts simultaneously, upsetting her bathing-suit top. "Now the other side." She turned Helen over, and removed the top entirely. Slowly and methodically Lydia rubbed her friend's back, soothing the muscles, massaging the backs of her thighs, sliding her hands under the suit bottom, manipulating, squeezing. She rubbed for many minutes, enjoying the tactile softness of Helen's skin, the contours of her body. Helen opened herself to Lydia's vigorous rubbing and gradually gave consent until she felt the bands of her suit slide down her legs. Lydia knelt and kissed her as Helen stared across the pool at the groomed green grass and the colorful oleander, feeling keen thrills in the heat of the afternoon, all of which, as they spent the next hours enraptured together, seemed appropriate to a certain balance.

HALLOWEEN 1994

*People Who Think They Look
Like Other People*

T he bar where Hugo and Robert agreed to meet was sponsoring a contest, and many of the patrons were dressed in costumes. Hugo, who didn't pay attention to dates, had forgotten it was Halloween, and the sight of makeup and masks surprised him when he went in. They sat at the bar, and a man standing near them in a big blue bonnet explained to the waitress, "I'm a Dairy Queen."

Robert Burton was Hugo's best old friend. The world opens its doors to certain persons, conferring a kind of diplomatic immunity, special license to visit its unsavory quarters unmolested, its grandest places by intimate invitation. Robert was among those so privileged, a man of action and intellect, who had bicycled through India, climbed mountains in Nepal, explored China in a small airplane with a colleague from the university, and after a stint in the military, had become a journalist who wrote spy novels on the side. "I just take the latest parliamentary dispute, create characters for each side, assign weapons and duplicitous motives, then let them go at each other. The books write themselves." A wild side beneath the studious facade made Robert mysteriously attractive. He once wired Hugo from Honduras: "Staying with Indians. Please advance one thousand dollars, I've run amuck."

Tall and slender, with straight dark hair, quick birdlike eyes, and pointed features, Robert Burton's aspect radiated observant confidence. Hugo looked up. The mirror above the bar hung at a slight angle reflecting the one opposite on the wall behind them, doubling their many mirrored heads to infinity. Hugo had just finished giving his friend an account of the fight with Lydia. He rolled up his sleeve. "Look at this. Can you believe it?"

"If the charm of youth is not knowing what comes next, the wisdom of age is the art of surviving surprises." Robert put out his cigarette. "Why do you continue?"

Hugo shook his head. "When the police came to the house, I knew it was over."

"That wasn't the first time."

"No. The first time she tried to accuse me of wife-beating."

"And?"

"They arrested her instead. I went with her to court. The judge forced us into marriage counseling."

"And?"

"We learned a few things. Lydia correlates pain with truth. I'm a pleasure seeker habituated to disappointment. I've moved out to a small place in Long Beach until I figure out what to do. I'm still on the water, but it's a different world. I'm thinking of moving to Manhattan."

"Under the circumstances I think it's wise that you moved out."

"Let me tell you about Sarah." Hugo told Robert how they met, their layovers, Rome, their flight in the Luscombe and their visit to his cottage at the lake.

"She sounds almost too perfect." Robert gave him a sharp glance.

"I know, but I have a feeling."

"What kind of feeling?"

"I know it's new, and my marriage is old, and it would be easy to confuse love with need, but it's not that. I have her blood in me. She's the sort of woman I'd be. I think she feels the same way, but it's at an incredibly inconvenient time for both of us. If it is happening, you know, if—whatever—I mean, it would be . . . Maybe I'm crazy."

The bartender, a young woman with a Raggedy Ann wig, put down cardboard Heineken coasters, took their order, and left to make their drinks. Early dinner guests began to arrive. Robert looked past Hugo briefly to watch a couple being seated; they were dressed elegantly as ghosts of the *Titanic*.

"I liked Lydia, Hugo; she was funny. Do you remember the Christmas party when she asked the piano player to sing 'Down on Your Knees" when she meant 'O, Holy Night'? But she was a particular sort of woman. You were never truly compatible."

"You don't think so?"

"She made you an adversary."

Hugo felt a bit defensive against Robert's candor. "In the beginning we had a lot of fun."

"You're the one who told me that she used sex as a shield."

"Great shield, though."

Robert laughed. Then he said, "I once fell in love with a woman, or thought I had, but she dumped me after two weeks. A love story: written, revised, edited, and deleted in four dates. I was hurt, but she was right. We had the feeling and the desire to feel it, and we wanted it, but that wasn't enough. It wouldn't have lasted."

"How do you know?"

"Because love and nothing else soon becomes nothing else. Be advised."

The bartender returned with their drinks. She put the glasses down and pushed a bowl of pretzels over. Robert raised his glass. "But what the hell. Here's to love. And nothing else."

"And never knowing what will happen next. Cheers," said Hugo. In the presence of his friend, early flying days were vivid in his mind once more, youthful enchantment and awe alive again.

Twenty years before, at Air Force Undergraduate Pilot Training, Robert would have taken first honors, since his flight scores were highest. But in the last quarter of training the commander changed ranking criteria retroactively from checkride scores to a sum of daily grades. Everyone knew that daily grades were inflated for the weaker students in order to give them confidence.

"Typical," said a furious Robert at the time. "Let's advance the blind and the halt and piss on the best and brightest." Hugo helped him to unhalter his parachute. They had just flown a mock dogfight; adrenaline was still pumping.

"You're exaggerating—and with your usual modesty," Hugo said. "Help me with this."

Robert held the risers at the shoulder of the pack and Hugo slipped out of his harness. They hung each chute carefully, side by side on the parachute rack. Then they took their helmets to the cleaning station in the corner. They cleaned the white fiberglass surface of the helmet with ammonia, then cleaned the visors with Plexiglas cleaner. Robert rubbed a spot at the top of his helmet.

"I'm an overachiever, Hugo, it's a family malady. I don't want to be mature about this. These commanders are morons."

Hugo laughed. "Tell me what you really think."

They put the helmets on pegs with the others that hung in rows on the wall like trophies. Robert pulled a cap from his leg pocket and put it on. They walked down the hall to the squadron room to fill out their flight record.

Robert held the door for Hugo. "George Buckley is ahead of me now. He can't find his dick with both hands. He led a two-ship formation through the departure track on his checkride."

"Mistakes happen."

"He'll be dropping bombs on friendlies if he ever goes to war."

"Buckley's got a reserve assignment. You'll still get first choice of aircraft, so he can't get in your way."

"That's not the point," said Robert adamantly. "They undermine initiative. They miss the point of everything. It pisses me off."

The flying day was over. Hugo and Robert filled out their daily reports and walked through the adjacent briefing room to the back exit. Base grounds appeared serene. They went across the macadam parking lot toward the officers' club on the other side of headquarters. Among trees and picnic tables, children played in the sun. Mothers sat nearby. In almost every aspect it seemed ideal, except that razor wire curled atop the surrounding Cyclone fence, armed guards stood at the gate, and everyone who worked on base wore a uniform. Identical blue sedans made an eerie impression. Each evening at sunset, like Moslems facing Mecca, soldiers and their kin stopped in their tracks as the entire base came to attention and paid homage to images of battle when amplified strains of the National Anthem played on loudspeakers as the flag was lowered. It was a scene of duty and obedience in a culture more than passing strange to those who were anti-doctrinaire civilians at heart such as Hugo and Robert.

As they crossed the main intersection by the base exchange, a sergeant approaching from the opposite direction saluted smartly. They returned the salute, though each experienced the same slight twinge of chagrin that came because neither subscribed to the rigid caste of rank sustained in the ritual. Both believed that brains mattered more than stripes or bars, and recognized that ultimately a system so rigidly conceived could only foster idiocy in the name of some loftier-sounding purpose, and manifest it in such scenes as the one unfolding across the street. A middle-aged lieutenant colonel was upbraiding two young enlisted airmen, whom he commanded to stand before him at attention in front of the movie theater. He lectured them sternly on the length of their hair as their dates stood by, embarrassed and baffled.

"Really, Robert, we have nothing to complain about," Hugo said. "Life here is utopian by every definition. We have leaders," he indicated the colonel with his thumb. "Our needs are met. We're told how to dress, what to think, where to be, whom to kill. And regulations are written down for us if we forget." Hugo put an avuncular arm around Robert's shoulder. "In a stray moment you may not remember, for example, how far below the top of the upper vermilion your moustache may extend. But reference material exists to give you guidance, manuals and codes, and real-life human beings who have made this their mission. Really, it doesn't get much better than this."

Two MPs walked together toward the headquarters building, their white riot helmets like smooth hydrocephalic skulls in bright late-afternoon sun. "You're right," Robert said facetiously, "I was confusing oppression with security."

Twenty years later Hugo and Robert could laugh about that year of training, but it was indoctrination to a world where a drumbeat sounded ceaselessly, and often pointlessly.

"The military taught me a chilling lesson," said Robert.

"Which was?"

"People crave to be ordered around, and they'll do almost anything they're told to do."

Hugo looked up at the mirror above him. He put his drink down and turned suddenly to face Robert, "Have you ever felt invisible?"

"How do you mean?"

"You look into the mirror and there's no coherence anymore, you can't see yourself."

"I felt that way in Vietnam." Robert began to notice with more interest the costumes all around them. The festive atmosphere of Halloween had grown in the last hour as more costumed people arrived for dinner. Several Rambos, an Elvis, a Batman and Catwoman, a hunchback, and the Unknown Soldier. The soldier had the bag on his head and had written "Unknown" on one side, and "Forgotten" on the other.

Hugo pointed to the soldier. "I remember my last day stateside before Vietnam, wondering how it could possibly have happened that I was being ordered out of my own country, banished from my home as if I'd committed some tribal atrocity." As he related the feelings and events of that afternoon, Robert nodded understanding. It was a time and circumstance alien to young Americans today, a choice of flight to another country, or war, or jail.

"After an afternoon of walking around I was so hot and uncomfortable nothing mattered. The war was closer to me. I went into— get the name—the Last Chance Cafe." Hugo continued the story.

Inside, the ceiling was low, forcing an atmosphere of intimacy. Small round tables and chairs surrounded a dance floor in a wide room. There was a bar on one side; on the other, The Enemy was tuning up on a small bandstand. His waitress introduced herself as Verlane Sharp.

"What kin I git you?" she asked, eyes alert with bright personal energy that didn't fake sincerity. Her face was youthful and pretty, but lines of a marginal existence were written into it, flesh was beginning to fall on her features like wax kept for years in rooms too warm by a degree.

"Vodka and tonic," he said. "Please."

The manner in which he said "please" was a civility she was unused to, but one that she appeared to appreciate.

"Vodka and tonic," she repeated.

"Thank you," he said.

Her eyes met his for an instant. "You're welcome," she said. Then she turned and walked away with just that shade of self-conscious poise with which women signal a favorable acknowledgment to men.

Meanwhile, he noticed that most of the patrons were monstrously fat. Florid men with bulging red eyes smoked incessantly and seemed ready to explode on their barstools; women whose flesh spilled out of tight clothing giggled grotesquely and fed on salted peanuts.

At the table next to his, a lone patron was turning pages in a magazine with small photographs of naked people and brief accompanying autobiographies. Hugo managed to read over his shoulder. Under a picture of a timid-looking man who, except for his nudity, might have been the mayor, was the following invitation:

"Male, 44, seeks understanding lady with one or more preadolescent daughters to share in the fulfillment of my fantasy to be the natural father of our grandchild."

And under the portrait of a smiling black man: "Near-Mensa Negro desires intelligent non-married women for clean discreet sex."

On the page opposite, a bovine woman with pendulous breasts wrote: "Rural ex-housewife, new to the city (Columbus), warm, wet, willing, experienced with animals, anxious to meet men."

Verlane returned with his drink. And a bowl of peanuts.

"Thank you," he said. She put a cocktail napkin down, and then the vodka. Wordlessly, she slouched, reached down, and stirred the drink for him, which in the language of small gestures had large significance.

More men and women streamed in after the swing shift at the refrigerator plant. The Enemy began to play an agreeable honky-tonk. Couples danced, lost in the low light, smoke, and din.

He went to the men's room. The stench was awful. The small unventilated room reeked of mortal urgencies. The floor was foul, and walls were written in scrawls of meager rebellion—LBJ PULL OUT LIKE YOUR FATHER SHOULD HAVE—and from the heart of secret cravings—I SUCK COCK. It was a place where you held your breath for as long as you could.

The last several drinks had come without request. They had appeared; she put them down and walked off, swaying confidently. Occasionally their eyes met while she worked other tables across the room. She knew he was waiting for her. The band finished their last set and the lights went up. The guitarists unplugged. The drummer began to break down his set.

"Wait here," she said, "I'll be done in a little bit."

Hugo nodded.

He got into her Plymouth Valiant, littered with plastic coffee cups, popcorn, fast-food wrappers, yesterday's newspapers, and an Odor-Eater long past its useful life hanging from the rearview mirror. Her car smelled of automobile old age, scorched fabric, oil, and gasoline fumes. She drove.

The road cut along ridges in the higher country away from town. It was pitch-dark outside, and he saw no evidence of other people anywhere. She began to tell him about her life in a drawl that was seductive and profane.

Her skirt was high up on her legs. In the faint light of the car she seemed younger, less tired, almost a teenager, with a wise teenage girl's peculiar mix of ingenuousness and precocity.

"I just got real tired of it," she said, of a marriage she'd left, of a job she'd once had, of a town where she'd lived. He put his hand on her knee and she moved it up onto her thigh. Then she put both hands on the steering wheel and smiled out the window. In this way they drove in the night through Tennessee back country and he was in the South of his imagination, a South that had always been asquirm in cabins, moaning in monosyllables, bleating from shadows alive with the hoot and holler of lustful wrongdoing.

A tale of her first husband degenerated suddenly. "When you get right down to it, most men are just a bunch of fuckheads." Hugo took "most" to mean that he was an exception.

"Why do you say that?" he asked.

"Are you married?"

"No," he said, chilled by the voltage and suddenness of the question.

"Good," she said. "I don't really give a shit if you are or not. We're both adult human beans. I just hate lies, is all."

"I have a girlfriend," he said in a seizure of imbecile truthfulness.

Her aspect darkened. "Well that's just fine, and I just bet she's your fiancée, too." With rude violence she threw his hand off from the place where it was happy and warm. Shit, he thought. It was dark outside on the lonely road they traveled, patient darkness waiting for him.

"I'm being honest," he said, unconvinced himself. Honest about what, with whom, to which purpose? The eyes of his college sweetheart shone in his mind. They'd talked of marriage and pledged fidelity, undying love.

"How long have you been engaged?" she asked.

"I'm not engaged," he said, recovering into untruth. All sacred vows swept aside in any case, if sex with Verlane was his only object, why be honest about anything? What was a stitch of truth worth in a main fabric of mendacity? These were not words in service of integrity. He told her the truth to begin with because he didn't want to be viewed in a poor light, counted by her among that other class of men who were fuckheads.

"Well that's just fine," she said again, not alluding to him particularly.

An offensive parry was called for. "Don't ask questions if you're afraid of answers," he told her.

"I'm not afraid of any damn answer," she snapped. Then her manner changed once again into the lustful country flower of the moment before. "Hell, I'm married," she laughed.

A prudent silence followed. Hugo raised his eyebrows. The moon appeared for a moment behind thickening clouds.

"Don't worry, he's away," she said, throwing him a sidelong glance with a faint smile.

He hoped so. He took that comment as an invitation to resume her thigh. Verlane's language carried words in queer syntax; they seemed to slide through her Southern lips slowly, then piled up against harsh expletives. He didn't want to talk about marriage anymore. They followed the curving road as it moved in the beam of her headlights.

"I like it when you do that," she purred, "it feels real good," and her arms stiffened against the steering wheel. "Let me feel you."

She made a sharp turn and they were bouncing down a dirt road deep in the country. Two dilapidated barns stood in a wild ungroomed swale. Tall grass tufted around boulders heaved up by years of frost and thaw; they stood in the moonlight like ancient neglected graves.

His mind fought with different images—at the bar where she worked while he waited until closing, and now as they drove to the place where she lived—in lust and anticipation, he thought of his girlfriend—his fiancée really—of what she might be doing, of how horrified and hurt she would be if she knew what he was up to with

Verlane; that he could so casually, and with such panting eagerness, forget entirely for a night recent betrothal and a true love that he held dear, and bed down with a stranger. And enjoy it. He sat beside Verlane, pressing closer to her as they drove deeper into the woods.

"It feels real good," she said again, and again her arms stiffened against the steering wheel. The road was rough; they seemed to be careening, and he was playing under her skirt with desire sprung from sardonic hope, from loneliness, from boredom; she responded with shivers and the kind of bitten thrall that has always loved to say yes to men.

"We're almost there," she said.

She turned into a narrow drive, and Hugo looked up. He saw a large old farmhouse, a barn, and a shed or small detached garage. The car stopped abruptly when they reached the yard, skidding on pebbles in the dirt, raising dust in the dark. A porch light glowed weakly above the front door. Evidence of electricity, at least, he thought.

"It's my granddad's house," Verlane said. "My cousins live here with him. I'm staying here while my husband's away." They got out of the car. He could hear the metallic ticks of the engine cooling.

"Over this way. I've got my own door."

She took his hand. He followed behind her in the near-absolute darkness like an obedient blind boy, stumbling in chuckholes.

Crickets squeaked from invisible places in the tall grass and cicadas rattled from trees at a volume strong enough to convince alien ears that, on earth, insects were rulers of night. Verlane opened a side door and they were inside at last.

Warped floorboards, peeling paint betrayed its age, but the house had a certain charm. She turned on a small table lamp with a tattered fringed shade and Hugo could see how she lived. The room was large enough to have a couch and a table. It was clean, uncluttered; in fact, it looked like a small apartment. This was her familiar space.

"I've got some beer in the kitchen," she said, but as she tried to leave the room he caught her by the hand and pulled her onto the couch. Her arms fell around him and their legs kicked out the coffee table. A picture of her husband, PFC Emmett L. Sharp, in his olive uniform with marksman's medal, toppled to the floor. Clothes flew from them. She led him from the couch to her bed.

In darkness beneath the blankets with Hugo, a sensitivity and a hunger for the physical grew. Verlane lay back while Hugo stroked her hair, caressed her breasts, and kissed her gently on the face, and he enjoyed doing these things for she was a remarkable lover, soft, intuitive, tactile, rich with the scent of sex. Finally, kneeling with head bowed, Hugo performed intimate devotions while delicious minutes passed, she moaned and twisted and stiffened with escalating pleasure, but Hugo would not unfix himself until rather violent muscular leg spasms threatened to crush his jaw, but by then she had placed hands on him like a priestess, and began to moan affirmatively, giving blessing from one who takes up snakes to one who speaks in tongues.

"Jesus!" she said. For several minutes she stared open-eyed at the ceiling. "That was world-class, Buck." Verlane reached for her cigarettes, but the pack was empty. Hugo offered her one of his Viceroys. She took one, tore the filter off, and lit it with a wooden match she scraped along the steel bedframe.

Soon it began to rain. It thundered, and it rained hard for a while, stopped, then began suddenly again. Hugo stroked the back of Verlane's head with the calm, even strokes of an old voluptuary, eyes agaze at the smooth lean lines of her back, the curve of her legs and their seductive tuck, her hair. He let his sight absorb the details of her room, her couch, her television, her clothes scattered on the floor with his, the walls in need of paint, a print of Millet's *The Angelis,* and another of a horse, and a large poster of James Dean near the refrigerator.

He lit his cigarette from hers.

Darkness and the sound of rain made them feel warm and secure, and the night had mystery.

Then she was animated and began to stroke his leg under the covers. Desire grew again in both of them. She took him by the hand and they got out of bed. She led him into the chair across the room and made him sit. Then she went to the dresser and took something out of the drawer, but she kept it hidden from view. She went over to the bed and brought back another glass of wine. Kneeling beside him, she made him sip while she held it. Then she lit a second candle and put it on the floor by the chair. Their shadows jumped on the walls in animated exaggerations. She walked behind him. She bent over him and he was looking at her face upside down.

"Feel this," she said, and a glove appeared as though floating in the dark. It felt like living flesh. She put it on and knelt once again beside the chair. It fit her hand tightly, like a second skin.

"Sit back," she said, and walked on her knees until she faced him then spidered the gloved hand along his leg until she seized him with a squeeze. Then she began to whisper insanely to the glove, ordering it to perform certain gentle caresses, coaxing and admonishing it into stroking, praising its efforts with coos and smiles and kisses as she read pleasure on his face, a demented little girl playing puppets.

Where am I? he thought. Suddenly none of it made sense. I'm buried on a farm in Tennessee, in the woods, in the mountains. He felt outside his own experiences. Yet in another way it made eminent sense. His longing of the afternoon had been answered by her need to have a man beside her this night. What was complicated about that? He felt the dim presence of deep resentment for a world that savaged such simple pleasures.

"It's funny," Verlane said, when they were back in bed. "I kinda feel like I've known you all my life, and I never seen you before tonight."

Hugo smiled at her. It seemed to be true for him, too.

"It feels good. Peaceful like. I guess I don't feel that too often. Most times men are just a bunch of—"

"I know, you told me."

"They don't know what a woman likes. Pretty things. Soft things that make it feel like when you was just a little-bitty kid."

"Like Christmas."

"Yes!" She turned toward him suddenly, nuzzled his shoulder. "You're soft." Her hand held him.

"Thanks a lot."

She began to giggle. "I mean you're gentle."

"Sometimes." He reached for his cigarettes on the bed table, got one, tossed the pack which bounced and landed upright. Verlane lit it for him.

"It's not like you're trying to prove something."

"What would I be trying to prove?"

"I don't know. Men are always going about trying to prove themselves—leastwise, I think so. Fightin' and all. Drinkin' themselves silly, as if that's a big deal. Going to war, too, and thinkin' that's somethin's gonna make them a real man. Shit, a man ain't afraid of a bullet as much as he's scared of a woman."

Hugo exhaled smoke toward the ceiling and watched it dissipate, become invisible in the dark. Every sense was satisfied. "Everyone's afraid of something, I guess," Hugo said.

"Women aren't afraid of much, leastwise women aren't afraid of the things that scare men." Verlane became earnest; she sat up against the pillow.

"What would you say men are afraid of?" Hugo asked.

Verlane looked down at him over the side of her shoulder. "Afraid of losing something, losing a fight, losing a girlfriend, losing a job. Afraid of not being a man." She took his cigarette and had a drag, then gave it back. "Afraid of not being a man, mostly." She began to draw circles on his chest. "But that's what women are for."

"What?"

"To stand by your man. Like the song says. You know that song?"

"Yes, I know that song." Hugo put his cigarette out and rolled over to lean on his arm while he talked to Verlane. She began to tickle his shoulder. "I don't think men are afraid of women."

"Bullshit," she said adamantly. "You're all he-man woman-haters amongst yourselves until you're alone in the dark. And then you want us—oh, do you ever—especially when the world ain't working right, but you hate us for knowing it."

"I don't believe that." But he did.

"Hell, I listen to the bullshit that flies between soldiers around here before they go to get their heads shot off," Verlane said with convincing authority. "It don't take brains to see they're scared. They talk up courage, that's all. Can I have a cigarette?"

Hugo passed her one from the pack. She decapitated it and put it to her lips. Hugo lit it for her.

"Women don't talk up courage," she continued. She exhaled an authoritative jet of smoke. "It's inside them from having to deal with men."

"What are women afraid of?" he asked.

"Of not having one," she said.

"What?"

"A man."

"You mean a woman needs a man to know she's a woman?"

Verlane laughed. "I don't think so, Buck." She turned to face Hugo. "A woman always knows she's a woman from the day she's born. And men know she's a woman. But there's a big difference between men and women. Men know what the difference is but they don't go deep with it."

"Why do you say that?"

"Because they've got to go around and *prove their damn selves*. All's that matters is that. To them." She looked at Hugo directly. "Men will never be mothers. That's why you're going to Vietnam, Lieutenant. The country's run by men and they want to show off how great they are. Why not beat up on slanty-eyes?" She turned and looked straight ahead and had another drag of her cigarette. "Women don't vote for wars." She exhaled. "Shit."

Often, when he felt alone in the world, or amazed at its stupidities and cruelty, Hugo would meet someone who shocked him into awareness of how others met life on its own terms with courageous acceptance. Verlane, he decided, was Fate's angel on an existential errand; she wasn't offering lessons or solutions; she wasn't on the side of sin or virtue. For that matter, she wasn't an angel at all, rather an episode summarizing life as he knew it, resonating truth in a part of himself that felt fearful.

They sat against pillows and shared the cigarette without saying anything, like an old married couple. It was very late. Suddenly, Hugo was exhausted. The silence was comforting. He reached over and turned out the light. She took his arm, put it around her waist, and held it there until she fell asleep.

In the morning when they woke, the rest of the household was up and about. The storm had cleaned the air. The sun was climbing in a clear sky; it hit the ridge in a slant from just above a hill to the east where starlings crowded into apple trees near a big rock and made a musical clamor; chickens pecked at the ground in the yard by the cars. Hugo got dressed while Verlane disappeared into another part of the house. Outside, Verlane's cousin, a young girl, was bringing her great-grandfather out to his chair on the porch.

Verlane came back and told Hugo to go outside and have a look around and she'd be right behind him. Hugo left through her door and stood in the drive, leaning against the hood of her Valiant.

The old man was seated on the porch by this time, and the young girl brought him a blanket for his legs, and now she was shaving him with an ancient electric Remington cordless that sounded like a frantic giant bee. She moved it back and forth across his chin. The old man's face was blank. She moved around him and changed the position of his head to shave his neck. Hugo watched her. She paused and squinted into the sun, not noticing him. The smell of earth and animals came up because the sun was warm and rising fast. He looked at the old man's face and began to think he saw certain faint expressions cross his features, feelings that worked to the surface as though from a great dark distance. The girl stepped back and held his chin while she surveyed his beard. The old man dribbled slightly and his tongue moved, and then he swallowed.

"I'll leave you the blanket, Poppy," she told him, making another adjustment, making sure he was comfortable. "You'll be fine here for a while."

The old man looked up at her throat, at smooth young skin that disappeared into her cotton dress where full recent breasts pressed their visible outline.

Hugo looked around. Verlane came out of the house. She called to the old man and waved, but he didn't move. His eyes stared ahead. In daylight, as they drove up away from the house, the whole property—the fallen barns, rusting machinery, neglected fields, the sagging porch and the tiny figure of the motionless old man in his chair—presented a view of unrejuvenated Dogpatch. And Hugo wondered if, in the old man's staring eyes, there wasn't something of anger and disappointment in the view that each day gave testimony of a once well-worked property gone to seed directly following his own decline. But then he thought that maybe the stare was the old man's last rebellion, his way of maintaining dignity, facing each day without regret, complaint, or apology.

* * *

"That was nearly twenty years ago, but it's as clear in my mind as if it were yesterday." The din of cocktail hour had abated somewhat but the festive atmosphere of Halloween remained unsullied. Hugo paused, and had a sip of his drink, then said to Robert, "You don't know when the last day of childhood happens, or the first day of adulthood, but there are days that reach moments when you know afterwards your life is different. I knew that going to war meant leaving the life I had come from forever, and that there was no going back to it."

A man dressed as Richard Nixon sat down next to Robert and gave the bartender his famous two-handed victory sign. "I cannot tell a lie," he said, "I didn't do it." Hugo looked up and caught a glimpse of his doubled reflection in the mirror above the bar, an accordion row of hundreds of himself, an image of his million moments.

arah sat on the living-room couch barefoot, legs tucked under her, with her second cup of coffee. In the yard, the clamor of lawn-mowing stopped abruptly and the morning returned to peaceful silence. The neighbor boy dragged his mower from the far end of her yard to the driveway by the back door. Sarah got up, went to the kitchen, and opened the door as he approached.

"Is six dollars okay?" Wide, dark, boy eyes petitioned her hopefully.

"Here's eight, Drew," she said. "Come back whenever you think it needs a trim." The boy smiled broadly and left.

She had been on the phone with her mother all morning.

"I'm still in shock." Her composure began to break. She fought it. "I don't want you to worry about me. I'm fine. I just need time alone to think."

"Sarah," her mother said, "won't you give some consideration to what we discussed?"

"Resign? Mother, I . . . You *really* don't understand." Sarah's voice trailed off. It was just the sort of aggravating suggestion that hampered their relationship. Her mother lived in the world of daytime television; she never had and never would understand what flying was, how it felt to fly, the reality of it, what Sarah's life was like. "Yes," Sarah had said finally, "I will give it thought."

If the crash had wrecked comfortable assumptions, clarity had come to her as well, a passive saneness that saw average events as miracles. She sat on the couch, safe, silent, surrounded by her familiar things, her logical mind bewildered by events. Until the accident there had been no tragedies in her life. All at once she was a vulnerable mortal creature with a measurable number of days left to live. She couldn't waste them.

The accident accelerated a fretful thought process begun soon after she had met Hugo. During October and November she'd come to believe that Hugo was a fine last fling before the serious business of life should begin. He was married, he was safe. They flew a trip to London in December, and met for dinner in New York on two occasions, but she spent Christmas with Michael in Vermont, and on New Year's Day, he'd asked her to marry him. She had not given an answer, but she did call Hugo to end their relationship. Her call came as a shock.

"You're married."

"What?" he said.

"All our moments are stolen," she said.

"I can't talk about this on the telephone," he said.

"That's what I mean. Isn't it obvious?" Nothing was obvious.

"Can we talk tomorrow?"

"Are you listening to me?"

"I'm listening. Meet me tomorrow."

"I don't see—"

"At the Indian place."

"What time?"

"Two o'clock." She had not wanted to meet with him, but yet found it impossible to be harsh or unreasonable.

It was a restaurant in Queens where they had taken meals after flying in from Europe. Hugo sat alone at a table in the corner. It had begun to rain. He saw Sarah walk past the window quickly, holding an umbrella. The sight of her sent a nervous shock through him. He stood when she came through the door. The place was empty, and when they sat down together, her restless glances and evasions hardened into a dour aspect.

A waiter brought them a menu and a carafe of wine. Hugo declined the menu. "She'll order for both of us." The Indian smiled and bowed politely. He handed her the menu then poured some wine in her glass. She approved the wine and he filled both glasses. He nodded again and disappeared.

Hugo leaned across the narrow table. "How well do you think he knows you?"

"How well do *you* think you know me?" Love made it impossible to know anyone.

Hugo's voice lost its edge. "Why are you doing this?"

She leaned into the space between them. "I can't lie anymore—" She cut herself off, then shook her head and sat back, looking him squarely in the eye. "I can't keep this up. And why should I?" Her prickly manner put him in mind of a racehorse balking at the gate, restless, assertive, poised, magnificent. The waiter reappeared and put down a plate of seeded wafers and several pepper sauces.

"How hot is it?" Sarah asked.

"Very hot, madam, today," he said. "Perhaps you prefer something milder?"

"No," she said, then turned to Hugo. "Try this."

She took a wafer and filled it with pepper sauce and handed it to him. He put it whole into his mouth. The taste acted quickly, his tongue caught fire and his eyes watered.

"Hot?" she said.

"Very."

Now he made one and fed it to her. They both took wine. The peppers were hot and good and they finished the plate and called for more and for more wine. Sarah took a cigarette from her purse and lit it. No words passed between them. Outside, the rain began to come down hard. The waiter watched them from a corner. It was early, and, because the restaurant was deserted, they were the object of his boredom. Hugo watched Sarah finish the cigarette, and still they did not speak. Then he noticed all at once that the silence had salutary meaning, that there was nothing awkward about it for either of them, and that in fact they were negotiating not the end of their relationship, but the beginning! He saw it clearly; was it possible she didn't know?

"Is that why you called? To tell me you're marrying him?"

"Yes."

He had a picture of Michael from her occasional comments. Stolid, conventionally accomplished; at thirty-eight, divorced, a man with the usual run of disappointments.

The waiter approached their table. "Are you ready to order?" he asked, pen poised, standing upright in his dinner jacket, dark, patient, not contemptuous but sour somehow, irritated by some private matter, aggravated by the early dinner hour, the emptiness of the restaurant, or, Hugo thought, oddly, by their presence.

She ordered their dish.

"And the sauce, madam? How would you like it? Medium hot?"

"As hot as you've got."

"Very good," he said.

Dinner was labored; it came as a relief to both of them when Hugo called for the check. Sarah wouldn't let him pay the bill. He shrugged and took her hand across the table. "Is this it, then?" he said.

"Yes."

"We're finished. You won't see me?" He watched her closely.

"No." Her eyes did not look up.

"And you're going to marry Michael?"

"Yes." Now she looked at him. "And please don't call."

He put his thumb under his chin and began to tap his lip in concentration. They fell silent again. For the moment he was willing to accept that she thought this was the right thing to do. He needed time to think. They stood, he held her coat, she slipped into it, he handed her the umbrella and they kissed once more at the door, a cold, thin kiss. "You go first," he said. He watched her umbrella open and she stepped onto the sidewalk under it, and the umbrella went past the window, then she was gone.

Later, he was sure she had been asking him a question: How do you feel and what are you willing to do about it? There was also a second issue: Time counted. Her feelings for him, however strong, could be put aside if she didn't believe in his sincerity. Past a certain point, she would be lost to him. Hugo thus brooded over his feelings for Sarah and his sense of the situation until, one evening he suddenly got up from his chair and, amazed at his resolve, full of what he later thought of as mad confidence, he left his home, took a train to the town where Sarah lived, and walked from the station to her house.

There was a sharp chill in the air. His mind revved with excitement. I have to see her. The problem is she's afraid of me, afraid of my attachment to her, but maybe it's the other way around; I mean, it's fantastic and I think, LOVE, then, well . . . but she makes me feel both ways, I don't know. He heard his footsteps echo on the empty sidewalk, the buzz of a transformer overhead as he crossed a street.

Her window shades were down. A car went past as he walked between houses to her back door. The air was crisp, full of winter, his feet snapped small sticks as he stepped into her yard. High up and far away he heard the sound of an airplane flying in the night sky. He stepped up on the back porch and waited until the sound faded, then he breathed deeply the cold January air that brings longing for intimacy and desire for warmth. He knocked sharply on the small windowpane and peered into the kitchen through the narrow space where the curtains were drawn together on the door.

Suddenly, it all felt wrong.

He knocked on the door again. She was too long in coming. He knocked again, but as a blind man can sense silent threat, dread began to collect in his gut. She came into the kitchen in a robe. Her hair was uncombed. She recognized him but she wasn't smiling; she opened the door, but only a crack. Her eyes fixed on his with shock and anger and hurt and also something accusatory, restrained, but furious—it was the look of a woman submitting to violation.

"Why are you here?" she said in a cruel harsh whisper. "I have company."

Company? he thought. . . . Company?

Paralyzed, stunned for several moments, his mind began to dissolve. He couldn't swallow.

Had he been wrong?

His sense returned, recording in a blinding instant every excruciating detail of what he experienced as betrayal: over her shoulder he saw wineglasses, and the living room beyond bounced in candlelight, with harsh leaping shadows on the wall that seemed to mime demented laughter. In the weak light he could see clothing thrown over the arm of a chair, socks lying on the floor. But oddly, most exasperating to him, the door to the freezer compartment above her refrigerator was slightly open. Plumes of icy air slid down like escaping ghosts. He had an urge to burst in and slam it shut. She wouldn't open the door.

You see—wasn't it splendid?—Company was here, and she was indisposed, entertaining. The exclusion was absolute. His thoughts ran on.

She turned her head away from him and looked to where he saw the shadow of a man's head.

"I have to go," she said, meaning, *You have to go*. "I'm sorry."

"I've got to talk to you," he said urgently, almost hysterical. "Please."

It was the only thing he could think of to say. He was clutching her screen door, talking to her through the chain lock and the small space it allowed. He was breathless with anguish. He tried to think of something to do. I'm a maniac, he thought.

"I'm sorry," she said again, and this began to outrage him because her words did not mean "I'm sorry" at all but *Please leave now*. He turned to leave, hesitated, and turned back again, but the door was closed and there was no crack in the curtain. He could see his breath.

He was calm, calm as a man who murders his children on a holiday; calm, like a helpful pedestrian who in the next hour is a suicide. He stepped off the porch into the dark yard. He was calm. Creature marking territory, he felt a sudden need to urinate and stood under the tree where he watched and listened to his water fall among the leaves. Then he walked back between the houses past the light behind her window shade and walked off, entirely without direction, confused, whistling, delirious.

He began a purposeful stride, to all eyes a man intent on his destination. Outwardly, he laughed at his own misery, inside he felt like the aftermath of a bombing.

My face is a mask, he thought. I would happily watch a car crash, or a building burn, lob a rock through a window, or start a fight. A bicycle went by. You little fuck, he thought. His eyes met the eyes of a man in a car. He smiled. Good evening. Cocksucker. He was courteous to an extreme, just a snatch from criminally insane.

It was eleven o'clock. He came to the end of the street, crossed, reversed himself, walked back, turned and slammed a stop sign with his fist, then continued on, relieved somewhat, mumbling unintelligibly. In this numb state he walked out toward the edge of the town proper where two roads merged to make a three-cornered cemetery. He hurdled its fieldstone wall where, invisible in the shadows of tombstones, he paced in silence until his mind calmed down and he could think. He did not feel the cold until the first paroxysm passed, when his anguish retreated as spasms subside between bouts of violent nausea. Lucid, he listened to the sound of his halting breath, alive to his own emptiness.

He could hear movement all around him, the scuttle of rodents in dead leaves, an imagined wind, a sibilant clamor of ghosts in unquiet graves, but he was fearless. Suddenly he was on his feet again, walking, nearly running. He sailed over the cemetery wall, and carried by blind impulse he wandered again to her familiar yard where he stayed, waiting in agony until her lights went out, waiting still when the sun came up, watching the door as her company left, and then walking, circling, killing time until a decent interval had passed and he could return to salvage his relationship with her. Memories crowded his mind, images of tender moments, of Rome, of the Luscombe, of lovemaking at the lake. He knew he loved her, and if that's what she wanted him to know, he was certain of it now. He loved her and he needed her, and because he needed her, he was vulnerable to her, and because he was vulnerable, he resented her. He straddled the thin troubled line between aggression and submission.

At eight o'clock in the morning, under a gray lusterless sky, he walked up the drive behind Sarah's house. He saw her on the small porch hugging her knees. She seemed wistful, as though expecting him. When she saw him she stood up and managed a faint smile. He approached slowly, resolutely.

"I'm sorry, Hugo," Sarah said. She sat down again. He remained standing. For a long moment he stood over her in exasperated silence. She waited. He didn't know what to say. His anger bewildered him.

"Do feelings count?" he said.

"Maybe only yours do." She faced him.

His aspect darkened. "I can't turn feelings on and off, Sarah. Out of nowhere, you called me up to tell me to forget everything. What kind of bullshit is that?" Yet while he said these things, another part of him noticed that anger was an intimate form; she watched him closely, and even if words tumbled from him stupidly, incoherently, her hurt eyes drew him into her calm, and they seemed together there, untroubled, while the clash of their personalities swirled.

"Why did you come over last night? We had an agreement."

He picked up a stone and threw it across the yard. His attention strayed to other goings-on: pigeons moaning in clusters under the garage roof, a dog in the next driveway tearing at a stick, trees with thin limbs scratching a colorless sky.

"You had no right to come over like that. I needed time away from you."

"To get married!" Hugo said, exasperated.

"You told me you'd respect that."

"Well, I don't."

She turned away from him. She wheeled around suddenly, and shouted, "Fuck You!"

Her words hit like a fastball right to the nuts. The dog's ears went up.

Hugo had come to claim her. They both knew that, and they both knew that behind it all was a trial of passage and some kind of sexual thrill. The sun vanished entirely behind thickening clouds and the sky turned darker. Every living thing on earth was giving testimony to spiritual poverty and cruelty and something ignominious in its nature. He felt the sex of words and how they cause pain; he wanted her to feel something from him.

Sarah's eyes narrowed at the sky, and when he sat down beside her she looked at him squarely: "Do you love me? Do you really love me?"

He said nothing.

"You do, don't you. That's it, isn't it?"

His expression softened. "Yes," he said.

"Then tell me. Say the words."

"I love you!"

They faced each other silently.

"Why didn't you say that sooner?"

"I didn't know myself."

"I knew. I've always known."

"But you would have married Michael."

"I might have," she said.

He believed her. She turned and walked toward the door and he followed her.

Sarah's black cat, Pearl, appeared at the windowsill, crept down onto the chair below it, and lay curled, resting in a blade of sunlight there. That morning was their true beginning, and Sarah was astonished at how quickly life had changed. Fate evolved from choices made in an instant, bewildering alternatives that seemed to spring up suddenly from nowhere demanding decisions. And then there were the large unexpected events.

The portable telephone lying on the couch beside her rang, startling her. She reached for it.

"Hello. . . .

"Yes, Mr. Latimer. Yes, I know, Hugo said you spoke with him. . . .

"About what? . . .

"I spoke to them about it. About a month ago. It's ridiculous." She went into the kitchen to a calender on the wall by the refrigerator. Turning back the pages she put her finger on a date. "We were together. Yes. That was the night before we flew to London. I can assure you neither one of us was drinking. Yes, absurd. I thought it was a dead issue. . . .

"I see. No, I understand. I'll tell him. Good-bye."

She went back to the living room. The incident made Sarah furious because somehow she knew that Lydia had made the call. What amounted to a cheap shot could have larger implications in light of the accident. Sarah knew that she and Hugo would come under close scrutiny. They remained on paid leave until after the NTSB board of inquiry completed its investigation. But, finally, there was nothing to do but wait. In the meantime, she would spend her energies productively. Her heart and will were committed to Hugo's healing, this was her immediate concern, and she made a resolve to focus on preparing for his release. Still, this sort of slander enraged her.

She got up from the couch once again and went into the kitchen to put water on for tea. She filled the pot with tap water and turned on the gas burner. Standing by the stove, her thoughts were moving in a certain direction, but where? She seemed closer to a central insight having to do with Hugo and a view of her own life and how it had changed. From childhood forward, she had sought the world, places beyond the backyard, a point from which to find in one transcendent view some sense of life and recognize it as her own. Flying stood for yearning, the pursuit of something tantalizingly beyond reach, yet so close she could believe that another flight or a little more speed would put her in touch with whatever it was. Then it came to her at last, subtle and obvious—it was life itself she yearned for, chased after, sought in the skies, and in books she read, and in art she loved—her own life she pursued while in possession of it, only . . . only she had failed to appreciate its *magnitude*. The horizon she so often saw from a privileged altitude was the place on earth like the place in the mind where the world and wonder meet, where imagination shines for a while on the edge of vast darkness. She stood by the stove, waiting for the pot to boil, staring into the sunbathed yard.

MARCH 30, 1995

At the same time, Hugo began to feel some similar effects of the accident, the sudden horror had disoriented him. He was unused to physical injury and confinement. A nurse called the room to tell him that his wife was on her way up. He received the news with a mix of curiosity and indifference. Immobilized in plaster and attached to his bed, he felt extracted from his life, removed from its past and present.

Lydia came into the room from her own oblivion dressed a bit too formally, Hugo thought, in a rather funereal black. She fingered her pearls nervously. Her sunglasses were the sort that darken in daylight. She wore them indoors, a pretension that irritated him.

"How are you feeling?" she said. The question was ridiculous, and she knew it. He looked like a broken marionette.

"Fine."

"I brought you these, where shall I put them?"

Awkwardness ruined her poise. She strode around the bed to the window; he followed her with his eyes.

"What are they?"

"Daisies. Shall I call the nurse for some water?"

"Just scatter them on top of the bed, that will be fine."

Lydia frowned and sighed. "That's what's unfair." She put the flowers on the windowsill unceremoniously. "I came to visit because I feel sorry for you—"

"Lydia, don't feel sorry for me." Hugo spoke abruptly.

"I didn't mean it to sound insincere." She turned, craning her neck at the window, her back to him.

"I'm sure you didn't." Hugo laughed sardonically. You brought flowers."

"Yes."

"Thank you. What kind? Daisies!—as in, 'I wish you were pushing them up.' Am I misreading the message?"

"Hugo," she said, turning caustic, "you're unwell."

He looked at his left arm, extended and hanging above him. "Yes, Lydia, I am."

She walked to the foot of the bed, facing him. "I can't say or do anything right as far as you're concerned."

Hugo changed his expression. "I'm sorry. Honestly. I appreciate your coming." He tried to shift slightly but couldn't manage it. He banged his elbow and cursed. Lydia went over to the bed and put a pillow under his arm. Hugo's eyes softened; he felt suddenly nostalgic.

But his words were wrong, feelings seemed filtered through a crazed prism. "I can remember caring about you, Lydia, actually liking you."

Lydia had been leaning against the table at the end of the bed; she stood up suddenly. "Listen to how *that* sounds. 'I can remember *caring* about you, Lydia, *liking* you.' Spare me your warm memories, Hugo. I can't remember ever liking you, how's that?"

"We used to laugh," said Hugo wistfully, not now sure himself if this was satire or sincerity. He drummed his fingers absently on the elevated cast. Lydia's eyes darted. How separated he felt from her! After ten years together he knew less about her than he had at the beginning, as though they had met as intimates and over ten years had evolved into complete strangers.

Lydia turned toward the window. Hugo watched her. "I'm sorry for what happened to you, Hugo, I truly am. I was in California with Helen when I got the news."

"Again?"

"I didn't know how to think about it. I didn't know what to do. I should have called you. I should have done something." Her fingers began to fidget at the flowers.

"How's Helen?"

"Divorcing."

"Really!"

Lydia stood motionless for a moment, then said, "I wonder why couldn't we discuss our relationship."

"Which relationship, yours with Helen or with me or with yourself?"

Lydia, who had resisted his implication, wheeled around and glowered. She took a deep breath then smiled like a big benevolent nurse. "I've talked to my attorney," she said. "He'll set up a court date after you're discharged."

"For?"

Lydia cocked her head. "The divorce, Hugo. We don't have to talk about it if you'd rather not," she said.

"No. Sure, why not. What about it?"

"I want to be fair."

"So do I," he said, adding, "want you to be fair."

"You make more money than I do."

"This is true."

"I'm going to need some of it to live on."

"Then I think we should sell the house."

Lydia grew adamant. "Never."

"Part of it is mine, Lydia, don't you agree? Or is marriage a stewardship?" He gestured with his right hand, the rest of him was rooted in plaster.

"The house is mine, but you can have the air rights above it," she muttered, then laughed in spite of herself. Hugo laughed also, though he knew she was serious.

"I've talked to my attorney," she continued, "and he says—"

"Lydia, please." He was tiring rapidly. "I was wrong, Lydia. I *don't* want to talk about this now. I'll be out of the hospital in a month. I'll see an attorney. We can talk then."

"All right," she said. An awkward silence ensued. Lydia fingered her purse.

Hugo's spirits began to sink. Suddenly, as it had begun to in recent days, the shadow of the crash and the fact of his injuries, uncertainty about the future, gripped him in the pit of his stomach. Lydia went over to the sink on the other side of the room and had a drink of water from a small paper cup, then spoke to him in the mirror. "I really am sorry I haven't called or come to visit." Her reflected eyes were oddly dark and luminous, then, looking away into the distance, she said, "Did you ever think you might have done this to yourself?"

"Excuse me?"

Her eyes traveled the chrome assembly. "You've always been self-destructive."

"Lydia, *you've* always been self-destructive, not me. You're the one who—"

"Hugo, you're the one who is always reading into things, who says nothing just happens."

"This isn't something that 'just happened,' Lydia; there are reasons why it happened."

"That's what I'm talking about."

"You're implying—"

"I'm just making a statement. I'm saying that you have said 'things just don't happen,' and I'm agreeing with that."

"Stop it, Lydia."

"Don't start, Hugo."

"What am I starting?"

"You overreact and become defensive and start calling me names. You fly off the handle."

"Do I look like I'm about to fly off anything but this bed onto the floor?"

"It's the violence in you, Hugo. That's what I told the therapist. My brothers see it. Helen sees it. You have violence in you."

No one had the gift for raising ire in him that Lydia had.

"You say words that you don't mean, or don't understand, or if you understand and mean them, they are only meant as a trigger for argument. You don't love, you incite. You don't think, you argue." He paused, staring hard at her. "I'd like you to go away now and leave me alone. I'm tired, Lydia, and—" He tried but failed to resist the urge to scream. "You're annoying me, Lydia! Get out!"

Lydia huffed, picked up the daisies and threw them at him. "Rest in peace," she said and left.

Inspired too late with words he might have said, Hugo's mind entertained witty rejoinders for hours after she left. In this way Lydia lingered vividly in his daydreams. But why was he upset? Could she be right? It was a huge thought. How far backward could a line be drawn from the night of the crash into his past, and how many lines might there be? His leg began to itch feverishly under the cast.

Alone in the hospital room, whether he laughed or cried, it meant the same thing. A fly appeared above his bed again. It buzzed in circles against the ceiling. Hugo followed its crazed movements. At last, it discovered a view of the familiar world through the window. It flew in a straight line at full forward velocity toward the sunlight until it collided brutally against the glass. He watched the fly repeatedly bash against the invisible barrier in bewildered angry confusion.

At first the fight against pain absorbed his energy, the shock of injuries numbed his emotions. Then, as the boredom of hospital confinement took over, specifics of the crash began to preoccupy him. The accident loomed larger, anxiety and depression crept into his thoughts.

"Are you awake?"

Hugo had been dozing. He turned his head. Sarah's face smiled from the doorway. Dressed in blue jeans, boots, and a leather jacket, she looked healthy as an ad for cigarettes. He shook himself. "What time is it?" he asked.

"Three-thirty."

He raised his eyebrows as though confused. "I've been asleep." He squinted at the clock. Sarah came to the side of his bed, kissed him, and sat down.

"The routine is killing me. Everything is regulated. I can't move."

"You need a change of scene."

"To say the least."

"I'm having the apartment done for us." She arranged the sheet neatly at his chest.

"Decorated?"

"It will be ready when you get out."

"The cast comes off in four weeks," he said, tapping his left arm. "They're going to put a smaller cast on my right leg. I'll be on crutches but at least I'll be out of bed." He paused, shook his head. "Lydia was here today," he said.

"Lydia?" Sarah sat back, surprised.

"Yes."

"Why did she wait so long?"

"She came to talk about divorce."

Sarah leaned forward. Her expression hardened. "Latimer called me this afternoon."

"What did he want?"

"The board of inquiry is going to convene next month."

"I'll be ready," Hugo said.

"He told me something else." Sarah sat straight up in the chair to put a slightly greater distance between them. She didn't want to upset Hugo, betray her feelings, but Hugo noticed her changed aspect and said warily, "What?"

"A week before our accident, the FAA got an anonymous call on their hot line. A woman claimed you left her house intoxicated, to fly a trip after a night of drinking."

"*What?*"

"He's going to call you about it."

"An *anonymous* phone call?"

"They called Danielson. He called Latimer. Latimer called me."

"I've talked to him several times since the accident. Why hasn't he brought it up?"

"He just learned about it. He wanted to get the facts. I told him I was with you that night, which I was, and that you were stone sober, which you were. He's concerned that your name had surfaced, that's all."

"Christ."

Sarah spoke softly. "Do you think Lydia is capable of something like that?"

"Lydia?" Hugo shook his head.

"Ex-wives and girlfriends are high on the list, disgruntled neighbors. The feds are obliged to investigate every allegation. Latimer doesn't want you to be sandbagged at the inquiry."

* * *

Hugo turned to look out the window. Bound in a cast from hip to toe, immobilized and burdened with responsibility for a fatal accident, he began to question the underpinnings of a life he had taken for granted. Every day he spent in the hospital made the past seem more remote and less familiar. There were worse days ahead. Hospital smells. He hated them. The itch in his leg was maddening now. His head ached. The fly, so energetic for hours, had given up. It clung motionless, a speck on the glass, exhausted.

The board of inquiry was scheduled to begin in four weeks. His thoughts regarding the inquiry had been few, but now he began to dwell on it. He turned toward the window. Outside, the sun shone brightly, but its brilliance was absorbed by a high, thin skein of cloud. Recalling Lydia brought back painful emotions. Suddenly he was tired. He rang for the nurse thinking that perhaps she could get him a wire hanger to fashion a scratching tool, and another pill for pain. Clouds were moving in from the west; their great shadows stole the sun. His mood darkened.

Hugo dozed.

He dreamed of himself in supersonic flight, tumbling through aerial ballet, and he heard the sound of his own breathing through an oxygen mask, felt the throb of his heartbeat, velocity, freedom. He rolled inverted at the speed of sound and lowered his canopy to the cloudtop where he saw what eight hundred miles per hour looks like from an inch above a surface upside down.

He woke slowly. I was only twenty-one years old, he thought. Then the thought dawned that one day his life would end, as one day it had had a beginning. In confusions of half-sleep, his love of velocity seemed to stand for the sweeping curve of the present moment, forever arcing over past loss and future uncertainties.

The door opened and a nurse came in carrying a bedpan.

MAY 3, 1995

The large immobilizing cast was cut away and a new one was made with a rubber step that enabled him to walk without crutches, but the awkwardness of the gait made him feel self-conscious, so he took them up, though without entire dependence. Crutches or not, he was glad to be leaving the hospital. He spent hours getting ready on the day of his release, a blue blazer, red tie, and gray slacks made him feel civilized again, resurrected from his long imprisonment in bed.

"What do you think?" He straightened his tie.

"You look wonderful," Sarah smiled. The old Hugo grin came back at her.

"Let's get out of here."

He grabbed a small bag on the bed and Sarah took the larger one. They went to the end of the hall where a wheelchair stood waiting for him by the nurses' station near the elevator. He said good-bye to the nurses, and when the elevator door opened downstairs his doctor was waiting for him in the lobby. "Go easy at first," he told him. "You'll be back flying in no time." They shook hands and he waved as the electric doors swung open, and for the first time in six weeks Hugo Price felt the world again.

"Wait here," Sarah said, "I'll get the car."

"I'll walk with you."

Hugo managed the crutches tentatively, without complaint. Relieved to be free, and absorbed in thought, he didn't say much on the drive into New York City, and Sarah didn't intrude on his silence. They crossed at the Triboro Bridge to avoid construction on the West Side, and when the Roosevelt Island cable car passed above them at 59th Street, he watched it drift across the river with the fascination of a child. Sights and sounds of the city stimulated senses hungry for motion and color, and the animated scenes of daily living brought the world back to his deprived experience.

"How do you feel?" she asked.

"A little disoriented," he laughed. He laughed, though he was also close to crying. They continued down FDR Drive to 14th Street, where just past the turnoff three fire engines surrounded the front of a building. Firemen stood in a circle looking up at a woman above on the fire escape waving down at them cheerfully. Once across town in the West Village, Sarah pulled up in front of their apartment building at the corner of Horatio Street and Greenwich Avenue. Hugo got out, crutches first. Sarah took his suitcase out of the backseat and put it by the front door. "I'll be right back," she said, turning, but Hugo caught her arm and he kissed her gently before he let her go. When the car disappeared, he looked up and down the street, a little amazed that he had come to the city after nearly ten years by the shore, that this was his new neighborhood on a fine afternoon, these buildings and sidewalks, shops and restaurants—city air itself, the smoked scent of scorched meat and sweeter savors of fresh bread signifying a different life, a reincarnation. In a few minutes, Hugo heard Sarah's steps; she came around the corner walking briskly, happy.

"What a beautiful day!" She picked up his bag and together they went inside.

They took the elevator up to the tenth floor. "Wait here," she said. "I want to make sure everything's right." She went inside while Hugo stood alone in the hall, noticing that the odor there was what passed for fresh in older buildings, a not unpleasant combination of industrial antiseptic and drying paint.

"Now you can come in."

A smile broke out on his face as he walked into the living room. A broad low couch below the picture window faced his favorite paintings on either side of built-in bookshelves, the books arranged according to his peculiar system, by author and category in subjective positions of prominence. Sarah had put down her blue-and-red Chinese carpet. Potted plants in the corners, and a large potted ficus tree at the far end of the room brought life to its spaces, and she had filled the room with objects and art of her own taste.

"It's fantastic."

"You relax," Sarah said. "I'll open a bottle of wine."

Hugo lay his crutches on the floor. He let his right leg stretch out and rubbed his eyes. The past six weeks dissolved in the light, fragrant spaces of these rooms, his new home.

"Latimer called me with a final word on that anonymous call to the FAA."

"And?"

"According to him it's a dead issue."

"I don't believe that."

"Why not?"

"Because the accident will bring it to life," he said with sudden resignation. He waved his hand, dismissing the subject for the time being. For a short while, at least, he wanted to indulge in the freedom he had so looked forward to, and save the serious issues he faced for a later time.

"I'm going out to get a few things," Sarah said, when she felt he was settled. "Do you need anything special?"

"I've got everything I want." He looked at his watch. "How about dinner tonight?"

"I thought I'd make something for us here."

"Do you mind if we go out?"

"Are you up to it?"

"I want to feel human again. It will be good for both of us."

When Sarah left and he was alone in the apartment, Hugo began to feel the gravity of a grim fact looming on the horizon: the real possibility that his career was finished.

You were only as good as your last landing. Since the airline's pioneer beginning as a mail carrier in the late 1920s, no Nation Air captain involved in a fatal accident had ever regained his command as a line pilot. In Hugo's first year on the line, Captain James Bradley slid off the runway at Logan Airport and nosed a 707 into the freezing Boston Harbor. Four passengers drowned. The accident was attributed to a freak ice-fog that glazed the surface. It could have happened to anyone, but it happened to Bradley, and his unblemished record of twenty-five years was unable to stand against those fatalities. He was abruptly retired at age fifty-five.

In contemplating his status in the corporation, Hugo had no illusions. His father's experience had convinced him that a corporation was really a voracious abstraction, a collective Id that fed relentlessly on human spirit and excreted money. "When you get into business . . ." was his father's favorite preface to bad advice, a likelihood as remote as had he said, "When you shoot your first African elephant . . ."

"I will never 'be in business,' " Hugo told him, but flying airplanes was a strange vocation to his father, who had once counseled him to enter dentistry.

Management faced a public-relations nightmare. If Hugo felt the strain of his own ambivalence, he could be sure that corporate carnivores would seek a scapegoat. No one was immune to the cold dynamics of corporation machinery. Certainly the chief pilot and chairman had conferred about the crash. Danielson had made no allusion to such a conference, but sooner or later the chairman would directly involve himself in Hugo's fate, and it did not console him that the current conceit of corporate leadership was a spiritual connection to martial fiends of history.

As a matter of present fact, at precisely this moment such a meeting was taking place less than three miles away from where Hugo sat.

Captain Danielson stood as the chairman approached and they shook hands like old friends, corporate old friends, which is to say, not friends at all but unequal sibling rivals, even outright enemies. The chairman was a famously aggressive man with a sanguinary appetite for success who had, in his ten-year tenure, taken the airline to the top of a fiercely competitive field. Classically schooled, rapaciously articulate, notorious for savaging his adversaries, he had brooded over this accident, and as the NTSB inquiry approached, had ordered a meeting with Danielson in New York at the Union Club. He wanted a feel for the chief pilot's impressions. Their conversation began with ritual solicitations on family and health, but soon the chairman came to the point, for he was not a man to waste words or time on phony sentiment.

"Dan," he said, lighting the first of many cigarettes, his voice sharp and nasal, his pronunciation jabbing and with a slight lisp that retained an unmistakable touch of the street, "are you familiar with the myth of Sisyphus?"

"No, sir."

The chairman smiled enigmatically. "Sisyphus was made to roll a stone uphill, and when he got to the top, the stone fell to the bottom again, and he was condemned to roll the stone up the hill forever. It was his eternal punishment."

The chairman dragged from his cigarette deeply and exhaled through his teeth. He leaned forward. "I feel like Sisyphus, Dan, condemned by irrational events to battle endless antagonisms. Bankrupt airlines that continue to operate, upstart carriers, crippling fare wars, union intransigence—for Christ's sake, a hailstorm in Texas cost us fifty million dollars!—and on top of this the Triple-Five disaster. We were on the threshold of real profitability." The chairman finished his cigarette thoughtfully. "I'm at the bottom of the hill again."

He lit another cigarette and inhaled with a ferocity of disgust. "I have tremendous respect for our pilots—which, parenthetically, I think the union leadership underestimates." He stabbed the air.

"The pilots respect you as a worthy adversary."

"Sometimes we disagree, Dan, but we look to the same horizon. We're stuck with each other."

"I think that's true, sir."

"Our reputation rests on service and safety. We're a first-line carrier. Our customers expect more from us." The chairman sat back, jutted his jaw thoughtfully, and drew on his cigarette. "Let's grossly oversimplify: I deliver the strategy, you deliver the safety. You have the most modern fleet, the best technology, the finest training facilities and maintenance in the business."

"Agreed, sir."

The chairman flashed a cold grin. "We *had* the best safety record."

"The circumstances of Triple-Five were unique."

Coldly ironic, the chairman chuckled. "Every fuckup is unique, Dan. We can't afford to kill our customers. What have you got to present to the NTSB?" He crushed out his cigarette and lit another.

"Did you get my report?"

"I want to hear it from you. What's your strategy?"

"We'll let Captain Price testify to exactly what he saw in the cockpit when the engine lost pressure."

"What exactly did he see?"

"Low oil pressure, high temperature. He had to turn back."

"Why did the engine explode? In your opinion."

"We don't know."

"Is that what you're going to tell the board?"

"The engine people will make that determination, but it really doesn't matter for our purposes why the engine exploded as long as it wasn't a result of operator error."

"Was it?"

"No. Not as far as we can tell. Captain Price did a good job."

The chairman brought his fingertips together and stared at his chief pilot. "Landing in a swamp is missing the point of our commitment to service."

Danielson stood firm. "I think if we keep the focus on what went right, we'll limit our liability for what went wrong."

"How will that be done?"

"I'm going to emphasize training. His decision-making process was correct, all of his cockpit work was by the book, and I think if we stand behind him one hundred percent it will work to our advantage."

"What you say may be true," he said, the tone of his voice conciliatory, eminently reasonable. "But I'm afraid someone has to bleed for this one." The chairman sat back, diamond-eyed, preternaturally at ease, smiling again, enveloped in smoke.

Sarah came in, her purse on her shoulders, holding a bag of groceries. Her return brought Hugo out of a declining mood.

"I made reservations at the Black Goose for eight o'clock. Are you sure you want to go out?"

"I do, yes," he said.

But by the time they got to the restaurant equivocation had entered into his manner. His eyes looked past her shoulder uneasily, and he would begin to light a cigarette, and then stop, or light it, and put it out immediately. He patted his jacket, looking for a lighter.

"It's here." Sarah pointed to where it lay on the table by the candle in front of him.

They sat in a raised alcove off the main room facing the bar. The slight elevation gave the table an advantage over all the others in the room.

"Do you really like the apartment?"

"I love it," he said.

"Will you be happy in the city?"

"Will you?"

"It's a new beginning for us. I'm excited."

Hugo smiled. "Once I lived in a house that looked perfect from a boat," he laughed. "It wasn't. I used to look out across the water expecting to see something, maybe find an answer. I didn't. Here, I look at all the lights and imagine that everyone else is having a better time. They aren't. I don't think it's where you live, but how you feel."

"How do you feel?"

He took her hand into his. "The next couple of weeks are going to be hell, you know that."

"Would you care for another cocktail, sir?"

"Some water, please." His throat was dry.

"Have some of mine." Sarah pushed her glass across the table.

Hugo took a sip and felt better. "I read over the voice-recorder transcripts this afternoon."

"They're eerie," she said.

"It brings back the experience."

"Completely."

The restaurant was filling quickly and the voices of other people around them rose. Words floated from the din and were lost again. Who are these people? Hugo thought. The room began to heave and unexpectedly his mood turned dark. Unused to crowds, he looked around with a stab of panic, looked at plates of food with incomprehension, and the idea of dining repulsed him all at once; he couldn't view eating steak as anything but cannibalism.

"Menu?" The waiter stood before them.

Seized with revulsion he threw his napkin on the table. "Sarah, can we leave?"

She sensed his discomfort. "Of course."

"I'm sorry," Sarah said, "may we have a check? It's not a problem here, we just need to leave." The waiter bowed and withdrew. Then she held Hugo's arm while he got his crutches and together they walked across to the other side and up to the entrance at street level. Outside the air was cool as they stood together on the sidewalk. Hugo took a rubber ball from his left jacket pocket and began squeezing it, a therapy for his atrophied arm.

"I'm sorry," he said. "I had to get out of there."

"Hugo, I understand." Sarah buttoned her jacket, a pale purple silk. A taxi stopped in front of them but Hugo waved it on.

"Let's walk for a while," he said. "Do you mind?"

"Are you all right?" She leaned forward a little to catch his eyes squarely, and he smiled and then he looked up to the part of the sky where the moon was visible. They walked slowly down the residential street and pale light gave mysterious distinction to each property. Ironwork on the border of tiny yards made jagged patterns against ivy that grew out of the shadows along the fronts of town houses. Occasionally a car went by fast, then slowed to stop at the light where the traffic traveled northbound. It was springtime, Thursday before Memorial Day weekend, a warm and humid night.

"Companionship," Hugo said, voicing his thoughts. "It takes root quietly. There's a real mystery in it, Sarah. I didn't know anything about it."

Hugo looked ahead as they walked, seeing not the sidewalk and the street, but himself amid flames and terrified people. Since the night of the crash his life seemed to circle and search; among the living again, he couldn't forget the dead.

"Sarah, I——" He faltered.

"What?"

"I've always felt, you know, somehow more fortunate than most people," he said. "When we met, I was strong. Even during the worst times with Lydia, underneath I felt whole. Now, suddenly, I feel—— I've never felt so——" He searched for a word, "——futile."

Sarah listened.

"When I knew we were going down, my life passed before me, like they say it does. Afterwards, nothing seemed real. Since then, I've felt like a ghost in the world." He turned and began to walk again. "Even as a ghost I don't seem to make a great difference. I haunt myself."

The vision of that night, of losing it, the feeling of losing it, replayed in each of their minds. The tail hit first. Then the secondary, violent crash of the cockpit came as the nose gear sheared. And then it was dark, and they slid in darkness as the plane disintegrated. The sound was deafening and terrifying, a prolonged, searing roar, an explicit splintering thunder like the falling of a giant tree, earsplitting, huge, inescapable, fatal. He could recall a strange exhilaration that came with a rushing sense of the end, and deep regret. Then it stopped. He felt no pain. They weren't moving—it was a miracle they were alive.

Hugo unbuckled his seat belt and shoulder harness.

"Sarah," he said. "Sarah! Are you all right?"

Certainly he was shouting, but his mind remembered it as a whisper.

"Sarah?"

Her eyes were wide open. The cockpit was intact. He climbed out of his seat and reached across the center console to shake her. "Sarah. Sarah!" Then the sound of muted screams came to his awareness. It will explode, he thought. We've got to evacuate. "Sarah, wake up." But she didn't move. He went to the cockpit door. It was jammed tightly and could not be opened. With the slow deliberation of one whose mind is moving faster than its capacity to think, he felt for the crash ax under the circuit-breaker panel. Then, with manic strength, he ripped the ax from the wall. One stroke broke through the door.

What he then saw was a sight that didn't make immediate sense to his shocked mind: a scramble of figures moved in the semidarkness of the wreck, but now there was no screaming. Like the second phase of a complicated dream, it appeared at first like chaos, but in fact, it was a movement of figures, an improvised logical motion imposed by contingencies of survival. Through gaping holes in the fuselage, through exits that somehow managed to open, through torn metal and debris, one passenger followed another up, over, around, and out of the airplane with the deftness of cats. Seconds had the magnitude of years. Flight attendants called out the way. Survivors helped each other with quick common sense, holding hands for balance, the way children will suddenly hold hands and tiptoe through puddles. It didn't immediately strike him as odd that so many had survived. It had happened too suddenly to be credible; all movements were reactive. He went back into the cockpit for Sarah. By then she had recovered from the shock and she was climbing out of her seat.

"Quick," he told her, "this way." She followed him through the cockpit door into the cabin. The rest of what happened, their escape, the explosion, was gone from his memory.

* * *

The accident was a shared experience that seemed to insist on interpretation as an abstraction, but both Hugo and Sarah resisted this. It was a material event with material consequences, something that, like the death of a friend, the mind could grasp but the heart refused to believe. They continued walking to the end of the block, then Hugo signaled for a cab. When it stopped, Sarah took his elbow.

"Let me help you."

"No, I'm all right."

Sarah held the car door open for him. He leaned on the roof and tossed his crutches into the back, then did a half turn and lowered himself onto the seat. She helped him lift his leg in then closed the door and went to the other side.

Hugo watched the passing scene as they moved south down Seventh Avenue: a black man waving a bottle in one hand staggered down the sidewalk screaming at the top of his voice to no one.

Hugo was suddenly weary. The cab slowed rapidly as the light changed to red. Sarah, turning toward him, said, "Has Latimer said anything else about the anonymous call?"

Hugo shook his head. "All he said was that an inspector named Gary Simmons had talked to Dan Danielson. Danielson assured him that he'd interviewed both of us and that the call was a hoax. He dropped it. Latimer is satisfied, but I don't like it."

Three well-dressed young couples on a frolic walked across the street in front of the cab. On the opposite corner a drug deal was going down, three men with their heads huddled making an exchange. The light changed; the cab lurched forward.

The cab turned west at 14th Street and then onto Hudson Street and stopped in front of their apartment. Hugo handed the driver six dollars through a bulletproof divider. "Keep it," he said.

Sarah helped Hugo out of the backseat. They stood together on the sidewalk for a moment as couples strolled past. A tall thin man in a Yukon cap and shirtsleeves was walking four dogs. City life was new to Hugo, another change, but not a bad one. They went into the lobby of the apartment as an approaching storm rumbled distantly.

Sarah handed Hugo a vodka and sat down opposite him on the couch in the living room. Outside, the sky grew sulfurous above buildings across the street and fat raindrops began to fall on the warm stone ledge by the open window, filling the air with a sweet smell of spring rain.

"When you told Michael you were leaving him, how did he take it?"

"His pride hurt more than his heart."

"Do you think he loved you?"

"Why do you ask?"

"I guess I've been pretty cavalier about that part of your life. I'm sorry about that."

"Don't be," Sarah said. "Michael would have been a mistake."

Hugo picked up his drink again and turned to look at the rain on the window and drops adhering to the glass. First they were stationary, then, slowly, they began to move, a race of raindrops, one after another, downward like a thing born that grows and moves swiftly through the span of a lifetime and then dies.

Sarah crossed her legs under her and sat against the corner of the couch. "Hugo, how do you feel?" she said. "I mean, how do you really feel? We have a lot coming up. Are you all right about it?"

"I don't know," he said. "I guess I'm afraid." Sarah reached over and took his hand. He made no protest. "In my life I've been good at one thing. And now everything's changed. I must have made a mistake somehow but it's unclear to me." He turned toward the window, and then toward Sarah; his eyes petitioned her. "Did I make a mistake? You can fly for years and nothing happens. Nobody knows or really cares how well you're doing the job, then something goes wrong, and all of a sudden another whole environment wrapped around the one you work in becomes visible. The flight recorder replays every movement you made, the voice recorder replays every word you said, satellite photographs show the weather exactly as it was—they could probably find you flying in it if they had to. Then you're called to a formal hearing to explain why you did what you did to a group of people who have had months to speculate from the safety of a desk. 'Captain Price,' they'll say, or 'Sir, would you mind telling us why . . .' and you can feel something seething in them, and it's like the furious part of yourself."

"We're going to go through it together, Hugo." Sarah had strength where Hugo faltered. While resisting a judgment that would find him at fault, he fought to unearth the real truth of his situation. His pride was that he faced truth, any truth, even at pride's expense.

Lightning struck nearby with a violent crack like a cannon shot, startling them. Hugo got up and went to the other window. Rain was falling hard. There were no people in the street, only cars, and those moved slowly. The sidewalks were empty.

Pearl leaped up from behind the couch and when Hugo sat down again she climbed into his lap, where she curled up and began to purr as he stroked her gently. "She seems comfortable in her new palace."

He tried to remain positive about the hearing, believing that its clarification would bring peace of mind. He wanted to believe in himself once again in the familiar way, he wanted to rediscover his confidence and reestablish the balance of caution and risk that had been his pride and had made his life worthwhile.

PART TWO

MAY 19, 1995

The trees on the main avenue of the small village in Nassau County, New York, were thin and undernourished, but they were high and wide and healthy behind the town and along roads beyond it, giving shade and concealment to the side streets. The Flight 555 Board of Inquiry was about to convene in what a local hotel was pleased to call a "conference hall," a convertible room with collapsible walls, folding chairs and tables furnished from pallets wheeled in from storage. A public-address system and recording equipment were set in place, and microphones stood on the tables at each member's seat.

Captain Hugo Price and First Officer Sarah McClure stood together in the hotel lobby. Music leaked from ceiling speakers like the last thoughts of Lawrence Welk. Sarah, dressed in a blue suit with a high-buttoned white silk blouse, drew approving looks which she ignored utterly. A sign at the far end of the lobby directed them to the conference room where members of the board were already gathered. They went in. Hugo's nerves were taut, sensibilities raw, perception keen. They were looking for Edgar Latimer.

Hugo took private note that as a group these engineers, investigators, and enforcers, all specialists of the aerospace industry, were of a general profile that reminded him of his Air Force days. Many of the men were overweight, a corpulence of exasperation, he thought. On the other hand, a few had the trim builds of evangelical fitness, and eyes of the zealot, which, to Hugo, amounted to the same symptom. He began to perceive a distance between what they stood for and who he was, symbolized by dress. Here were short sleeves and brown ties, belled cuffs, and an array of fabrics with a chemical signature unknown before 1970. These men represented order and conformity.

Hugo could feel the room awaken as an evolving organ of authority. The board represented the thread of a narrow logic that stitched a quiltwork of cause to effect and truth to blame. It took its formal mandate from a love of closed circles, and its reconstructions looked for failure.

At last, on the other side of the main entrance, Sarah saw Edgar Latimer and Chief Pilot Dan Danielson enter through a side door. Latimer came over to them immediately and greeted them warmly, his familiar face full of confidence and cheer.

"Sarah." He shook her hand. "Hugo. How have you both been?"

"I'm glad to see you, Edgar," said Hugo.

"How are you feeling?" said Latimer, putting a hand on Hugo's shoulder.

"Nervous."

The attorney laughed. "It's perfectly normal to feel nervous."

"Good to see you, Hugo," said Dan Danielson, extending his hand. They shook hands with a fraternal emphasis that conveyed, airman to airman, support and confidence. "I'll meet you at the table."

He nodded in the direction of their chairs. "Edgar wants to have a few private words with you." Danielson took Sarah to their seats and left Latimer and Hugo alone. Edgar put his arm around Hugo's shoulder, moved him a few steps to the right, a gesture that simulates privacy in a public place.

"The microburst did not appear on the radar," said Latimer. "I checked the records. There was no rain, and therefore no radar return. It shot out the top of a thunderhead like a fountain of cold air. It was a dry burst. You can't stay away from something you can't see," said Latimer, winking, aware of Hugo's unease. "Try to relax."

Dan Danielson motioned to Edgar. Hugo tried to think. He tried to reason and remember. Latimer caught him by the elbow. "We should be seated. Adams is about to open the hearing," Latimer said. The din lowered with anticipation. They took their seats.

"Good morning and welcome," said a long and lanky Midwesterner with high, hollow eyes. Hugo had seen him drinking coffee in the lobby.

"This hearing will come to order," he continued. "I'm Clinton Adams, a member of the National Transportation Safety Board and chairman of this board of inquiry. At this hearing we are considering an accident which occurred on March fourteen of this year on approach to New York's John F. Kennedy Airport. Of one hundred ninety-two passengers and crew, forty-five people aboard were killed."

Adams' head hung forward a bit. His jacket was pale blue plaid, and his tie, a beige knit, was held to his white shirt with a gold tiepin.

"This hearing," he continued, "is being held for the purpose of supplementing facts, conditions, and circumstances discovered during the investigation of the accident scene. This process will assist the Safety Board in determining the probable cause, and in making recommendations to prevent similar accidents."

Hugo watched, listened. This room, he thought, had the feel of a functional space, like a church, or a funeral home, and he felt precisely the anxious alienation that greeted him at those doors. Chairman Adams continued his preamble in a manner that, to Hugo's sense, combined the folksy nonchalance of Will Rogers with the menace of Rasputin.

"Parties present today include representatives from Nation Air Lines, the Federal Aviation Administration, the Air Line Pilots Association, and General Technologies Corporation, manufacturer of the power plant. Thank you all." Chairman Adams shifted in his seat and adjusted the microphone. He shuffled through some documents and asked an inaudible question of Dr. Alvin Crosley, who sat on his right. Dr. Crosley nodded, a man of medium build with a graying flattop and large square eyeglasses. The personality of the man was lost behind his lenses and under the severity of his haircut. Crosley murmured something, and then Adams said: "At this time I would like to call the first witness, Mr. James Hogarth. Mr. Hogarth was the investigator in charge of the on-scene investigation. You may testify from your seat if you wish, Mr. Hogarth."

"Thank you," said Hogarth, a jowly and dutiful eager good soldier, thought Hugo. Accident investigation required a certain obdurate enthusiasm, postmortem fascination.

"I arrived at the crash site shortly after eleven P.M. on the night of March 14," said Hogarth. "I and four other members of the NTSB GO Team secured the site. A full investigative team later arrived from Washington. The voice recorder confirms statements made by the captain that both engines were running at the time of the approach, although the left engine was at idle thrust, due to a low oil-pressure problem that will be explored later. At 2236 hours and 43 seconds, flight 555 was cleared for the ILS 22L approach. During the descent and initial approach, the aircraft experienced moderate turbulence. The turbulence increased in severity below two thousand feet, and the aircraft encountered severe wind shear at an altitude of nine hundred feet. The captain has stated that he brought the left engine to maximum thrust and commenced a go-around maneuver. The violence of the wind shear was pronounced, with a sudden loss of airspeed in excess of forty knots. At a point several seconds before impact, the left engine failed catastrophically, and the aircraft impacted the ground some twenty-two hundred feet short of runway 22L. As previously stated, forty-five passengers were killed. One hundred forty-seven survivors successfully exited the aircraft as it began to burn."

Hogarth's words, though accurate in their form, were inadequate to the images in Hugo's memory. He sat silently. Again, while he listened, an unfamiliar emotion swelled in him; not anger—it was more consternation, and fear.

"A line of severe thunderstorms had passed through the area forty minutes prior to the approach flown by flight 555. Three airplanes landed ahead of flight 555, and at least one report of wind shear encountered was given to the tower.

"At this time, Mr. Chairman, I'd like to enter into the public record the exhibits that will be used during the testimony here. Rather than read them, the list will be available from the court reporter. That concludes my statement. Thank you, Mr. Chairman."

"Thank you, Mr. Hogarth. Now, ah, Mr. Hogarth, in your capacity as Hearing Officer, why don't you go ahead and call the first witness."

"Captain Hugo Price," said Hogarth. "Come forward to the witness stand, please."

Hugo rose from his seat and buttoned his jacket. Using his crutches, he walked around the evidence table to a chair designated for witnesses. As he was sworn in, he felt absorbed into the indistinction of this bland hotel ballroom, its collapsible walls, its folding chairs and tables.

"Captain Price, will you please state your full name and business address for the record, sir?" asked Hogarth, in the same simple mo-

notone which a moment before he used while describing an air disaster.

"Hugo Bennett Price, care of Nation Air Lines, 445 Second Avenue, New York, New York."

"And you are employed by Nation Air Lines?"

"Yes, that's correct."

"Will you please give us a brief description of your aeronautical
experience and training background?"

"I am a licensed Airline Transport Pilot, and former Air Force
pilot."

"And what aircraft type ratings do you hold?"

"L-300, DC-9, B-727, and G-660."

"Can you tell us how much total flying time you have?"

"Roughly, twelve thousand hours."

"And how much total time do you have in the aircraft type you
were flying on the night of March 14?"

"Six-hundred twenty hours."

"Thank you, Captain. I have no further questions. I believe Dr.
Crosley will proceed with the questioning."

"Thank you, Jim. Good morning, Captain." Crosley remained
seated at his table adjacent to the witness stand. He had a number of
notebooks and papers in front of him, and he fussed with them
conspicuously. Thick glasses gave contradiction to a conceit of the
careful observer.

Hugo interlocked his fingers to appear composed. "Good morning," he said. He rested his hands in his lap. His eyes occasionally met
Sarah's.

"Sir," Crosley began, "were you the captain and pilot in command
of Nation Air flight 555 on the night of March 14 of this year?"

"Yes, I was."

"Can you hear me okay, Captain?"

"You're a little difficult to understand," said Hugo.

Crosley gave him a thin, comprehending smile.

"Perhaps you both could move a little closer to the microphone," said Chairman Adams.

"Captain," said Crosley, passing a paper to the witness stand, "this is a copy of Exhibit 3C on page seven of the exhibits document. You may refer to the document. Could you identify it, please?"

Hugo read it. "Yes," he said. "This is the station-copy flight plan of flight 555, dated March 14 of this year."

"And is that your signature at the bottom of the flight plan?"

"It is my signature."

"And it is your understanding, is it not, that this document, with your signature on it, constitutes a Flight Dispatch Release Acknowledgment?"

"It is."

"And what does that mean to you?" said Crosley.

The questions moved like a catechism. Hugo answered patiently.

"It means that I have reviewed the criteria for dispatch and accept release of the aircraft."

"Does a Federal Aviation Regulation state that you, as pilot in command, are wholly responsible and the final authority as to the operation of that aircraft?"

"FAR 91.3 establishes the captain's sole authority and responsibility, yes."

"On the day before the accident, you were off duty, is that correct?"

"That is correct."

"Could you go back, sir, and briefly recount for us your activities of that day?"

"I spent the afternoon at home."

"Was there anything unusual about that afternoon, anything out of the ordinary?"

"No."

"Did anything unexpected happen?"

"Not that I recall."

"Captain," continued Crosley, "how would you describe your relationship with First Officer McClure?"

Hugo looked directly at Sarah. "It is a good relationship."

"How would you characterize her flying skills?" Crosley bunched his lips and raised his eyebrows, facial punctuation of the rhetorician.

"She is an excellent pilot. Her systems knowledge is well above average, and she is procedurally correct in all phases of flight. She's by the book. But on the other hand, she isn't rigid. She's knowledgeable, but flexible and highly skilled."

"Who was the pilot flying that night?"

"I was the pilot flying."

"Was there anything unusual about that night before your engine problem?"

"Nothing unusual that I recall."

"What about the beginning of the flight. What was that like?"

"There was weather along the route farther north and east. We requested and got an amended clearance. It was a typical departure."

There was always a quality of the surreal to departure. He recalled the setting sun shining up against the overcast. It made the underside of clouds glow bright orange. New York City shimmered ahead in fiery silhouette. When they were cleared for takeoff, Hugo triggered the TOGA switch on the thrust computer and the auto throttles moved to takeoff thrust. The jet engines spooled up into a steady whine, and the aircraft began to accelerate rapidly along the dashed runway centerline. At rotation speed, Hugo eased back on the yoke, lifting the nose, and they were airborne. Sarah raised the landing gear at his palm-up command. The air was smooth. Tall buildings that seemed ablaze in the last minutes of sun lost their height as the aircraft climbed above them. Hugo turned south over the ocean. Sarah programmed the flight management system for their departure track. Hugo flew manually to the navigation commands of the flight director bars on the primary flight display. They continued to climb, and when they penetrated the overcast skies into clear twilight above, the city was gone from sight, but it glowed beneath the clouds, something golden, giant, and alive.

Voyaging the skies was given only to twentieth-century man to live. In an age of miracles, this was the highest magic. Hugo's hands held the controls of a jet airliner. Somehow he'd learned to fly, and that acquired knowledge now had the character of instinct. He had adapted to the iron and flint of his epoch, found in its high science a kind of perfect poetry, and lived his dream.

"Storms are forecast to the north and south of our route," he said, reaching for the printout of weather forecasts attached to the master flight plan.

The aircraft shook slightly and returned to level flight. They were just north of Boston, heading northeast past Nova Scotia toward Sable Island, their last landmark in North America. A dense fog blanketed the coastal cities from Boston north, but now the undercast began to break up beneath them. They were flying over water, moving fast. The moon was higher in the sky, its reflection shone on the ocean. Hugo squinted into the darkness but saw no indication of bad weather near their position. The radar painted a clear picture.

Sarah dimmed her instrument lights and leaned forward to look out at the dark horizon. The moon and stars were still visible ahead and far in the distance the lights of the north coast could be seen through the fog. In the moonlight below them, fishing boats were strung out in long linear formations creating the appearance of false shoreline. Farther out, in vaster isolation, the lights of rogue vessels shone below the indistinguishable horizon like fallen stars.

"It looks like we may have a quiet crossing," Sarah said.

Hugo raised his eyebrows in provisional agreement, looked at his watch, and checked the fuel. The engines were running smoothly. Reflexively, he scanned the entire instrument panel. One inconsequential switch was out of place. He moved it to its proper position, then reached forward and changed the range on the radar to 260 miles. No returns. Once again he peered ahead at the darkness. Weather in the North Atlantic was changeable.

Hugo banked to the east and checked the coordinates of their next waypoint. Sarah reported their position and made notations in the flight log. On course, on time, on fuel. Then she returned her attention to Hugo. An airplane moved in one direction on a linear path with fixed positions along the way. Life seemed to move in opposite directions simultaneously. Silent for some time, Hugo shifted in his seat, signaling the end of a private reflection.

"Nation Air Triple-Five, Boston Center." Air-traffic control was calling.

Sarah responded. "This is Triple-Five, go ahead."

"A line of storms is developing faster than expected along your route of flight. I can reroute you to the southeast and keep you clear."

Sarah queried Hugo with her eyes. He nodded.

"Keep us clear," she said.

"All right, then, pick up a zero-eight-five heading for now and I'll have clearance for you momentarily."

"Roger, zero-eight-five the heading, and we'll stand by for clearance. Do you have any ride reports?"

"An American flight reported occasional light chop."

"Roger."

Hugo picked up his chart and the flight plan. "They're going to keep us east of course then turn us north until we pick up NAT track X-ray. The winds are stronger than forecast, though, so we shouldn't lose any time," he said.

At their current position the air was smooth and the ocean calm.

That was unusual in the North Atlantic, Hugo reflected, especially in March. The hum of the cockpit was constant and reassuring, soothing as the sound of a heartbeat to an infant. They flew on as though dreaming their way.

"Nation Triple-Five, Boston."

"Triple-Five, go ahead," said Sarah.

"ATC clears Nation Air Triple-Five from present position to position N4200 W6000, thence direct position N4200 W5000, N4500 W4000, N4600 W3000, N4700 W2000, flight planned route, maintain flight level three-five-zero."

"Roger, Boston," said Sarah, and she repeated the coordinates and altitude.

"That's correct. Contact New York Oceanic now on frequency 3016."

"3016. Roger, good night."

"Good night. Have a safe journey."

Now they had clearance to cross the Atlantic. "May I see the flight plan?" Sarah asked.

Hugo handed it to her. Sarah wrote down the new coordinates on the master flight plan. Then she reprogrammed the flight management computer with the new clearance. Together they rechecked each coordinate verbally and made a notation on the master flight plan that the check had been completed. When that was done, she and Hugo selected "map" mode and scrolled their course visually on the navigation display, checking for discontinuities. There were none. Sarah took note of wind direction and velocity displayed on the primary flight display and compared these with the forecast winds, then made note of their remaining fuel and put the flight plan on the console beside the throttles.

"How are we doing on fuel?" asked Hugo.

"We're up a thousand pounds."

"And we're coming up on our next reporting point at five-eight. I'll give the report to Gander Oceanic."

"You mean New York."

"Right, New York. Good. And ask them for pilot reports along our new route, if there are any. With these winds we ought to make Paris on schedule," he said.

Hugo scanned the instrument panel and once again reviewed the flight log. He did this instinctively. A habit of vigilance fought complacency. Repetition, the repetition of checklists, repetition of flight profiles, the repetition of successful performance in the past, put a mask on complacency, and it could creep into habits of thoroughness and sound airmanship.

"Watch this," said Sarah, who seemed to be looking for something out to the southeast.

She moved the function selector switch to "position" on the inertial reference system (IRS) and displayed their current latitude and longitude, which was south and east of their original course. Then she changed modes, from automatic to remote. The remote mode of the IRS functioned as a kind of scratch pad. Any point on earth could be plotted; the computer programmed to display bearing, time, and distance information to that point from the aircraft's present position along a great circle route. She programmed new coordinates—N4144 W4956—and entered them, a position slightly south and west of where they were. The distance read six miles.

"Look over there," Sarah said. "Where the moon is shining on the water."

Hugo leaned over to look out his window, stretching to see the moonlight.

"We're six miles from the *Titanic*. That's where she went down."

Beneath the moon was a wide expanse of water, a huge emptiness where one night the great liner had heaved up and vanished from life. The survivors were left in frigid waters to live through childhood's greatest fear. They didn't abandon the ship, the ship abandoned them. Somehow, he felt, the *Titanic* sinking stood in the imagination for betrayed faith—of God to man, and man to himself—and upheld the chill logic under which a person is born into the world against all odds, the logic by which, against all hope, it will be lost to him.

"They didn't know what was coming," said Sarah. "They thought they were on the safest ship in the world."

Hugo turned to her. "They were."

Storms to the north were growing visibly; lightning flashed inside the clouds. On one side a towering nimbus seemed to boil. In another quadrant stars shone brightly in a clear black sky. Often Hugo felt like an interior voyager traveling above his own unstill emotions.

Hugo plotted their position on the plotting chart, took a wind reading, and recorded their fuel and the time, then drew a line to their next position. He threw the chart down on the console and looked out the window thoughtfully. Then he turned to Sarah and said, "I was served with divorce papers this morning."

Sarah, surprised that he hadn't mentioned it until then, looked at him curiously.

"You were out."

"Why didn't you say anything?"

"I guess I wanted to keep it to myself for a while."

A minute passed. "So tell me," she said finally, "what upset you so much about being served with papers?"

"Nothing really," he said, shifting in his seat. He turned his head sideways, reached up to the eyebrow panel and turned the light-intensity rheostat down. The NAV display dimmed. Then he looked at her squarely. "It's just that one part of my life is over and another part is about to begin." Hugo laughed, shrugged, and reached across the console. He took Sarah's hand affectionately into his. "I guess I feel I'm at a crossroads, and I couldn't be happier."

The master-warning aural alert chimed and the red emergency annunciator flashed. Hugo immediately silenced the chime and turned full attention to the electronic centralized aircraft monitoring system—or ECAM—CRT display. A checklist had already appeared on the monitor.

"It's a low oil-pressure warning on number one," said Sarah calmly. The indication was confirmed by rising oil temperature.

"Shit."

"What was your position when the low oil-pressure indication illuminated?" Crosley asked. He stood up, and came out from behind the table. He was holding a yellow pencil in his right hand and gestured with it as he spoke.

Hugo referred to notes. "We were at N5232 W3344 on North American track X-ray. A voice-recording exists of our position report and subsequent communications with New York Oceanic Control. They gave us a phone patch to Company. We were thirty minutes short of our equal timepoint."

"Would you define the equal timepoint for us?"

Hugo shifted slightly in his seat though he felt comfortable with this line of questioning. "The equal timepoint, or ETP, is the point along a course over water when the time to fly to destination alternate equals the time to fly to return alternate in event of a loss of an engine."

"And while you communicated with company dispatchers, you made the decision to return to New York at that time?"

"No. I determined a course for the return to a coast-in point off Nantucket. The engine temperature remained within limits at idle thrust. The pressure was marginal but indicating. As long as I could keep the engine running at idle, I postponed a destination decision until we made landfall. The airports along the Canadian coast were fogged in. I wanted to wait for updated weather."

"I have no further questions at this time," said Dr. Crosley. He walked back to his seat without looking up.

This abrupt end of Crosley's interrogation surprised Hugo. He sensed there was a standard method to these proceedings, a movement based on feint and fake, like football. Hugo remained on the stand while Chairman Adams addressed the table of technical representatives. He spoke directly to the power-plant specialist from General Technologies, the engine manufacturer.

"All right," said Chairman Adams, "I think Mr. Castor has some questions for Captain Price. Jim, will you come up here?"

Among all of the engineers at that table, James Castor struck Hugo as the most well rounded, and probably the youngest. About forty years old, with the white freckled complexion of redheads, he had light eyebrows that made his eyes seem to bulge, sausage curls receding slightly on the sides of an otherwise full hairline, and an aspect of good humor. Hugo felt a certain immediate affinity with the man which experience had taught him was usually mutual.

"Thank you, Mr. Chairman," said Castor, who stood and came forward. "Good morning, Captain."

"Good morning," said Hugo.

"Captain, we found a very curious and somewhat rare malfunction that might have been the cause of the engine explosion. But before I go into that, I'd like to ask you to recall if you can the oil pressure, temperature, and quantity reading after the engine was retarded to idle."

Hugo felt curiously at ease with Castor, not the antagonistic edge that, real or imagined, he felt with Crosley. One is always, he had noticed long ago, at greater ease with a peer in age.

"The pressure held at between ten and twelve psi. We accomplished ECAM items and then went through the flight manual Section Twenty Abnormal Procedure for Engine Oil Pressure Low Light On / Oil Pressure Gauge Low. The N2, or second-stage compressors, were steady at fifty-four percent. That's about normal for idle. The oil temperature was high, close to redline, variously between one hundred sixty-five to one hundred seventy-two degrees centigrade."

"Are you aware of the maximum oil-temperature limit?"

"One hundred seventy-five degrees centigrade."

"But there is an operational limit, is there not, for continuous operation of the engine above one hundred sixty degrees?"

"That's correct."

"And what is that limit, Captain?"

"If the temperature is above one hundred sixty degrees for fifteen minutes, it is recommended that the engine be shut down."

"Did you consider a precautionary engine shutdown?"

"No, not with a steady reading. We were prepared for a shutdown if it became necessary. The temperature held at the limit."

"Past the limit for continuous operation," said Castor, who touched the bridge of his nose in a way to modify the baldness of the statement.

"That is a recommended limit," said Hugo forcefully. "We were eight hundred miles from land. I made a decision to run the engine at idle thrust because the temperature, though high, was stabilized. Emergency command prerogatives supersede book recommendations." He felt a surge of confidence.

"The captain has absolute authority, that's quite true." Castor looked at his shoes and smiled faintly.

Hugo sensed no malice in Castor, merely thoroughness. Findings would hinge on the board's perception of his judgment and Hugo felt he had made an important point.

"Do you recall the oil-quantity indications at that time?" Castor continued.

"Only that the quantity was not unusual. It wasn't low. I thought we might have a clogged oil filter, but we didn't get a warning light. I tested the annunciators to make sure the light was working."

"Did you feel any engine vibrations?"

"None."

"Let me, if I may, review the situation as instrument indications presented it. You had low oil pressure, marginal but acceptable for continued operation at idle thrust, high oil temperature, above recommended maximum for continuous operation, but not above the maximum of one hundred seventy-five degrees centigrade, and normal oil-quantity indications. Is that correct?"

"That's correct."

"Do you recall fluctuations of any kind in the oil-quantity indicator?"

"Not really, no."

"You monitored it throughout the return to New York?"

"I monitored all of the engine indications. My main concern was temperature and pressure, because they were close to redline."

"Let me submit our analysis of the number one engine and instrument indications taken from the wreckage," said Castor, who passed a folder to the chairman. Adams flipped through the pages. "Briefly, what we discovered was a number one oil-quantity indication that was frozen at twenty-two quarts, which was curious because, according to records, the aircraft was dispatched with only nineteen quarts of oil. In essence, oil was added in flight."

Clinton Adams became instantly curious. He leaned forward and exaggerated an already cartoonlike posture of an eavesdropper. "What does that mean, Mr. Castor?" he said.

"It could mean this. As you know, cold fuel, chilled by the frigid temperatures at high altitudes, is heated to make it volatile before combustion. This is accomplished by means of an elegantly simple device, the fuel/oil heat exchanger. Hot engine oil is fed through coils around fuel lines forward of the second-stage engine-driven fuel pump. This system simultaneously cools the oil and heats the fuel. Now, the oil system is a sealed system. If the quantity indication that we found can be believed, it is possible that an internal leak developed in the fuel/oil heat exchanger. If that was the case, raw fuel replaced the oil in the bearing case. Because of its different density, the pressure indication dropped. The temperature was high, but remained within tolerable limits. The quantity indication rose to maximum because it reads the volume of fluid, which had, in fact, increased."

A chill ran through Hugo as the significance of this analysis sunk in. From his first flying lesson he was taught to trust his instrument indications. Relationships existed among the various monitored systems, and an unusual reading on one instrument could be confirmed or rejected by analyzing its correspondents for a specific problem. But here was something insidious; several related instruments, as if in conspiracy, sustained a false message.

"We were a time bomb," Hugo said, incredulous.

"Yes," said James Castor. "Essentially, that's true."

They faced each other in silence.

"That's all I have, Mr. Chairman," Castor said, turning to address Adams. He walked back to his seat.

"Captain Price, you may step down," Chairman Adams said.

Hugo stood, favoring his left leg. The chief of hotel security, a tall thin man in a dark double-breasted suit, handed him his crutches. Hugo felt the faces of strangers, every eye in the room, watching him. A walkie-talkie hissed electronically. The eyes of faces in the gallery met Hugo's with a kind of expressionless fascination, with sympathy, he thought, though this unnerved him. Sarah reached to touch his arm. She wanted him to look at her but he felt abashed and looked past her as he took his seat. He squeezed her hand.

Latimer leaned across Sarah to speak to Hugo. "Good work," he said. Hugo patted Sarah's knee, looked at her and nodded cryptically.

Chairman Adams looked through some papers in front of him for several moments, then leaned over and whispered to Crosley. Crosley nodded, wiped his glasses, and put them on again. Adams looked up and addressed the gallery. "Let's take a ten-minute recess, and then I'd like to call the first officer to the stand." He rapped his gavel and the room dispersed.

Edgar Latimer handed Hugo a glass of water. The lobby was congested. They stood off to the side.

"That was a bombshell," Latimer said. "Have you ever heard of a fuel/oil cooler malfunction?"

Hugo took a sip of water. "I saw a procedure for it once in a DC-10 manual. It's rare."

"Do you remember what the procedure said?"

"Shut the engine down and land at the nearest available airport."

MAY 19, 1995

During lunch Hugo began to sense the magnitude of the inquiry, the impact it would have on his career. Such intense scrutiny distorted his view of things, and he became suddenly keenly observant, finding in the immediate environment an analog for this distortion. He watched a fat man emerge from a corner restaurant. His jacket was brown and far too small for his enormous bulk; his tie was green and wide and it fluttered from side to side as he walked. He walked swiftly, in a determined stride, with that remarkably repulsive alacrity that fat people frequently exhibit in short bursts. He went on for a half block and then disappeared into an insurance office. Hugo tried to extract something from the scene. He could only imagine that the man was running away from the scene of his latest gluttony. Something wicked in his mind drove him to eat excessively. It was the same thing that drove others not to eat at all, or to run themselves to rickets for the sake of health: the desire to be perfect; in one, answered with an obdurate obesity, in another by a discipline of starvation, and in a third by self-defeating goals.

On the way back to the hearing, he saw a doorman in a worn brown uniform with a tattered braid standing alone in front of a smaller hotel on the main street. The little doorman talked to himself, squinted at the sky, and then looked at his shoes. He paced back and forth in his uniform like a stray Napoleon, or like a deranged elderly Boy Scout. Two tired salesmen passed him on their way into the hotel. Hugo could feel their hollow weariness, their unrewarded fortitude, their longing for a drink. Their faces washed past his as faces flow by in a day, eyes that meet your own from a curiosity for recognition, or look away from fear. He was reaching for an explanation. "Experience . . . is the impression of an individual in his isolation, each mind keeping as a solitary prisoner its own dream of a world." A sentence remembered from he-couldn't-say-where, but it came to mind and matched his mood.

Chairman Adams rapped his gavel. "The board is reconvened," he said. "Mr. Crosley?"

"I call to the stand First Officer Sarah McClure," said Crosley, rising. "Would you come forward, please?"

Sarah walked to the witness stand and took her seat. She was asked to state her full name and place of employment, experience and background, just as Hugo had. But Crosley's initial line of questioning took a different tack.

"You were off duty the day before the accident, is that correct?"

"Yes, that is correct."

"Could you describe your activities of that day?"

"I was helping Captain Price move into his apartment."

"Helping him to move?"

"That's correct. He had taken an apartment in New York. I volunteered to help him move some small items, books, papers, that sort of thing. We met at ten o'clock in the morning and spent most of the day downtown. The moving company arrived after lunch with the furniture. They were finished by four P.M."

"Moving furniture, you say." Crosley gestured with his pencil. "That can be quite tiring. Were you tired by the end of the day?"

"It was a busy day, but I would say that we were both rested. We took a nap for an hour before leaving for the airport."

"Did you have adequate rest the night before?"

"I had adequate rest."

"How did you get to the airport from Captain Price's apartment?"

"We drove to the airport together in his car and arrived about an hour and a half before departure time."

Crosley made a few notations on a yellow pad in front of him. Then he looked up. Sarah remained expressionless. He stood up and walked around the table to the open area in front.

"Would you say that the preparations for departure proceeded in a normal manner? Were there any mechanical discrepancies in the log book?"

"There was one writeup, as I recall. The APU had been placarded inoperative for bleed air. We started the number one engine at the gate using the air cart."

"Is that the only item you remember?"

"That's the only item I recall because it involved an alternate starting procedure."

Crosley paused for a moment, put his pencil down gently on the edge of the table in front of his empty seat, and pursued a new line of questioning.

"How long have you known Captain Price?"

"Eight months."

"And you have flown together often?"

"Yes. Our seniority is compatible."

"Would you say that you are compatible partners in the cockpit environment?"

"I enjoy flying with Captain Price."

Crosley pursed his lips, as though weighing his next question. "How would you characterize Captain Price's flying skills?"

"Excellent."

Crosley, who had been pacing slowly across the floor, paused. "What sort of relationship do you have with Captain Price?"

Sarah had been coached by Latimer to expect questions of this sort. The object, he said, was not to probe their private lives, but rather to establish that there had been no conflict in the cockpit on the night of the accident. Still, the question had prurient resonance. "A good relationship."

"How so?"

"We work well together."

"There has never been a problem, expressed or implied, regarding . . . regarding gender? That is, are you satisfied that professional standards were never compromised as a consequence of your sex?"

The question irritated Sarah.

"How do you mean that?"

Crosley folded his hands in front of him and looked directly at her through his thick glasses. "I mean Ms. McClure, did Captain Price ever seem to you uncomfortable or in any way disturbed by the fact that you are a female pilot?"

"There was never a problem with sex," she told him. The gallery tittered.

"Ms. McClure," Crosley continued, referring to notes on the table in front of him, "you performed the preflight inspection of the aircraft on the night of March 14, is that correct?

"That is correct."

"The exterior walk-around inspection?"

"Yes."

"Did you notice anything unusual during your inspection?"

"No, nothing unusual."

"And the flight proceeded normally until the indication of low oil pressure in the number one engine?"

Sarah felt her focus gather. She wanted to be accurate in every detail, accurate and brief.

"We've heard Captain Price describe the first part of the flight as routine. Do you agree with that assessment?"

"Yes, I do."

"And yet there was weather along your planned route of flight that necessitated a change in plan."

"We diverted to the south of our planned course due to weather. Reports came to us via the ACARS printer and ATC pilot reports. We were well informed of changes in the forecast along our route. Captain Price decided to request NAT track Xray."

"A more southerly track."

"That's correct."

"You'd characterize that change in track as part of a routine flight to Europe?"

"Weather in the North Atlantic is changeable, especially in March. Decision-making is routine on every flight. Is that what you mean, Mr. Crosley?" Sarah tried to keep an edge out of her tone.

"So, in your judgment, Ms. McClure, as first officer, you would characterize the first part of flight 555 on the night of March 14 as entirely routine."

"The flight was not unusual."

Crosley paused again. Sarah sensed a shift in questioning. "Did you, Ms. McClure, at any time during the return to New York, suggest to the captain that Boston might be a better return destination?"

"No, I did not."

"And yet the weather in Boston was above approach minimums. Did you discuss it?"

"There was some discussion between us. I did not suggest either Boston or New York. I did get current weather. There was heavy fog all along the coast. A front was passing through New York. Logan was open for Category III Alpha approaches, but with weather so marginal on the bay, there were no guarantees; the visibility can go to zero at any time. I think we both tacitly agreed on New York."

"Tacitly?"

"The captain made a command decision. I agreed with it. We were very busy."

"Thank you, Ms. McClure. I have no further questions."

Sarah left the witness stand and went back to her seat beside Hugo. Latimer leaned back and gave her a wink of approval. Sarah leaned to Hugo. "He's a son of a bitch."

"There's an edge to him, yes."

"He made me angry. Did it show?"

"No. You were fine," Hugo said. She frowned and poured a glass of water from the pitcher at their table.

The rest of the first afternoon of the hearing was taken with technical testimony from power-plant engineers who described in intricate detail the design of the fuel/oil cooler. Hugo and Sarah listened with absorbed interest. Edgar Latimer took notes. The engineers were careful to emphasize the historical integrity of the system. The incidents of malfunction of the type suspected in the explosion experienced on Nation Air flight 555 were rare. That system, or systems similar to it, had been standard on jet aircraft since the 1950s. Simplified illustrations were offered as exhibits. Detailed maintenance records were submitted for study.

Hugo experienced this aspect of the proceedings like an audience-participation drama. Indeed, there were dimensions of tragedy here, and absurdity. The folding tables and chairs and folding walls of the conference room made a modern proscenium; the hearing became a secular drama of duties and responsibilities; it probed the relationship of human being and machine, underscoring that failure on either side had real consequences. Technology was not a shield against mortality.

The rapidity with which he'd been ripped from life as he'd known it continued to stun Hugo. His attention wandered. An exhibit was brought to the front of the room. David McDermott, from the Bureau of Technology, explained what amounted to basic aerodynamics, using a chart labeled "Airplane Forces." McDermott was a tall, reedy man with a slow deliberate manner that seemed to take its caution from experience in a world too slightly undersized for his height. Hugo imagined him not comfortable at a desk, more at home in a workshop alone, communing with the simple physics of broken things.

The chart depicted an airplane profile, with arrows indicating the four forces in play that affect flight: thrust, drag, lift, and gravity. Chairman Adams asked questions that McDermott answered for the benefit of those present. This explication would serve as a foundation to understand later testimony of Hugo's struggle to remain airborne in the last seconds before impact.

"Mr. McDermott, would you please explain for the record the terms we see on the chart?" said Adams, indicating the exhibit.

"Simply put, an airplane can only sustain flight if lift is greater than weight, and thrust is greater than drag." McDermott, wielding a chrome telescopic pointer, stood beside the large colored illustrations. "The arrow above the airplane figure pointing upward," he said, "indicates a lift force that acts perpendicular to the flight path, and which must be greater than the weight force, indicated by this down-pointing arrow here. The forward-pointing arrow indicates the direction of thrust, and the backward-pointing arrow indicates drag."

"And what is the meaning of that graph in the lower corner?" asked Chairman Adams.

"That graph indicates the angle of attack of a wing. Let me explain it this way: A wing can be compared crudely to a water ski. A high angle of attack creates high drag, requiring greater power to overcome it, in the same way a water-skier requires greater power from the boat towing him until his skis are flat on the surface, or until the angle of attack of his skis is reduced."

"And the meaning of the second chart?"

"This curve graphically demonstrates the coefficient of lift, or the lifting capability of a wing surface. The water-skier of the last analogy can maintain himself at slower speeds on the water when his skis are at a high angle, but sufficient thrust must be present. But see here how the drag curve peaks. Increasing the angle of attack at this point will not help, but in fact hurt the ability of the ski, or the wing, and require an escalating amount of thrust until, at a certain critical point, the aircraft will enter this region here, commonly called 'the backside of the power curve.' " McDermott pointed to a line that rose in a forty-five degree gradient, then hooked down suddenly.

"And what is the significance of this?"

"At this point, even with full power, drag will be greater than thrust, weight will be greater than the lifting capability of the wing, and the plane will not sustain flight."

McDermott moved to the other side of the chart and stood back so that Chairman Adams and the rest of the board had a clear view of the graph.

"This red square here indicates the onset of stick-shaker, which is one percent above stall speed. The blue squares indicate the point where buffet occurs, or the onset of stall. In the last seconds of flight 555, the aircraft flew into the buffet three times below five hundred feet, although here, at thirty feet, we see the beginning of recovery. The aircraft continued to descend slightly, however, even with full thrust on both engines. At engine failure, Captain Price was within eight knots of minimum controllable airspeed. At that angle of attack in violently unstable air, with full power on the remaining engine, the aircraft was very much in danger of exceeding the opposing roll and yaw forces, especially considering the drag of the failed engine. A power reduction at that critical moment was the only action that could prevent the aircraft from rolling inverted."

Hugo listened and recalled feeling in the flight controls precisely what the graphs indicated. As he watched McDermott's chrome pointer run along the profile, he was flying again, struggling to keep the plane airborne, holding the angle high until the stick-shaker vibrated the yoke, relaxing back pressure slightly until the shaker stopped, feeling the fragile, precarious balance of thrust fighting drag, lift fighting gravity, until the massive three-hundred-thousand-pound aircraft hung in such refined trim that an ounce of yoke pressure one way or another would shift its flight path significantly. And then the explosion, the loss of thrust, the change in feel and loss of balance, reflexes that had to accept impact as a bad trade for control, exactly as McDermott suggested.

But, God, this was a cold account of it.

"I thank you for your explanations, Mr. McDermott," said Chairman Adams. McDermott resumed his seat and a murmur rose in the gallery. Adams turned through some pages in a notebook, then went through some loose pages handed him by an aide. He checked his watch and whispered something to the aide.

"It's getting late," he said, looking up. "I think we'll break here for the day." He picked up his gavel and rapped it once. "Ladies and gentlemen, this hearing is adjourned until nine A.M. tomorrow morning."

The room rose as one and Latimer closed his briefcase.

Hugo was in a state of tense anxiety, though he wasn't clearly aware of it. He stared at a corner of the folding wall where the plastic paper had peeled. Sarah was exhausted. Like Hugo, she experienced the proceeding with a mix of anxiety and tedium. Who were these strangers, assembled to ask questions about an incident in her life that she hadn't fully absorbed herself, and might never? There was something disorienting about the power of judgment they held. Life was uncertain, unintelligible, hinged on chance so it seemed, and in an odd way immune to judgment, although she hadn't thought about it before. These proceedings had theatrical significance of some obscure range, otherwise the voices seemed unreal.

"Relax tonight," Latimer told them. "Have dinner out. Take your mind off things. Tomorrow they'll get into the specifics of weather. Have you got all you need, Dan?"

"Yes, I believe we're prepared," said Danielson. They rose and left the room.

Dan Danielson, Latimer, Sarah, and Hugo stood under the canopy at the entrance to the hotel. Danielson smiled and nodded to familiar faces who acknowledged him as they passed, occasionally stepping aside to have a few words with someone. Hugo watched this exchange of greetings with some interest. A chief pilot practiced politics with transportation officialdom in the same way the airline chief executive maintained a working relationship with Congress. A low-key affability natural to Danielson's personality could blunt the sometimes sharp edge of the bureaucrat. He maintained good relations with the FAA, and he was well known and respected in aviation circles, having saved more than one pilot from disciplinary overreaction in the course of his tenure.

"They'll have you testify early tomorrow, Dan," Latimer said.

Danielson nodded. "I'm prepared for whatever they'll want to know about our flight operations." He turned to Hugo. "They'll talk to me first—about training and the general management of the flight department. That's the usual procedure. Then they'll call you again for further testimony." He opened his hands frankly. "Just tell it like it was. Straightforward answers. As I said, your procedures were by the book, and that is absolutely of the first importance. But they're going to sniff for pilot error. The feds will be attentive to everything they hear, believe that."

"Can I give anyone a lift?" said Latimer.

"No, thank you, Edgar," said Hugo.

Danielson and Latimer walked off to their cars, while Hugo and Sarah went in the other direction. The crutches were cumbersome, but he could move in a steady rhythm without appearing awkward. They stopped at the corner and waited for the light to change. "What did you really think?" Hugo asked.

Sarah gave the question considered thought. "Accidents should be investigated, and they seem to do their job in a fair and thorough manner. But everything finally comes down to ego and politics somehow. I guess I feel naked, and sense something lurid in their curiosity."

"We're under a microscope, aren't we?"

"It sure feels like it."

MAY 20, 1995

E   dgar Latimer's bifocals rested comically on the end of his
         nose. His briefcase was open in front of him. "Danielson
will testify first," he told Hugo. "They want background. Then
they'll call you. You'll be asked further questions. In addition, there
are a number of survivors present to give eyewitness accounts of the
evacuation." Survivable accidents, he explained, were studied in detail for clues as to how those who survived had managed it, and what
actions or safeguards might have protected those who did not.

    Some surviving passengers had written letters to both Hugo and
Sarah, thanking them for saving their lives. The letters depressed
Hugo. There were other communications critical of the airline, of
Hugo, calling for criminal charges, turning every bitter personal
grief into wild allegations.

    There had been phone calls, anonymous calls, and these had a dev-
astating effect. Sarah had found Hugo one evening with his head in

his hands. "Don't listen to them," she had told him. "Hang up." The calls continued until she got an unlisted number.

"This hearing will come to order." Chairman Clinton Adams rapped his gavel.

Sarah observed that the chairman's hair was cut too short to be combed, and too long to be brushed. It stuck out in unruly spikes like fur on a frightened beaver. A dark brow and a slightly extended jaw gave his expressions a sometimes comic aspect of muddled concentration. There was a plodding quality to him in pace with the tedious business of formal investigation.

"Dr. Crosley, call your next witness."

"Captain Dan Danielson, please come forward."

Dan, who was sitting next to Hugo, stood, buttoned his jacket, and walked to the witness stand. Dan knew that questions directed to him would be a prelude to the interrogation Hugo would undergo regarding the final minutes of flight 555, and he was well prepared. When he was seated, the oath was administered, and Crosley began his questioning.

"Captain Danielson, what is your present position with Nation Air Lines?"

"I'm the Eastern Regional Director for Flight Operations. That's a fancy title for regional chief pilot."

"And among your responsibilities is management of the Flight Safety Division, is that correct?"

"Yes."

"What are some of the functions of this division?"

"There are four primary functions of the Flight Safety Division," said Danielson, his hand held up, counting on his fingers. "First is accident prevention. Second, is to collect and analyze safety information. Third, to act as a liaison to training and technical departments.

And fourth, to develop emergency response procedures."

"When you say 'flight safety,' for purposes of clarification, do you also mean ground safety? What are you describing?"

"We're concerned with every aspect of the operation of an airplane from the moment the crew enters the cockpit for the purpose of flight until the completion of the Parking checklist. There is also a Maintenance Quality Control Division, but that's something separate."

"Would you briefly mention some of the activities that the Flight Safety Division is concerned with in the four categories you mentioned?"

"To enhance accident prevention we have a hot line established at all downline stations as well as an eight-hundred number so that safety issues can be immediately debriefed. Supervisors are also available to discuss issues of immediate importance. We get calls from Air Traffic Control, the FAA, the NTSB, NASA, even the military. If these messages can be addressed from a flight safety standpoint, we investigate and pass the information along to the appropriate authority. For example, hydraulic fluid was packaged in containers very similar in design to cans of oil, and in one case we learned that hydraulic fluid had in fact been mistakenly used in an oil change. We changed the procedures for stocking and procuring the fluid, and then went to the manufacturer to request that they alter the colors on their packaging to make the mistake less likely to happen again."

"And you mentioned that the Flight Safety Division acts as liaison to technical and training divisions. How so?"

"We meet with fleet captains twice a year, and check pilots on a continuing basis. Roundtable discussions frequently identify areas where improvements in standard operating procedures might be indicated. Sometimes there are very gray areas. But if we think a procedure should be changed in the interest of safety, we'll meet with the training division, and recommend the change."

While Danielson spoke, Hugo doodled squares on a legal pad

that he turned into cubes, which he then shadowed as though light was falling down on them from the left. He turned to a clean page.

"All right," continued Crosley, his thick glasses making him appear alternately highly intelligent and retarded. "Let me ask about the training at Nation Air Lines. In an earlier discussion I had with you, I think we agreed that roughly eighty percent of accidents and incidents in aviation are attributable to human error."

"Worldwide, yes, that's an accurate figure."

"How does your training division approach that sometimes nebulous term, 'human error'?"

"Human error can be something simple to analyze and address, or very difficult to identify. Years ago, a pilot forgot to put his retractable landing gear down. After a number of such incidents, engineers designed a warning system that would alert the crew on final approach that their gear was not in a position for landing. That system virtually eliminated a safety hazard attributable to human error. But often it's not so simple. A nuance of inattention may develop insidiously over time, a series of small errors or lapses can begin to lay an intricate trap. The modern cockpit can seem impregnable. Yet a decade ago a Nose Gear Down light did not illuminate which drew the attention of the crew, who then failed to notice when the autopilot inadvertently disengaged. Final determination: They descended into the ground because a ten-cent lightbulb had failed and distracted them from their main concern. Over the years technology has sought to combat the potential for human error. But flying is a complicated skill. The seriousness of an emergency can't always be immediately apprehended, and emergency situations can deteriorate with alarming suddenness."

"What kinds of simulators does your training division use?"

"State-of-the-art Phase Three simulators, FAA-certified for landings and type ratings."

"The simulators are very realistic, aren't they?"

"Well, I guess they are when a pilot can be trained so effectively that the first time he flies the real airplane it's on the line with passengers. To answer your question, yes, the simulators are very realistic. By the time a pilot is a type-rated captain, he's seen about everything he's likely to see in the real world, and a few things he'll probably never see."

"Could you give us an example of one such exercise?"

"Well, we'll jam the hydraulic controls entirely and see how well the pilot can maintain flight with power only. It can happen, it has happened. A blown pressure cone wiped out hydraulics on a JAL 747 a few years ago. That pilot finally lost his struggle to keep it in the air, but he never gave up working with what he had. And, of course, the United DC-10 at Sioux City was a similar situation. The captain landed in a cornfield with no flight controls whatsoever. These incidents point to the fact that anything can happen. We do our best to prepare the cockpit crew for any eventuality."

"So, Captain Danielson, you would say that the simulator training is the most valuable training a professional pilot gets."

"It's one of several important training phases. When you're concentrating, you forget a simulator's not the real thing. I've seen pilots come out sweating and shaken. It's a very serious training tool. And I might add that all our pilots are required to fly the NASA windshear profile created from the Delta flight 191 flight recorder in the Dallas accident of 1985."

"Captain Danielson, in your estimation, could simulator training, because of its remarkable approximation to the flight environment, at some point become a detriment to safety?"

"How do you mean?"

"The flight environment, dynamic and variable as it is, might be taken for granted. Isn't there a saying, 'Flying is safe as long as you remember it's dangerous'? Could simulator training lull a pilot with a false sense of security he might then bring to line flying?"

"No, sir. I disagree. The sole purpose of simulator training is to expose the pilot to unusual situations so that he or she will be prepared to cope with real contingencies."

As Hugo listened, he recalled older pilots' initial resistance to simulator training. They resented simulator sessions in lieu of practice in the actual airplane, claiming that the "feel" was different and therefore not realistic. But they were wrong—their complaint was actually against its realism. Hugo agreed that the feel was slightly different, perhaps more sensitive—simulated approaches were slightly more difficult to fly because a computer-generated picture had no depth perception—but on occasions when he had flown actual instrument approaches at night in heavy rain and fog, forced to let down on altitude callouts because the smeared erasures of wiper blades obscured the ground, he had found simulator training invaluable. To cautiously descend an airliner into a spreading trapezoidal geometry of lights was an exercise only a simulator could safely recreate without hazard.

"Do you have a cockpit resource management program in your training division?"

"Yes, we implemented it last year."

"Captain Danielson, would you describe the training emphasis of cockpit resource management for us?"

"Briefly, it's an evolving program that addresses the realities of human nature in the special context of the cockpit. It insures a clear division of labor, and tries to target the psychological blocks to critical communications that might compromise safety. Accidents result after a sequence of failures: failure of the pilot flying, of the pilot not flying, failure of the air-traffic controller handling the flight, almost always a failure of communication. We try to build in safeguards. Cockpit Resource Management is a program of awareness. We want our pilots to know what resources are available to them for the safe management of flight, and offer guidelines for utilizing them. And in-

cidentally, I'd like to comment here that the voice recording taken
from flight 555 indicated to me that both pilots were performing their
duties in accordance with principles of CRM."

Hugo's glance met Sarah's. They had always thought as one at
work, which made their flying together so effortless and pleasurable.
A contrary personality could easily break down the smooth flow of
information and response. In those cases, captain's sovereignty overruled objection, but, in the modern cockpit, that was a last and worst
solution.

Crosley shifted his stance and put his hand on the table in front of
his seat, seeming to balance himself with his fingertips. He appeared
to be considering his next question.

"Captain Danielson," he said, "does the ground school include a
discussion of extreme weather phenomena?"

"Do you mean does the ground school include training on wind
shear? Yes."

"But there are other weather anomalies that can affect safety of
flight, isn't that correct?"

"Yes, that's true. Clear air turbulence is common on the perimeter of the jet stream at certain altitudes. Thunderstorms, of course."

"And pilots are given training in these phenomena?"

"Yes. Thorough training."

"And how would a pilot be made aware of unusual weather that
has developed along his route of flight after the departure?"

"There are a number of ways. Air Traffic Control will issue ride
reports based on communications with other aircraft along a route at
a certain altitude. There are high-frequency weather stations that report conditions on an hourly basis. In addition, our aircraft are
equipped with on-board ACARS, or airborne communications computers and printers. Significant weather is monitored by our meteo-
rology center. Any change from the forecast appearing on the
captain's dispatch report is sent via the ACARS computer as a mes-

sage. The crew receives the message in flight and acknowledges in code. It's a thorough communications system."

"Thank you, Captain Danielson, for your testimony. I have no further questions." Crosley took his seat.

"Anyone else?" said Chairman Adams. He turned to Danielson. "We very much appreciate your participation, Captain. Thank you."

Hugo followed the line of Crosley's questioning, he knew he was building a foundation of testimony. He recalled receiving two ACARS messages from flight dispatch regarding the line of thunderstorms passing through the New York area on the night of the accident. They were turbulence reports. Moderate turbulence below ten thousand feet, and moderate, occasional severe turbulence reported by a 747 climbing out within ten miles of a cell. Still, that wasn't unusual for that sort of weather at that time of year. Turbulence was a fact of flight.

Hugo felt that his task here would be to represent accurately, to a group of individuals who had not lived it, the difference between his actual experience and their denatured description of it. Of his fight to maintain airspeed on that night, his struggle for balance in a tumble of violent air, what could they know? This proceeding could do nothing to reverse what had happened, nor could it remove the perils all pilots contended with, nor could it attenuate nature, change the caprice of fate, nor bring those who were lost back to the world of the living. It went against the grain of technological achievement to accept that marvelous inventions could be vulnerable to the deadly whims of "nature." The instinct was to look for human error, to identify an individual responsible for every disaster. Modern man could not look into the abyss and see himself. Hugo sensed that tomorrow would not be an easy day.

MAY 20, 1995

Hugo waited to be called again to testify. From one view, he thought, there was a hint of madness in the proceedings. He could feel it in the air, a kind of mild hysteria. He looked for further indications of it in the sober deportment of the board, but found nothing to validate what he sensed. Slowly it dawned that these feelings were his own.

He listened to Danielson's testimony and recalled the disasters he had mentioned; the JAL captain manipulating his engines frantically for thirty minutes before losing control, enough time for some passengers to write final notes to their families, later found. Another aircraft in recent memory had suffered explosive decompression; passengers were sucked from their seats, later to be euphemistically referred to as "debris" that caused the number three and four engines to fail. This secular reduction of horror to statistics had elements of the obscene in it.

"Mr. Crosley," said Chairman Adams, "would you like to call another witness at this time?"

Hugo expected to hear his name.

"I would, Mr. Chairman. I'd like to call Malcolm Dunn to the stand, please."

"Mr. Dunn?" said Chairman Adams, as a man rose from the gallery and walked to the front of the room to be sworn in.

Mr. Malcolm Dunn gave the appearance of being able and successful. Dark hair worn longer than average made him seem younger than his roughly forty-five years. His eyes were dark brown and capable of strong concentration. He took the oath with a somber sense of duty. Whether earned or born to it, Dunn had the presence and demeanor of a man long used to luck.

Mr. Crosley addressed the witness: "Mr. Dunn, you were a passenger on flight 555 on the night of March 14, is that correct?"

"That's correct."

"Would you please, for the record, state your full name and business address?"

"Malcolm James Dunn, 145 Greenwich Avenue, Greenwich, Connecticut."

"And your occupation, if you would?"

"Senior partner at Commercial Finance Corporation. We're capital investors."

"You also have a pilot's license, is that correct?"

"That is correct."

"Could you tell us something of your background in aviation, the type of experience you have?"

"I have a commercial license and an instrument rating. I own a twin Beechcraft Baron that I use for business and pleasure."

"And how many total hours do you have logged as a pilot?"

"In the neighborhood of two thousand hours. All of it in light airplanes. Mostly single-engine."

"Mr. Dunn, where were you sitting on this flight?"

"In the last row of first class. Seat 12A"

"A window seat on the left side of the aircraft?"

"That's correct."

"Was there anyone occupying the seat next to you?"

"Yes. Carl Gross. Another partner in the firm. We were flying to Paris on business."

Crosley paced the length of the chairman's table, as though giving consideration to his next question. Then he turned and said, "Could you describe in as much detail as possible how you experienced the final approach, and then the impact and your escape?"

Dunn leaned back in his seat, tugged at his trousers, and leaned forward again. He looked over the heads of those in the gallery to the far wall, where his sight fell on a rip in the wallpaper. The room was silent as he began to speak.

"It was turbulent. The captain told us that we were about to make our approach, and he said it might be rough, that is, that the air was choppy, and I think he said he was going to have the flight attendants take their seats early. We were told about the engine problem several hours earlier, when we reversed course, but I wasn't concerned. It was more an inconvenience than anything.

"As we began the final approach I heard the landing gear go down. I always listen for the landing gear. I guess it's a habit from my own flying, to make sure it's extended. Then you know you're about to land. Outside, I saw lightning. There was one very bright fork of lightning to the ground. We started to shake quite a bit and at one point we dropped suddenly. The shaking was severe, but it stopped almost right away. Then it was smooth for a few seconds and I could see the ground. It looked like we were somewhere below a thousand feet when the plane seemed to rock. Actually, it wasn't rocking, that's not the right way to describe it. It was a feeling that we were being thrown around. Then it got very severe, and I knew that the captain was going around because suddenly the nose went up and he tried to climb. The engines began to whine the way they do at takeoff. We were shaking because of the turbulence and I couldn't see out the window. Carl looked at me. He seemed extremely concerned. He said, 'Are we in trouble?' Then I saw a flash and fire under the left wing. That was when the engine exploded. There was a sound, but I don't remember it, either because we were shaking and my attention was fixed on whether we were in control, or because the crash came just after that. The captain was trying to keep it in the air, but he couldn't.

"Believe it or not, it did enter my mind that we might turn inverted. When you're trained on twin-engine airplanes, even light airplanes, you learn that there's a minimum controllable airspeed for continued flight on the operating engine. If you go below that speed, the flight controls can't keep the plane straight against the thrust of the operating engine and the plane will turn over. That night everything happened so fast. The nose went up and we sort of balanced in the air. But the engine exploded, and then we started sinking and I knew we were going in. I said to Carl, 'We're not going make it.' I could feel it. Carl said, 'No, no, it can't happen.' And I said, 'Get down,' and he said, 'What?' and I put my head down and grabbed my knees and then we hit. It took all of five, maybe six seconds."

Crosley leaned against the table, listening intently. The room was nearly still. A fascinated attention held it under a spell. Hugo was thinking: There's something almost sacred in this curiosity. It was a solemnity that felt like church, or an execution. And then he realized that this sense of the sacred was present whenever human beings gave formal testimony to their mortality.

"It was a violent impact, and we were sliding, and then the lights went out. I was rattling between the armrests in my seat, we were all like dice in a throwing cup. You couldn't see anything. We slid and slid. The noise was tremendous. I knew that flames were on the outside of the plane because you could see the flashing and flickering light against the darkness, but I couldn't see fire. Then the fuselage broke apart behind us. Not all the way, but I did see that it broke apart. Then flames and thick smoke rushed forward from the rear where the fire was. I couldn't see anything. It was like being blind. I guess we had stopped when I unbuckled my seat belt. Nothing was visible. Nothing. I held my breath and headed in what I thought was the direction of the break. I knew that there was an emergency exit ahead but I was afraid that it might be jammed, so I went toward the rear. There were other people at the hole climbing out. It was like a fire drill in grade school. Only faster. And then I was on top of the plane, and I jumped. When I was outside, I felt safe again. I felt it was over. Other people were running by me. I wasn't in their way. I paused for a second, amazed at the devastation. Then I heard someone above say, 'Hey!' Like on a basketball court when you're a kid and then someone tosses you a ball. I looked up, and this other man was holding a baby, holding it out right above me. As soon as he knew he had my attention he dropped the baby. There was no time for thinking. So I caught the baby and he jumped, and I gave it back to him and we both ran away from the plane. Later I learned he'd found the baby in the aisle. He had flown out of his mother's arms when we crashed. Then, unbelievably, we found her, the mother, outside. She survived. He recognized her. She was in shock anyway, but when he handed her the child, and she saw it was safe and unharmed, there was a look of disbelief that I think I'll remember until the day I die. Nothing about anything that was happening was ordinary. None of us had been through anything like this before. One minute we were in our seats thinking about the delay, and about what flight we were going to catch in the morning, phone calls we'd have to make, that kind of thing. The next minute we're standing in a marsh next to the blazing wreckage of our airplane knowing that there were other people inside that didn't make it.

"I was standing back. We were in a kind of circle, a wide circle toward the nose of the airplane. Nobody else was coming out, and nobody had come out for about a minute, I guess. Then two people appeared, the captain and the first officer. You could tell by their uniforms. They seemed to be struggling a little getting through the broken fuselage. They took a few steps and then stopped. The back of the plane was on fire. One of the flight attendants ran toward them, I think she tried to get them to move faster away from the plane. They started to run. Then it was like a bomb. The whole thing exploded. I saw a rush of flames along the top of the fuselage. The only thing you could see above was thick black smoke. If anybody was left inside that plane you knew it was over for them."

During his testimony, Malcolm Dunn looked at no one. He kept his eyes fixed on the torn wallpaper while indelible images of that night materialized with intense vividness. A sense of the plane going out of control, a final warning to his colleague, the crash, his escape, the voice calling, "Hey!" and the almost casual toss of an infant into his arms, it was all extraordinary. Yet in retrospect, how readily those who survived adapted to the urgent measures required. Out of necessity an etiquette of escape evolved in seconds. There were many stories of instant assistance and miracles of good luck. There were also stories of wrong choices.

"Mr. Dunn, during your escape, did you notice any emergency-exit lights?"

"No, sir. The heat from the fire was intense. And the smoke. You have one thought only, and that's, 'I've got to get out fast.' But you don't say to yourself, 'Let's see, the emergency exit is eight rows back on the left.' "

"We know that Mr. Gross, your business partner, did not survive the accident. Do you know if he tried to exit the aircraft?"

"The last time I saw Carl was just before I put my head down between my knees. Just before we crashed. After that I can't remember clearly what happened, only that once the plane came to a stop, I was moving fast, fighting my way over bags and seatbacks to get to where I knew the hole in the fuselage was. I had one sight, like a snapshot, of people still in their seats at the center of the airplane as flames came down the aisle. Then nothing because of the smoke, and then all of a sudden I was outside."

"Did you notice anyone having trouble or difficulty getting out of their seats?"

"I'm a little ashamed to say that until I knew I was about to get out, I only had one object, and that was self-preservation. I didn't see, I felt. I went on instinct. Every part of me was focused on escape. My movements were in inches, not feet or yards. I know I was moving quickly, but it seemed too slow, like dreams when you can't move. It's not a memory of images. It's a memory of feeling terrifying strong emotions in a very short time span that seems to last forever."

"How long would you estimate it took you to evacuate?"

"I would say no more than ten seconds, fifteen tops. I don't think more than fifteen seconds."

"What were your observations of rescue personnel after they arrived at the scene?"

"I think they did a fabulous job, but it was frustrating. Those of us who got out were running back and forth helping others to get away from the airplane. The left side toward the rear behind the wing was on fire. The flight attendants were directing some of us to hold the forward slide, and then others of us were trying to find stragglers. They deserve recognition for being cool-headed. Most of the people left the airplane through splits in the fuselage, and so it was quite a drop, and those of us who weren't injured helped to catch them. Then the heat got to be too much, and nobody else was getting out. That was the frustrating part. The fire trucks, the medical teams, all of us had to stand and just watch it burn. They sprayed it from every direction but it was just too much to do anything about. I don't think anybody got out the rear emergency exits. I just don't think they had a chance."

"Thank you for your testimony, Mr. Dunn," said Crosley. "I have no further questions." Dunn was excused.

"Would you like to call another witness at this time, Mr. Crosley?"

"No, Mr. Chairman. Not at this time."

"Mr. Jenkins?"

"I would, Mr. Chairman," said Ben Jenkins. "I'd like to call Captain Price to the stand for further examination."

"We want to hear Captain Price's testimony, but I think at this point it's a good time to adjourn for the day. We'll convene tomorrow at nine A.M. Thank you, gentlemen."

MAY 20, 1995

Hugo put another pillow behind his back. He had been restless all evening and continued to toy with the sheets, twisting them around his index finger while he spoke. Sarah caught his hand and stilled his fidgeting. Her book lay facedown between them.

"I knew there were storms in the area. Maybe I unconsciously took a risk."

Sarah's aspect grew stern. "I was with you, Hugo. You heard Latimer. The microburst was invisible to radar."

"If the engine had held for two seconds longer we might have made it. We were hanging on the edge." He shook his head, exasperation overtook his expression. "The truth is, we should have gone into Boston."

"New York made more sense. It was a safer choice given what we knew. You're not being fair with yourself. Or with me." Sarah spoke adamantly.

During the next minute they were both silent.

"I feel like I've been sleepwalking all my life," he said.

Sarah lay her head on the pillow facing away from him. "You haven't," she said to the wall.

Hugo turned the light out and for a long while he lay silently in the dark. When he heard the sound of Sarah's even breathing he felt better. Tension dissipated. Soon he too fell asleep. But sleeping was no escape. He began to dream, an epic dream with tangible geometries and strange melding images. He dreamed of life, and he dreamed of death, in vivid metaphors. The face of his mother appeared as he was lounging in the garden of his childhood. Lush perfumes of growing things filled warm still airs with the sweet scent of lilac and white rose. He sat in the shade of a Dutch elm. The sun shone with unfiltered intensity on the green lawn and on the scarlet plumage of a bright azalea; it threw out dappled shadows from the hedgerow, and amplified the richness of natural hues, bringing even to stones a brilliance that nearly solved their essence. The sky was bluer, the grasses greener, the forsythia by the house more radiantly yellow, the yard itself taken all in tints of Eden, so that finally in this midst, against such light and color, the flowers of the red azalea stood blazing.

Then sense and sensation were numb and he seemed suspended between waking and dreaming; something was very wrong, a weariness gripped him that he felt as a failure of will, and he was lying in a hospital bed.

"He's delirious, Doctor," said one of the nurses.

He could hear himself, see himself, feel himself laughing. Laughter as a summary of spirit, wild, profound, ironic, paradoxical laughter, laughter that was crying, laughter that was screaming, laughter recalling every howl of pleasure, celebrating all the joy, grief, pity, and hope that living was; laughter at every slight and intimidation, every resolve to excellence, every failure, achievement, desire, and betrayal, laughter that beheld pettiness, every human contriving to exhort against frailty, against mortality. Laughter at the brevity of life on earth and its passing, how madly funny it all was, after all. Only slowly did the laughter abate, fading as the answer to life that vanishes with waking.

In a far quarter of his mind he stood apart from himself and remained resolute. He saw that he was caught now in something larger than his will, a mistake. He hadn't meant for it to happen. His elaborate emotions were projected onto the wind and sea, a tumbling current swelled and curled, and a sky strewn with feelings signaled a gathering storm. He stood on a sailing ship. The edge of blue sky to the northeast disappeared. The absence of sunray on the horizon made the air feel colder. Waves slapped against the hull with untempoed percussive claps. The wind was high but steady, the sailing good, the water turbulent and dramatic. The sailboat cut a path through the swells and left a wake that lasted on the whitecaps. The waves rose and broke over the bow as the sky darkened and the horizon gradually disappeared into the mist.

"Ready to come about?" a voice called.

Hugo, smiling, uncleated the port jibsheet, held it fast, and wrapped the starboard jibsheet loosely. "Ready," he said.

"Coming about!"

The bow moved through the line of wind and the sails luffed until the boom moved from port to starboard across the deck. The jib shifted and he tightened the sheets. The sails filled once again, becoming taut and still. The ship heeled to starboard and rapidly increased in speed. The wind was stronger now.

"I made a mistake," said Hugo, words almost inaudible in the rushing air. "Something went wrong."

The wind began to gust, shocking the sails and driving the gunwales into the waterline. The drama that outwardly riled held his most troubling apprehensions suspended from him for a while. Fear was outside him now. A bond between mind and spirit was struck on a solemn reflection of death, and he was left to face the horizon alone. But he had something that would help him with what was next; an attitude, not tangible nor even articulate, except as sunset is articulate, or the way wind whispers when the earth lends its living essence to an unanswered wish, and you feel religion in it.

Finally, he felt peace advance. He was flying again, and all of the passengers were safe, and Sarah was next to him in the cockpit, and this was flight 555, and nothing had happened.

Landfall. The lights of the Irish coast were apparent below breaks in the clouds. There is always a hint of relief at the sight of land after a crossing. At mid-ocean, imagination feels the spirit's isolation in a vastness. The mind knows that it is alone, and life can sense its vulnerability to a fragile sustaining balance. Then landfall. Something inside rejoices.

The first indications of dawn were apparent in the northeast. The earth below was dark, but a faint light, low on the horizon, appeared as a dim glow. They flew on. The light grew in intensity until it caught the cloudline above it and drew broad red lines on the sky. These were the first traces of morning. Soon the sun would rise, and the moon would set, and, on the western horizon, Paris would appear as dawn broke in the east.

Then it began to happen, and clarity came to an understanding of what his voyager's life had been. Just as when we stand before great art and see with the artist's eye the thing in his work that brings us into the mysteries of his vision, so in the act of flight had he always seen his world with the Creator's eye, and, with the many-mirrored spirit of a dreamer, found in the haunting regularity of sunrise and sunset intimations of immortality.

H is dream had had the force of an actual event, and left him with an emotional hangover.

"Mr. Jenkins, do you have some questions for Captain Price?" asked Chairman Adams.

"I do, Mr. Chairman."

"You may proceed."

Edgar Latimer leaned over as Hugo rose and said, "Give him straightforward answers, but don't offer him anything he doesn't specifically ask for." Hugo nodded. He resumed the witness stand for the second time.

Ben Jenkins was the National Transportation Safety Board's general counsel. A man of medium height, balding, and close to sixty years old, his hands were small and his cheeks were jowly. He had the patient, self-possessed look of a man who enjoyed the opportunity to exchange wits in a public forum.

"Captain Price," said Jenkins, "we heard Captain Danielson describe the insidious nature of some emergencies, and also how human factors can affect performance. It seems evident that your flight encountered a wind shear, or microburst, below one thousand feet on the approach to runway 22L on the night of March 14. Did you or your first officer anticipate at any time the probability of such an encounter?"

Hugo crossed his legs and sat with his hands folded. He spoke clearly, without hesitation. "A storm system had swept through the area that night. We observed cell activity on our radar. It was turbulent throughout the descent from ten thousand feet; I'd say steady moderate turbulence. Under such conditions you anticipate unusual winds of some kind, and possibly wind shear. Wind shear had been reported on the approach."

"So you would say that you were prepared."

"I was advised and aware of conditions."

"Did the fact that your left engine was, for practical purposes, unusable cause you any concern, given those conditions?"

"Any unusual configuration is cause for concern. Was I bothered by the turbulence, is that what you mean?"

"Were you bothered by the turbulence?"

"No. Only insofar as it was uncomfortable. It didn't hamper our operation of the aircraft. That was my only concern. I did, however, plan to use more airspeed than normal, twenty-five knots, I believe. This was a pad against the reports of shear, and in consideration of our single-engine status."

"How familiar are you with the phenomenon 'microburst'?"

"All pilots at Nation Air Lines are given training in microburst escape procedures. The simulators are programmed with microbursts of various intensities. I know that microbursts can appear wherever there is convective activity."

"And there was convective activity on the night of March 14?"

"Yes."

"Did you consider microburst a possibility?"

"In those conditions it's always a possibility."

"Did you, at any time, consider landing at another airport besides JFK?"

"Not after I made the decision to return to New York. Turbulence below ten thousand feet was reported at all the metropolitan airports as far south as Philadelphia."

"Behind the passing front, the weather was turbulent. But the front had not yet reached Boston. Did you obtain the weather at Boston?"

"Yes, I did."

"Do you remember the weather conditions at Boston as they were reported to you?"

"The ceiling was three hundred feet obscured overcast, visibility reported by runway transmissometers as variable between eight hundred and twelve hundred feet."

"Were there any thunderstorms reported in the area around Boston?"

"No. The line of storms was advancing from New York."

"Was there any turbulence reported in Boston?"

"Some light turbulence. Occasional light turbulence in the descent."

"And no convective activity?"

Edgar Latimer now stood and waved a pencil with a pointed flourish to get attention. "Mr. Chairman, I think Captain Price has demonstrated an awareness of precisely where the convective cell activity was. There is no need for reiteration."

"I'll withdraw the question," Jenkins said. "Captain, your operations manual instructs you to land at the nearest suitable airport in the event of an engine malfunction, is that true?"

"That's true."

"And what constitutes a suitable airport?"

"An airport with maintenance facilities that can accommodate the Gantry 660 aircraft. Ideally, a Nation Air Lines station."

"And is Boston's Logan Airport such a station?"

"Yes."

"In fact, Nation Air Lines has a terminal at Logan Airport, isn't that correct?"

"Yes, it is."

"Did you ever consider landing in Boston?"

"Yes, I did. At one point Kennedy was closed due to thunderstorms during our return. I spoke with flight dispatch, and we discussed Boston as an option. But the weather there, as I said, was marginal in fog. When it became obvious that the front would pass by the time of our arrival, I elected to land in New York."

"And why was that, Captain? The aircraft is certified for Category III Alpha autolandings even with an inoperative engine. Though marginal, the weather in Boston was adequate for an ILS approach and autoland."

"Would you fly an approach like that, when New York was clear?"

"The aircraft was designed to make very low visibility approaches, even with one engine inoperative."

"The weather in New York was improving rapidly with frontal passage. I didn't want to risk a missed approach."

Jenkins looked at the floor and walked from one end of the table to the other as though meditating. "I see. Were you aware that Boston was closer to your landfall than New York?"

"Not significantly closer."

"In fact, Captain Price, Boston was one hundred and twenty-two miles closer to your coast-in point than JFK. Did you receive radar vectors from air-traffic control as you approached the New York area?"

"Yes, we received vectors."

"And do you recall if those vectors were issued to keep you clear of weather? That is, were you vectored out of a normal approach routing specifically to avoid bad weather in the area?"

"Yes, in fact we requested diversions ourselves to avoid some of the weather we saw on radar."

"Do you recall in what direction you were taken to avoid the convective activity?"

"We diverted to the north and east of the normal approach into New York."

"Yes. Air-traffic control records have flight 555, at its northernmost point during deviation for weather, to have come to within eighty-five miles of Boston's Logan Airport."

"But we weren't landing in Boston," he said emphatically. "I had made the decision to land in New York."

Jenkins paused, turned, and paced the floor, as though collecting his thoughts. Then he went over to the table and moved his hand through papers there, pretending to read. Finally, after a certain period of time had passed, he continued.

"Earlier, Captain, you stated that there were reports of wind shear on the approach to 22L."

"That's correct."

"You had one engine virtually inoperative, yet you had no major misgivings about commencing the approach?"

"I had reasonable concerns."

"And what were those?"

"That we had an engine with a problem, that as a consequence the approach was abnormal, and that the weather, though not as bad as I've seen, was not optimum."

"You were not using the autopilot, is that correct?"

"That is correct."

"And why was that?"

"I could have used the autopilot. I chose not to. In this case, the turbulence was causing the autopilot to overcorrect. It can only keep up with so much variance. By hand-flying, you can attenuate the pitch and roll corrections and make the ride somewhat smoother."

"So this decision was made in the interest of passenger comfort?"

"No. In bad air, I like to feel what's happening to the airplane. It brings me closer to the situation. Personally, I want to feel in my hands what the turbulence is doing to the controls, how the airplane is responding, and what I have to do to keep it steady. I don't want to come to the final approach cold."

"Do you recall receiving pilot reports on turbulence below ten thousand feet?" Jenkins positioned himself in front of where Hugo was seated in the witness chair. This was to give emphasis to the sequence of questions he was now asking. He held papers in his hand but they were meant as props. He never looked at them.

"We received a report of continuous moderate, occasional severe turbulence below ten thousand feet," said Hugo.

"And, Captain, how would you define 'severe turbulence'?"

"By definition, severe turbulence can cause large fluctuations in pitch and roll movements, with occasional temporary loss of aircraft control."

"And at no time, in consequence of these reports of turbulence, did you consider changing your destination to Boston?"

"Airplanes operate in a fluid and dynamic environment, Mr. Jenkins. Experience in identical or nearly identical conditions indicated no unusual cause for concern. The front had passed, convective cells associated with the front were clearly visible on the aircraft radar, and our distance from those cells throughout the approach was adequate according to average operational parameters. Turbulence exists, it's part of a pilot's working environment, and occasional severe turbulence is common in the vicinity of thunderstorms. The weather reports we received that night were consistent with frontal passage. Other airplanes were landing. The visibility was good. We flew into

a microburst that had probably been developing in the interval between the last aircraft's landing and the beginning of our approach.
There were no radar returns. It was a dry burst." Hugo was silent for
a moment. Then he said: "It happened to fall in our approach path.
We were unlucky."

Jenkins paused. "Yes," he said. "Unlucky. Thank you, Captain."
Jenkins' eyes made momentary contact with Hugo's. He then turned
and addressed the chairman.

"I have some further questions, Mr. Chairman," he said, "but perhaps we can take a short break."

"Gentlemen," said Chairman Adams, "if everyone is in agreement, let's break for twenty minutes." There were no protests. The
room adjourned.

Hugo had answered all of the questions simply and honestly in an
even, steady voice. He was surprised at his own calm response. Yet
anger welled inside. He struggled to channel it while at the same time
trying to be sure that it was justified. As aircraft commander he was
responsible. He was accountable. But was he culpable? In dreams, he
heard Lydia's accusing voice. Was it poor judgment or bad luck? For
the dead, he thought grimly, it didn't matter.

Meanwhile, other meetings were in recess, and the lobby was filled
with refugees from a self-improvement seminar. Doughnuts, cigarettes, and happy greed for free air betrayed their vices. Dan Danielson looked at his watch. "I've got to get back to the office. Keep cool,
Hugo. Your testimony is strong. What do you think, Edgar?"

"You're doing well," said Edgar Latimer. "Just keep it up. I'm
monitoring the questioning. I won't let them lead you astray."

"The questions I have answers for don't worry me, Edgar."

Latimer smiled. Danielson and Hugo shook hands, and Danielson left.

"Captain Price?"

Hugo turned. A man shorter than himself was standing beside

him. He had sandy-blond hair thinning on top, blue eyes, and a wide mouth with thin lips. About forty years old, he had an athletic build, and wore a well-tailored blue suit. "I'm Inspector Gary Simmons with the FAA." He extended his hand. Hugo shook it. He recognized the face as one he'd seen in the gallery on and off during the proceedings.

"Why do I know your name?" Hugo wasn't sure he should be talking to anyone official without Latimer being present.

"You may have heard Captain Danielson mention me. I contacted him in connection with an anonymous call we received several days before your accident."

A shot of adrenaline rifled through Hugo's body. "Someone called your 800 line and accused me of drinking on a night before a flight. I remember."

"Could we talk privately?"

Hugo moved toward the corner of the lobby behind a column that gave them some concealment. "I told Danielson exactly where I was, what I was doing, and with whom on that night. I was told the matter had been dropped."

Simmons gestured with his hands, throwing them apart, then brought them together, interlocking his fingers. "We have a responsibility. You can appreciate that. You had an accident less than a week after we got that call. Some of the higher-ups wanted us to investigate it on our own. Look, I'm not against you. A few things have come to light that I want to talk to you about."

"Like what?"

"About a year and a half ago, a domestic incident landed you before a judge."

"My wife assaulted a policeman."

"According to the policeman's report, both of you had been drinking. She had called the police to make a complaint against you."

"My wife is an alcoholic. The charges were dropped."

"Yes, but the judge mandated a program for both of you to join, a kind of therapy, isn't that true?"

"Something like that, it was nothing."

Simmons touched his finger to his lips briefly. "But you see there's a problem connected with this," he said. "You never indicated the therapy on your flight medical application."

"What are you talking about?"

"FAA form 8500-8, sections 18W and 19 make it mandatory to disclose 'any court-mandated rehabilitative or educational therapy, and any visit to a health practitioner including a psychologist or clinical social worker.' A check of your medical applications in the last eighteen months shows no such disclosure. Technically—and I emphasize *technically*—you've made three fraudulent applications and your medical and pilot certificates have been invalid for over a year."

Hugo turned ashen. What next? The FAA held sole jurisdiction over certification, and since 1991 coercive regulations forced a pilot to sign a disclosure release allowing the federal government access to data banks throughout the nation that held personal records on everything from hospital visits to traffic court. Any pilot who refused to sign was denied his medical certificate and thereby lost his license to fly airplanes.

"I did not consider a month of marriage counseling to be significant. There were never any charges against me personally. What are you trying to do?"

"It becomes a delicate situation," Simmons said.

Hugo did not sense a predator in the man, but why was he telling him these things? Was it a warning, was he sizing him up?

"On the drinking allegation, we captured the caller's number. The call originated from your house in Connecticut."

"Inspector," Hugo spoke with commanding calm, "the accusation is false, and if it were true, it's not provable now. The other issue is a petty technicality. If you want to, I suppose you can ruin me and open the airline—the entire industry—to endless unnecessary law-suits. You want my breath, my urine, and my blood, and finally you want my career." He leaned into Simmons. "Well, I'm not going to give it to you. You'll have to take it from me."

"Captain, I—"

Simmons tried to respond but Hugo turned away and walked back to the center of the lobby where Latimer signaled to him and they went back into the conference room to the resumption of proceedings.

Hugo once again took the stand.

"Captain," resumed Jenkins, who kept his hand on a manual that was open for reference, "I'd like to go back to a previous discussion on training at Nation Air Lines, specifically, training in wind shear. Can you tell us a little about the training you've had?"

"In the simulator, we fly through various wind-shear profiles, in-cluding microburst, programmed from readings taken from actual aircraft flight recorders."

"According to your training syllabus, and it's even in your flight manual, there are three prime objectives to this training. Do you know what they are?"

"Yes, I know what they are."

"Would you mind telling us for the record what they are?"

"Prevention, recognition, and escape."

"What indications in flight would cause you to suspect wind shear? In other words, how would you recognize it?"

"Sudden or uncontrolled changes in airspeed or vertical velocity, a sudden change in heading."

"About how much change in vertical velocity would alert you to a problem?"

"Any change more than five hundred feet per minute—a sudden

increase to twelve hundred feet per minute or more, for example, on an otherwise stable approach."

Jenkins had been glancing at the manual as Hugo spoke. Now he looked up. His hands moved in slight gestures as he continued the questioning. "Microburst is considered wind shear, is it not?"

"It is an extreme form of wind shear, yes."

"Recognition is very important."

"Yes."

"And escape, of course, if it is possible, is important. The flight recorder taken from the aircraft indicates that you took appropriate action after recognizing the onset of the microburst. You flew the airplane with exceptional skill. According to our analysis, you kept it in the air right on the aerodynamic edge, fighting it all the way. This is commendable."

"Thank you."

Jenkins looked at the floor now and paced twice, back and forth, in front of Hugo. Then he stopped, and looked Hugo directly in the eye.

"But Captain, isn't prevention, or avoidance, isn't *that* the primary emphasis in your wind-shear training?"

"No one would knowingly fly into severe wind shear close to the ground," said Hugo. "Yes, prevention has an appropriate emphasis in our training."

"Appropriate emphasis. Yes. Because, in this tragic case, had you elected to land at Boston's Logan Airport, the recognition of wind shear, and your laudable but unsuccessful attempt to escape from it would not have been necessary."

"Objection," said Latimer. "Wind shear is only a contributing factor. The explosive failure of the number one engine has to be considered a primary factor, and that could have happened at any time according to previous testimony."

"Mr. Jenkins, please don't draw conclusions," said Clinton Adams, chairman of the board.

"It keeps coming back to me," said Jenkins, turning and lowering his head, and then raising it again, "that Boston was the nearest suitable airport, and that the presence of convective activity severe enough to cause Kennedy Airport to close for some forty-seven minutes might give pause to an aircraft commander in a crippled craft. Turbulence was certainly impressive by all reports. The thunderstorms in New York were clustered and severe. Yet in Boston, there were no reports of turbulence on the approach segments." Jenkins picked up a transcript from the table and began to read from it. "At an altitude of just under two thousand feet, according to the cockpit voice-recorder transcript, you said, and I quote: 'Look at that lightning! It was a fork, right to the ground. Did you see that?' Then the first officer said, 'I have a cell at nine miles south.' And then you said, 'I'm bringing up number one.' " Jenkins threw the transcript back onto the table, a gesture calculated to punctuate his line of questioning. He turned once again to face Hugo squarely. "Had you made a decision to go around at that moment?"

"No," Hugo said, a recognition dawning on him. "The turbulence was quite strong at that point. The lightning seemed to jump out miles across the sky. I became concerned, I suppose, because I brought the power up without thinking, that is, I wanted to have the engine spooled up and ready in case I needed it. Normally in the descent you use a fraction of maximum thrust. I felt that the engine could take it. I told the first officer to keep her eye on the readings."

"But you did not abandon the approach at this time."

"No."

"So you were thinking that at least there was a possibility of something unusual, wind shear?"

"I wasn't thinking of anything. I was responding to impressions. You don't think under those circumstances, not in the normal sense. Your mind is processing information and your hands and feet are responding in tenths of a second. I don't believe I was consciously aware of bringing up the number one engine. It was instinct. But if I hadn't brought the engine up when I did, we wouldn't have got power out of it in time to cushion the impact. We hit the burst at about eight hundred feet above the ground, and it was rough. The transcript gives you words, but you'll never—I hope you'll never—experience what we experienced."

"You seemed remarkably calm."

"Did I? I wasn't. There wasn't time for panic."

"The voice recorder indicates that you lost power in the number one engine at two hundred feet above the ground."

"We were just coming out of the burst. I had full power on both engines, and the speed had decayed nearly to stall. The stick-shaker was constant. I lowered the nose to decrease the pitch angle and we seemed to hover. The burst had stopped driving us into the ground, but I had almost no flying speed, and no altitude to play with. Then the number one failed. I had to pull back the power on the good engine and let it crash. It wasn't a choice. We were so close but I . . . I had no choice. And . . . we . . . hit."

Hugo sat silent for a moment. He was not at the hearing, he was back in the plane reliving the final moments. He felt every movement on the controls, saw every instrument; he heard the ground-proximity aural warning call, *"Sink rate,"* and *"Pull up, pull up,"* he felt the vibrations of the stick shaker, then the large, bright red light on the eyebrow panel that flashed, STALL, and the accompanying voice of the warning system call, *"Stall, stall, stall."* He heard again, on top of all of this, the strident ring of the fire warning bell, and the verbal warning *"Fire left engine, fire left engine,"* and saw yet another red light illuminate in the T-handle in front of him. As though computers could fear for their existence, their circuits flashed red cautions, their voices came alive with a chorus of emotionless warnings that were incessant and overlapped, and then the speaker boomed when the tower called, *"Go around, go around,"* and finally Sarah, eyes fixed on her instruments, only her mouth turning to register fear, imploring, saying softly, "Can you make it?" And throughout the tumble and the tumult, and the chanting computers, and the engine explosion, he flew from a reserve of instinct gathered from experiences of twenty years' flying. Then, all at once, time slowed down. The sounds of compressing crisis moved out of his awareness. As the ground rushed to meet the falling plane, a second flash of lightning struck, illuminating with chilling certainty the grim inevitability of impact.

Jenkins continued to thrust. "But Boston was your nearest suitable field. Your operations manual specifies that the aircraft commander will land at the nearest suitable airport. Why didn't you do that, Captain?"

Hugo discovered he was calm at his center. He felt no fear, he had grown used to being questioned and it no longer produced confusing anxiety. Clearheaded, neither angry nor apprehensive, the scope of the inquiry seemed suddenly simple, no longer intimidating, and he could speak his mind.

"Mr. Jenkins, I know about limitations and specifications, and suitable fields. In the last three days I have submitted to your questions with goodwill. I've had my judgment and professional qualifications questioned, and have been asked at length why I did this and not that, and what about this rule and that regulation, and I understand why these questions must be asked, and so I've been willing to answer to the best of my knowledge. But now I feel you pressing me, insinuating that I've somehow sinned against a sacred text, a rule of law, as though a complex activity can be reduced to a set of commandments. A wise man uses rules for guidance. The Federal Aviation Regulations provide that in an emergency the pilot in command may deviate from any rule to the extent required to meet that emergency: Finally, utterly, and absolutely, it's the captain's call. I made the decisions I made, and though I have wished that the outcome had been different, it was not.

"The rational process is not infallible. The responsibility for those who lost their lives is mine to bear, but I will not be judged to have negligently caused their deaths."

That was his last word on the matter. The hearing ended.

AUGUST 23, 1995

H ugo lost his license.

At the New York Port Authority complex at Kennedy Airport, where vision has been overwhelmed by politics, the FAA regional headquarters seemed to exist in a time warp. The building, and others like it, had the sterile optimism of postwar / Cold War America. Hugo Price and Edgar Latimer sat across a table from Field Inspector Gary Simmons, and his superior, William Cunningham.

Cunningham, the tall rangy ex-Marine, put on his glasses and read from a transcript of testimony bound in red ribbon that lay on his desk. "The NTSB final report on the crash of Nation Air Lines flight 555 cited mechanical failure of the number one fuel/oil cooler, and meteorological conditions, specifically microburst, as primary factors contributing to the accident. The captain's decision to divert to New York was not considered relevant pursuant to Federal Aviation Regulations with respect to captain's emergency authority." Cunningham ran his finger along the lines he quoted and then stopped at the place he wanted to emphasize. He looked up at Hugo and Latimer. *"His failure to shut down the number one engine when oil temperatures exceeded maximum continuous limits was listed among possible contributing factors to the engine explosion during application of Go-Around Thrust."* Cunningham paused and looked up. "The board-recommended fleet inspection of the fuel/oil cooler found to be flawed. No other recommendations were made." Cunningham closed the transcript and took off his glasses.

"But Inspector," Latimer responded, "the engine did not explode until Captain Price advanced the throttle during the attempted missed approach. Is it your contention that use of the engine under emergency circumstances was ill-advised?"

"The engine had a mechanical problem. The temperature was out of limits and it should not have been running in the first place. This has been testified to."

"But you suspended his certificate under Federal Aviation Regulation part 91.13, which prohibits reckless operation of an aircraft. I find that mystifying."

"This was a fatal accident."

"Not in any way due to negligence on the part of the captain and crew."

"Captain Price deliberately exceeded a critical engine limitation when no necessity or procedure justified such an action."

Hugo thought: You know you're in trouble when people around you talk as though you aren't there.

"Captain Price was exercising emergency authority." Latimer sat back slightly in his chair, reading glasses on the end of his nose, eyes fixed squarely on Cunningham. "The NTSB—"

"We conduct our own investigations," Cunningham snapped, territorial truculence standing against all argument. "We're not questioning the authority under which the captain chose to ignore the oil-temperature limitations. We're questioning the judgment therein." His use of the word "therein" carried an essence of the bureaucrat.

Latimer's voice remained calm and even. "In the interest of fair understanding, safety was primary in his mind. As his testimony indicated, two running engines are better than one. This is not reckless thinking."

Cunningham turned his head toward Simmons briefly, and held up his hands as though helpless to explain regulation and policy. Simmons' expression remained neutral. Cunningham continued. "The facts are these: Passengers lost their lives. This office is expected to take action in these cases, and we have. And let me tell you something else. I wanted to revoke this man's ticket and I could have; Simmons talked me out of it. We've saved the airline exposure to lawsuits by not pressing technicalities. If I were you, Captain Price, I'd smooth out the rough edges."

Latimer ignored him. "This suspension is unsupported by testimony at the NTSB hearing."

"We examine the rules and regulations that apply to a flight. If we find a violation, we are bound to take action."

"Reckless operation? That's a stretch, Inspector."

"Mr. Latimer, published guidance does not allow for the operation of an engine that has exceeded limits. That to us is a clear point. No published guidance exists to back up Captain Price's judgment. Without published guidance to support him, we have to conclude, given the consequences, that, faced with options, he chose wrong ones. Captain Price's pilot certificate is suspended for a period of six months. Period." And with that, the meeting ended.

Hugo stood with Latimer outside in the hot sun. He felt shamed and numb. He put his crutch under his right arm. "They had to have their piece of you," Edgar Latimer said, a tone of disappointment in his voice. "It could have been worse."

"How?"

"Cunningham is a stickler for rules, but Simmons is a good man. He downplayed the business of the medical disclosure and talked Cunningham into a suspension."

"Is the whole system run on technicalities?" Hugo said.

"More and more."

"What about the truth of things?"

Latimer rubbed his chin in his lawyer's way. "There's always a penalty to pay for bad luck, Hugo. It's a part of life as true as anything."

"To be honest with you, Edgar, flying has lost its savor for me."

"That's bullshit, Captain. How old were you when you began?"

"Sixteen."

"In this life, you are lucky if you find your thing to do. Most people don't." Latimer chuckled and put his arm around Hugo. "You'll fly again, my friend. You do it well. It's always been your dream, your thing to do. Don't throw it away."

Robert Burton ran his hand across his head to take the wind out of his hair. He held the door for Hugo then followed him into the bar where they had a drink while waiting for a table. Robert leaned forward, listening to Hugo's account of events.

"They suspended my license."

"An insidious engine problem and a freak wind, a mechanical failure and a microburst. Whose fault is that? You drew the short straw." Robert sat back abruptly and threw out his hands. "They had to do something to cover their political asses. You're not naive."

Hugo smiled thinly. He took a sip of his drink. "At the beginning, in the hospital when they knew I would live, they told me I was lucky. Can you believe that?" Hugo shook his head. He looked up at his reflection behind the bottles and then at Robert. "Everything I was disappeared into what happened that night. I don't recognize myself in the mirror."

Each time Hugo described the accident, he relived it with slightly different accents. Each telling was a purge; reiteration gave the whole and its parts fresh examination. Robert listened. He watched Hugo's expression become tense.

"You know, confidence is different from courage. I always thought courage by itself was a mask for fear, nothing behind it but desperation. Confidence, on the other hand, that's tied up with who you are and what you know. You've always had confidence."

Hugo knotted the plastic sip-straw in his drink. "I used to believe in something—I don't know exactly what, some kind of balance or purpose. I used to think I had a charmed life. I guess I've lost whatever that was. I don't feel the same about anything."

The maître d' called them to their table for dinner, and Robert paid the bar check. They walked past the end of the bar into a larger space at a lower level. It was cool and dark in the dining room; the ceiling was high; the area of the restaurant was sparsely and dimly lit.

Hugo observed a well-dressed couple walking to their table, the man comically large with a face like a meat cleaver, the woman oddly proportioned with a wide mouth and uneven eyes, yet the sort of face that salvaged beauty from ugliness in mysterious ways. Love, he could see, was always a favorable radiance to plain features.

Robert and Hugo sat down at a corner table and a tall, thin, pale, provocatively lifeless waitress appeared with a face painted in three shades of red. Her eyes were wide and round, her lips lustful and indifferent. She took their drink order with a bored expression, recited the specials, and walked away staring dazedly into the middle distance.

Robert put the menu aside and leaned forward. "You've been injured in a variety of ways, and recovery will not be automatic, but you will recover. Just remember, those who survived owe their lives to your skill."

Hugo mused darkly. "I used to laugh at people who stood in the rubble of their destroyed homes to praise God for sparing their lives. Why did the tornado, or flood, or earthquake hit the home in the first place? Was God responsible for that? Praising Him for creating the situation is lopsided logic."

"And who would God be in this analogy?"

Hugo sat back in his chair.

An art-deco mural on the far wall depicted a man and a woman formally dressed near a streetlamp, with towering city buildings all around. For an instant Hugo imagined himself in that painted world of stylish images, away from the present moment, and the real world of living consequences. He looked directly at Robert. "The truth of the matter is simple. I'm spooked. I've lost my confidence."

"Temporarily, perhaps," Robert said. A long silence followed.

Hugo shifted in his seat, "I can't remember how I was unafraid before."

"You'll get it back."

"I see airplanes flying overhead and I wonder how the pilot can assume—can presume—to be responsible for the safety of the flight. That's strange, don't you think? since I have been that person all my life."

"In the cockpit it will come back."

The waitress appeared again at their table.

"We'll need a little more time," Robert said.

"Oh, sure," she said, and walked to the other side of the dining room where she leaned against the wall with her hands behind her, a vacant look on her face.

Hugo stared at his hands. "The accident didn't bother me at first— I mean mentally, while I was in the hospital."

"You were traumatized."

"Possibly." Hugo shrugged. "When I got out of the hospital, as time passed, it began to hit me. The memory began to grow in me. I don't know how to describe it."

"Try."

Hugo looked up momentarily, trying to find the right way to explain himself. "It's not just what happened, it's what might have happened, and maybe what should have happened. I feel some larger significance about the whole thing, as if it stands for something else."

"Like what?"

"I'm not sure." Hugo thought for a moment. "I can't forget the feeling of falling out of the sky, watching lights ahead flatten as the ground came up. I can't get that sensation out of my head, or the sound of voices after the explosion. I was lying in the mud, not feeling pain at all, feeling shock and fear, and fear of reprisal. I was making excuses to myself almost immediately. Not very noble sentiments."

"I think you're taking a black-and-white view of things, Hugo."

"How do you mean?"

"Give yourself some latitude. When are you going to requalify medically?"

"The cast comes off in two weeks."

"When do you report for training?"

"Dan Danielson told me I could fly the simulator whenever I felt up to it." Hugo turned to look at the couple across from them. The man held the woman's hand tenderly. Hugo drummed his fingers on the table.

"You should."

"I've got to clear some things up in my mind."

"Fine. But why not go to Phoenix and play in the sim once or twice?"

"I might."

Robert saw Hugo eyeing his cigarette. "Want one?" he asked. He held out the pack.

Hugo put his palm against the offer and laughed. "I quit. I'm risk-averse, Robert. The new me."

"Listen to what I'm telling you," Robert insisted. "You're a little bit off in your own world."

"Am I?"

"Yes, somewhat. I'm not being critical, I just have a feeling your unconscious is working overtime. Maybe it's some kind of posttraumatic response. Nothing in your life could have prepared you for what happened."

Hugo didn't respond. He believed what Robert was telling him. Until resolved, these mechanisms from within would keep him grounded just as effectively as those from without had. And it was by no means assured that he would fly for Nation Air Lines again. Officially, he did not have a training assignment. He and Danielson had not had formal discussion about it, but he felt the time would come soon. There had been no word from corporate officers on his status, none as far as he knew.

The waitress appeared again. "Are you ready to order?" she asked. There were a lot of things Hugo wished he could order, peace of mind, for example—but he doubted she had it on the menu.

NOVEMBER 5, 1995

I t's no good."

"Hugo, I don't mind. I don't—"

"Let's forget it."

"Really, I don't care—"

"Lydia!" The wrong name ripped from him like a growl. A long pause followed.

Sarah spoke quietly. "Hugo, what *is* happening?"

"How about, what's *not* happening?"

Failure of sex forced him back, drove him down into himself. All he felt was a numb mortified retreating. A field of anxiety imprisoned him so that the closer Sarah approached, the greater he resisted. She touched him on the shoulder and he recoiled.

"I don't really want to talk about it," he said.

Sarah took up her book from the bed table and opened it without reading. At the hospital, Hugo had seemed altogether too removed from the emotional impact of the crash. Afterwards, during the days of testimony he had become quiet, withdrawn, sullen. He was awakening to it inwardly. She couldn't reach him.

Hugo got out of bed and went into the bathroom where sudden bright light made him squint. He studied his face in the mirror, staring at his eyes until they began to grow and change in subtle variations until he didn't recognize himself but got a glimpse of what he felt inside. When he returned to the bedroom Sarah's eyes followed him and her expression was concerned.

"When Lydia came to the hospital she implied—" He hesitated. "I think of Lydia and me at the beginning when it was good, and how it faded, and then the breakup. We didn't really hate each other, we didn't really know each other, and after all that time together the marriage seemed like a kind of performance. A career can be like that. In the hospital I kept thinking about the assumptions we make every day to keep terror back. My life is like the two-sided message. 'The other side of this is true, The other side of this is false.' I keep turning it over and over in my mind, waiting for an insight that can understand what happened."

"That the accident was *not* unconsciously premeditated. That's Lydia's insinuation. She envies you, Hugo."

"Envies?"

"Those calls she made to the FAA were meant to bait your fear. Lydia wants your life. If she can't have it, she'll destroy it."

Hugo sat back against the headboard.

"She wants you to feel her hate." Sarah switched off the bedroom light. Their view looked over a pleasing geometry of city rooftops. "I'm going down for requalification on Tuesday."

"Next week?"

"I got my schedule today. Why don't you come with me, fly the simulator for the heck of it?"

"I'm still in a cast!"

"So what. Sit in. Watch."

Hugo's eyes petitioned her earnestly. "Do something for me. Let me come back in my own way, in my own time. I'm not sure what the flight department plans to do. Do you understand?"

"I only thought—"

"I know. I appreciate that. But promise to let me do this without pressure."

"No pressure," she said, "I promise."

"Thank you."

They were silent in the dark, and then Hugo said, "I'm sorry. I've been avoiding the real issue."

"Which is?"

"Which is, Will I fly again? Can I? Will they let me?"

"Of course they will."

"If I had died, it would be different, dead men are forgiven."

"But they lose everything."

For many minutes Hugo lay in the dark thinking.

The Nation Air Lines Flight Academy was a sprawling acreage of modular cubes—classrooms and windowless simulator bays—in the flat arid wastes north of Phoenix, Arizona. A glass pyramid rose six stories above the surrounding complex and solved this Euclidian scheme impressively. Still, it might have been a settlement on the moon.

The office of the chairman of the board extended across the entire area of the sixth floor, a vast uncluttered space with three views through tinted glass that ran from floor to ceiling and gave the area a floating-cathedral effect. A large oval desk faced the central view. There were four high-back leather chairs and a long leather couch positioned opposite the chairman's desk, and these could accommodate nine or ten visitors. In addition, a conference table by the west window was available for formal meetings. The present neatness and silence of the office belied the tense level of activity and debate that raged on each day as strategies were formulated for the running of a global airline.

The chairman was reading the NTSB transcripts, waiting for Dan Danielson's arrival. He read rapidly with fierce concentration, turning page after page, making notes on a yellow pad as he went.

A tone sounded and a voice came over his intercom. *"A messenger from the legal department is here. Did you sign the documents?"*

"Come in and get them," he said. He took a folder from the corner of his desk, opened it quickly, and signed his name in a hand that moved in long sweeps, rapidly making letters like the voiceprint of a lion's roar.

A middle-aged woman entered the office and took the folder from him.

"Thank you, Rose. Call me when Danielson's here."

"He just arrived."

"Send him in."

Dan Danielson came through the double door and the chairman rose to greet him.

"Hello, Dan, come in, sit down. I've been reading over the record."

The chairman had a face like a knife and cold blue appraising eyes. He shook the chief pilot's hand with the amiable fellowship of a man who flagrantly enjoyed his power.

Danielson, in a blue suit, sat in one of the chairs; the chairman, in shirtsleeves, perched informally on the arm of the couch. Wasting no time, he threw out his hands in a gesture of bewilderment. "Why didn't he take it to Boston?"

"Judgment call."

"Bad judgment." The chairman smiled, baring his teeth which he brought down on his lower lip while he considered his thoughts.

"Bad luck," Danielson replied.

"You think he should stay?" The chairman fixed his eyes on Danielson.

"I do. He's a good pilot."

"The feds suspended his license."

"For six months. They had to flex their muscles."

The chairman stood up, walked over to his desk, and sat against it, facing Danielson but looking at the wall above him. He was thinking over the professional future of Captain Hugo Price. To fire him might cast a bad light on the flight department. To retain him might imply corporate laxity. The chairman looked up suddenly with a resolute expression, took a quarter out of his pocket and said, "Why don't we make a judgment call, Dan, heads or tails?" He flipped the quarter in the air.

"Heads," Danielson said reflexively. The chairman caught the quarter with his right hand and slapped it on his left forearm. When he looked at it, he smiled, and put it back into his pocket without showing it to the chief pilot.

"I want to see this guy in the simulator."

"You want to ride with him in the simulator!" Danielson was stunned.

"Dan, we spend millions on technology. Make a videotape. I want you to program the wind shear that brought down Triple-Five and have some of your best pilots fly through it. I want to see how they do. Then get Price in the simulator and give him the same challenge. We'll see what he's made of."

"Are you saying he's still aboard?"

The chairman stood, lit a cigarette, and waved the match as a shrug. He jutted his jaw. "We'll see. He won the toss, so maybe his luck has changed."

JANUARY 26, 1996

As though at a signal from some intelligence-gathering unit, within hours of Hugo's medical reinstatement, Dan Danielson called and asked him to come to the flight academy and spend a few informal hours at the controls of the simulator. His certificate suspension was due to expire in the following month.

"I want you reexposed to the flying environment. I'll ride with you myself," Danielson told him. "No pressure. We'll just play around in the box for a few hours, no flying lessons."

"I guess it's time."

"So I'll see you tomorrow?"

"Sure, Dan. I'll catch an early flight."

Hugo went into his study and sat silently for a long while. He could feel his heartbeat, and his hands trembled and he put them on the arms of his chair while he thought. Over ten months had passed since the accident. He was determined, on the surface at least, to go forward with his life in the same manner as before. The cockpit was his life, and he missed the familiar rhythms of fifteen years. He had spent a huge effort to rebuild himself physically, walking long distances each day, gradually eradicating a limp that caused pain in his back and bothered his pride. The clock ticking on the other side of the room became audible and distracting. Dan Danielson's call was a gentle prodding, but his suggestion was more in the nature of a command.

As he packed his bag, he marveled at names, faces, and situations that circled in his thoughts like obscure music. Verlane and that Tennessee night of twenty years before returned with astonishing vividness, and he thought how strange it was that such a short span of time so long ago could reverberate through a lifetime. Why, he thought, should I think of Verlane? And then he saw the parallels, his fear was the same: Then it was the war outside of him, now it was a battle within.

Next morning, Kennedy Airport was a sprawl of hurrying people and unceasing uproar. Big flakes of wet snow were falling and a thin layer covered the cars. Whirlwinds spun snow playfully above the ground as Hugo turned into the parking lot. He parked in his usual area, behind the blast fence at the maintenance hangar.

Snow had reduced visibility to less than a mile. De-icing trucks surrounded a 747 and men in yellow coats standing on cherry pickers sprayed high-pressure jets of glycol on the wings. He walked through another door under the gate and went upstairs to the concourse.

The storm had delayed some flights; a glut of passengers idled in the lounge areas. Phone banks were busy. A businessman cradled the receiver on his shoulder and fumbled for a pen and paper. An elderly couple sitting by the newsstand watched him pass. He felt self-conscious. He opened his overcoat. At the far end of terminal D, the flight to Phoenix was about to begin boarding. The gate agent recognized him as he approached.

"Captain Price." Her eyes were bright, her manner vigorous and cheerful. She smiled, ushered him to the side, handed him a board-ing pass. "I saw your name on the passenger manifest. How are you feeling?"

"I'm fine," he said. What was she thinking? Was she trying to be kind?

"Are you back flying?"

"Not yet."

"Are you going down to the academy?" For God's sake, why the questions, why all this grotesque curiosity?

"I was able to put you in first class." She winked.

"Thank you."

"Go right on board." She opened the gate with her key. "It's good to see you again. We wondered when you'd be back."

How much had she wondered? His mind magnified her presence fivefold as he walked down the jetbridge ahead of general boarding. Suddenly this familiar scene turned against his ease, his steps grew heavy, and he felt himself in triplicate; one part urged him on, another considered retreat, a third seemed to paralyze him on the spot. He continued on into the aircraft.

"Hugo!" A flight attendant came through the curtain at the for-ward galley, put her arms around him. Bright red lipstick on beestung lips, dark eyes that disappeared under hypoallergenic treatments of mauve and blue shadow, leggy height. All Texas. She kissed him on the cheek, leaving a vivid print of her lips.

"Hi, Lucille." He smiled as certain pleasant memories returned. She winked.

"I'll fix it." She daubed him with a hot towel.

"How are you?" she said.

"Better."

"How's Sarah?" Her inquiry wasn't entirely sincere.

"Fine. She's back flying again."

"I'll take care of you. Give me your coat."

Lucille took his coat and he sat down and looked out the window at the snow. Jim Miller was the pilot. Hugo knew him casually. He went up to say hello.

Hugo stood for a moment at the cockpit door. Jim and his first officer were busy with preparations. They didn't notice him but he watched their movements, setting the radios and checking the flight systems. They were busy with preflight duties and he didn't want to interrupt them so he went back to his seat.

When the boarding was complete a final announcement was made. The door closed and Hugo heard the bolts lock into place and for the first time the inevitability of the flight came to him. It never had before. Sealed fate. No protest could stop the movement of the plane to the runway, or the takeoff into variables of atmosphere visible and invisible. The engines started, the aircraft began to taxi. Hugo calculated the consistency of the snow falling, mentally timing the effectiveness of their de-icing. On a day like today, he thought, to get thirty minutes of effectiveness, the mixture of glycol and water would have to be . . . The plane moved slowly in the reduced visibility.

"I'll take your coffee cup," Lucille said. He had been deep in thought. She stood over him, smiling. He handed her the cup. For the moment he could not mentally see himself in the cockpit and it was an odd sensation, like being unable to imagine a loved one. He felt the plane swing into position on the runway. The engines spooled up, the plane began to roll, and he counted the seconds until they were airborne.

January in Phoenix brought cool air to a russet landscape that seemed to crave heat. A shuttle bus ran continuously from the airport to the flight academy, thirty miles away. Hugo watched the scenery pass, a primitive landscape that seemed to reflect the loneliness in his mood. Each day away from the cockpit had estranged him further from the life he only half remembered now.

The van turned off the highway and followed an access road to the academy. An original Nation Air Lines DC-3 in a 1940s paint scheme stood in noble restoration on a concrete pad just beyond the main gate. Three towering flagpoles at the base of the pyramid flew colors of the United States, Arizona, and Nation Air Lines.

Most of the immense compound was a high-tech schoolhouse geared exclusively for the training needs of Nation Air Lines' ten thousand pilots. There was a large indoor swimming pool at one end of the complex. A fuselage "mockup" on either side of the pool had doors that ejected emergency slides for ditching and evacuation training. Nearby, an auditorium could accommodate three hundred students for security briefings and other required operational films. The classrooms for the six different types of aircraft flown by Nation Air Lines were located in adjacent buildings. Classrooms dominated half the buildings, the rest were simulator bays. The pyramid was the home of corporate headquarters.

From the far end of each four-unit bay, the simulators looked like mechanical monsters. Roughly hexagonal, with a thick umbilicus of wires trailing underneath, they rested on telescoping hydraulic pistons that created illusions of motion. Inside each "box" was an exact working replica of the cockpit.

The simulator felt like an airplane, and this was achieved in several ingenious ways. To simulate acceleration, the front of the simulator rose slowly but steeply; the pilots inside felt themselves driven back into their seats, though their cockpit view indicated level takeoff. At liftoff the simulator swooped down and up in a rapid but gentle semicircular arc. A wrap-around cockpit screen projected a 180-degree detail of the programmed departure city, including bridges, buildings and highways, always at a pale electronic dusk so that lights deepened the definition of computer-generated forms. The result was full-blown virtual reality that responded visually, spatially, and physically to the pilot's input, bringing verisimilitude to each training exercise.

The van stopped at the base of the pyramid and Hugo got out, carrying his overcoat on his arm. The driver handed him his bag and he went up a short flight of steps and through the main doors. The scent of glasswax and industrial cleaner greeted him, an odor he had long associated with training. His steps sounded in the empty hallway.

When he turned the corner, Sarah was waiting at reception. "What are you doing here?" Hugo said, surprised but pleased. He kissed Sarah.

"Dan invited me down to surprise you."

Hugo logged in at the desk and, from habit, checked his activity report for the time and location of his simulator. The report confirmed a 1530 brief with 1630 simulator.

"So! Hugo! We were wondering when we would see you." He heard his name called, a familiar chirping German accent. Irma Lund's head appeared from behind a computer console. Small in stature, with keen birdlike eyes and a puppet grin, Irma had long been familiar with the problems, complaints, and anxieties of pilots.

"We knew you would be here soon."

"Are you ever surprised?"

"Never, of course."

Hugo liked Irma. Longevity accorded her access to everyone of importance and she was famous for small favors.

"Captain Danielson was here earlier. He said you would have some fun together in the humiliator."

Hugo turned to Sarah. "Fun is a versatile noun here."

Irma knew nearly every pilot at the airline; they all passed her reception desk at least once during the year during training cycles. Her office in back was a small museum of photographs, artifacts, and appreciations from cockpit crewmembers going back thirty years. She stood across the reception desk from Hugo continuing to talk while she leafed through the daily activity reports for the training division. She pointed to Danielson's name on the instructor pilot daily itinerary. "Here it is. Simulator complex one hundred thirty-five at three-thirty."

"Thanks, Irma," Hugo said. "Let's go upstairs," he said. Hugo and Sarah walked together down the long corridor.

"What did you think when you first saw this place?" said Hugo.

"So this is hell," she said.

"Not many women here."

"I felt conspicuous."

"You were."

"High visibility is not what you need in a place like this." Sarah shivered recalling it. "They put pressure on you, you put pressure on yourself, and some don't make it."

As they walked down the glass-enclosed main corridor, pictures on the wall gave a photographic history of the airline: a pilot unloading mail from a biplane of the late 1920s, a woman waving from her berth on a DC-3 sleeper, Nation Air's fleet in military colors during the Berlin Airlift, and a 707 crew smiling after a record-breaking coast-to-coast flight. Each era of airline travel advanced safety and comfort; from props to jets to the computer-managed glass cockpit of Hugo's day, aviation seemed the only twentieth-century miracle where the golden age was ongoing.

They walked past classrooms in session, then out across a quadrangle to the simulator buildings, through the ground-floor corridor past the "iron kitchen" where pilots and instructors drank coffee during breaks in training. Sarah noticed a changed manner in Hugo as they went, subtle but discernible. He was growing enthusiastic. They stopped at a door marked ENGINEERING PERSONNEL. Hugo opened it. "Take a look."

The shiny gray floor smelled of antiseptic and electricity. Simulators bobbed on their hydraulic legs like terrestrial robots. Dan Danielson had just arrived and was leafing through a curriculum in the briefing room. He was dressed informally in a white shirt and blue jeans, and shook Hugo's hand warmly. "Welcome back."

"I'm not back yet," Hugo said, but the place was familiarly oppressive. He could hear the buzz of high technology. An instrument checkride in a simulator, compounded with engine failures and systems malfunctions, was the most stress-producing two hours considered to be routine in the professional pilot's career. "This is just practice, right?"

"Absolutely," Danielson said. "I have no specific profile in mind. It's up to you. We can fly a few visual patterns, shoot an instrument approach or two, whatever you want to do."

"Fine with me."

"You might as well fly the right seat, Sarah. I'll sit behind you."

A bell sounded as the transom dropped like a drawbridge and the simulator door opened. Dan Danielson opened the gate. "Let's do it." Hugo, Dan, and Sarah walked across the transom, entering the mirror world of the modern flight simulator.

Flight simulation had evolved from a tub on crude springs, to a device of eerie sophistication. Once strapped into the cockpit, familiar instrument presentation and a convincing sense of movement lulled skepticism. Once under way, a menu of emergencies kept the pilot far too busy to wonder where he was. Illusion became reality in a looking-glass world and every flight took a tour of limitations. "Utterly existential," as Hugo described it, "a personal voyage to nowhere."

Hugo and Sarah strapped into their seats and began their predeparture preparations. Hugo's hands felt for the switches instinctively. In the living room of his apartment during months of absence, the cockpit had seemed an alien place. But now his living room was impossible to imagine. Fears in abeyance, he became absorbed in the moment and forgot his misgivings.

"I'm going to turn on the motion now," said Dan Danielson. The warning bell sounded outside as the transom raised; the simulator settled slightly as the hydraulic pistons were activated. "I'll position you at the departure end of runway 31L at Kennedy Airport." Danielson programmed the position and New York City materialized in front of them. The long runway narrowed to a vanishing point two computer-generated miles away.

Danielson sat behind Sarah. He watched her and Hugo move through their preparations. Hugo was in the groove so he activated the video camera.

"Before Starting Engines checklist," said Hugo. Sarah began the litany of items requiring challenge and response. Hugo answered in the clear, unself-conscious voice of command that she knew well and had not heard for some time.

Log books—checked.

Flight forms—checked.

Rudder pedals and seat—adjusted and locked.

Oxygen masks and interphone—set and checked.

IRS—checked NAV.

Flight management computer—set and checked.

At the simulator control panel, Dan Danielson prepared the program he and Sarah had privately agreed to use at a particular moment. The program contained the vertical speed vectors extrapolated from flight 555's aircraft flight recorder. The shear had occurred in two separate events; entered initially as a headwind at eight hundred feet, it changed dramatically into a tailwind at three hundred feet as they flew through what amounted to a giant splash of air. Dan wanted Hugo to encounter the shear unexpectedly, as he had on the night of the crash, but he wanted him to experience it with two operating engines. If he passed through it successfully he would ask him to try it on one engine, voluntarily. Test pilots had tried the shear in the simulator months before to determine survivability under the conditions he had encountered. By measuring vertical velocity at impact, only one in ten approaches was determined to have been survivable. All had crashed. This was a fact that Dan had asked Sarah not to confide.

"Is everybody strapped in?" Hugo asked. All checklists were completed. He turned to Sarah to give her the departure briefing.

"Captain's takeoff," he said. "Any problem recognized prior to V1, call it out, I'll make the decision to abort if necessary. After V1, all failures will be considered inflight emergencies; if we lose an engine, we'll use eight hundred feet for cleanup and perform ECAM actions at that time. . . ."

As the words came from him, he was gripped with a sudden panic, which he concealed. A memory still vivid of the last time he and Sarah were together in a cockpit overwhelmed him for a moment. He thought with sardonic amusement, I'm getting a simulated second chance. The anxiety passed. In less than a minute they were airborne in a virtual atmosphere.

After takeoff the dark electronic evening was every bit as mysterious as a real night over New York. Hugo banked the simulator and saw Coney Island pass under the left wing. On Sarah's side, the Verrazano Bridge spanned the narrows from Staten Island to Brooklyn. North along the river, the prominent skyline shimmered in vivid definition. Hugo flew along the New Jersey coast. He could see the lights of Atlantic City in the distance. He began a lazy left turn to the east. "Why don't we go back to Kennedy and fly the Canarsie approach to 13L?" Hugo said.

"I'll put it in the box," Sarah said. She scrolled the flight management system for the VOR 13L approach, commonly known as the Canarsie, famous for its curving array of flashing lead-in lights that pilots followed along the Jamaica Bay shoreline in a continuous turning descent to touchdown. "Got it."

The approach appeared pictorially on Hugo's NAV display. He continued his turn until heading directly toward the initial approach fix, named ASALT, six miles southwest of the Canarsie VOR. Sarah requested approach clearance and a descent to three thousand feet.

"Nation Air 123, you are cleared to three thousand feet, maintain three thousand until ASALT, cleared VOR 13L approach, contact Kennedy tower on frequency one-one-niner-point-one." Sarah contacted the tower and received clearance to land, all air-traffic control voices played by Dan on the interphone.

Hugo flew past ASALT, and descended to fifteen hundred feet. In the descent he called for slats, flaps, and landing gear. Checklists were complete prior to passing Canarsie. The airport was in sight at his two o'clock position, and he could see the runway at the end of the sequenced flashers. He trimmed to the approach airspeed and set power for final descent. The turn to final was a graceful continuous bank; he rolled out at three hundred feet, on centerline. Sarah called out their altitudes: "Two hundred . . . one hundred . . . fifty, forty, thirty, twenty, ten . . ." The airplane touched down gently and rolled out to a full stop on the runway. An observer standing beneath the simulator would have observed only a slight momentary jostle at touchdown. He brought the aircraft to a stop on the runway.

"Well, you haven't forgotten anything," Dan said. "Let me reposition you for takeoff again. Set the brakes, please."

"Brakes set," said Hugo.

Danielson pressed the Reset button. A blur of light crossed the windscreen as though a sudden wind had blown New York away. Then they were at the departure end of runway 31L again. Suddenly New York City shimmered before them, restored, silent, and still.

Hugo reconfigured the plane for takeoff. He moved the flaps from forty degrees to fifteen. He reset the trim, and reprogrammed the flight management system for departure. Sarah watched him with fascination. He was utterly absorbed. This was the personality she remembered. He seemed to have come to life again, as though the doubt that had dominated him during his convalescence belonged to voices he could not now hear.

"Ready?" he said.

"Cleared for takeoff," said Dan on the interphone.

They moved down the runway, and Hugo marveled again at this technology for expanded experience; sometimes reality was just a perfect simulation of simulation.

They began to move down the runway centerline. Sarah made the callouts: "V1 . . . VR . . . V2," and they were airborne again.

"Nation Air 123 turn right, heading zero-six-zero." Hugo banked to the right. The lights of La Guardia Airport and the Whitestone and Throgs Neck Bridges came into view. The turn put them on a track up the north shore of Long Island, paralleling south-shore mainland coasts. A simulated airplane passed by and flashed its lights.

"Let's fly the ILS 22L," Hugo said. The vector suggested that runway; this was what Dan Danielson wanted. Sarah readied herself for callouts that would echo March 14.

"I'll brief the approach," said Hugo. "Initial approach altitude is two thousand feet, decision height two hundred fifty feet; that's on the radar altimeter. The bug is at two hundred fifty on the barometric. Missed approach is climb to four thousand and direct Colt's Neck, or as directed."

"Good," said Sarah. A silence came over them. She looked over at Hugo; he was staring straight ahead, his expression abstracted. She knew that expression.

"Nation Air 123, turn right to heading one-niner-zero, maintain two thousand feet, cleared ILS 22L."

The ECAM master warning sounded.

"Engine failure, number one!"

"ECAM actions," said Hugo. The plane yawed to the left and began to decelerate. Hugo disconnected the auto throttles and set power at max continuous thrust, or MCT, then backed it off to maintain 250 knots. He then engaged the autopilot. Sarah called ATC, advised them of the failure, and requested an extended downwind leg to allow time to run the emergency checklists. She and Hugo referred to the ECAM CRT, which enumerated each relevant procedure step by step in bright red print. As each action was performed, red changed to yellow, indicating completion. "Engine failure checklist complete," Sarah said.

"There were no unusual indications," said Hugo. "Let's try to start it again." If there was no obvious reason for the engine failure, a restart attempt was a wise course. Following procedure, Hugo had Sarah switch on engine ignition; she brought the number one fuel shutoff lever to the On position and the engine lit off. "We've got a restart," she said.

"Good," said Hugo. "Advise ATC, and request vectors for the approach."

The engine failure was an exercise of rather simple procedural steps in the air. A failure at takeoff was far more critical. Danielson had given Hugo the airborne failure to keep him occupied and to salt his confidence. He cleared him for the ILS 22L approach. As the plane swung onto centerline, he prepared to spring the wind shear.

"Runway in sight," said Hugo. "Flaps twenty, landing gear down." Sarah extended the flaps and gear and ran the landing checklist.

Altimeters—set.

Flight instruments and bugs—set.

Auto brakes—minimum.

Spoilers—armed.

Landing gear—three green, no doors.

Flaps.

Flaps.

Flaps forty.

Hugo disconnected the autopilot as the aircraft approached the glideslope. The flight director captured the beam and he began final approach descent. "Out of a thousand feet," Sarah said, "landing checklist complete."

The city was clear to the left. The shoreline ended abruptly as a string of lights five miles to the south. The descent went smoothly for the first thirty seconds. At nine hundred feet there was slight tremble. At eight hundred feet the plane began to yaw, slightly at first, then suddenly and sharply; the airspeed increased by forty knots and they began to rise on the glideslope. Hugo pulled the power back slightly and pushed the nose over. The cockpit shook violently. Then sudden turbulence rolled the aircraft forty-five degrees; they lost sixty knots of airspeed in less than a second and began to lose altitude rapidly. "Wind shear!" Hugo said. He jerked the yoke to the left and righted the plane. He shoved the throttles forward to the stops and pitched the airplane up to fifteen degrees. They continued to descend.

"Ref minus ten," Sarah called. "Minus twenty, minus twenty-five, holding—sink two thousand down." She watched the readings closely; the indications were difficult to read because the cockpit was buffeting.

"Five hundred feet, sink twenty-two hundred."

Hugo held the yoke back and tried to ride the wind by feel, but the buffeting was severe and the wings began to rock. The airplane held its own through the first stage of the shear; its powerful engines at emergency thrust fought for altitude against the violent downdraft. They entered the second stage at four hundred feet, and lost an additional twenty knots of airspeed. Hugo dropped the nose gingerly as the stick-shaker vibrated the yoke, indicating that the wing was running out of lift. He danced with the shear, his mind in focus on instruments, his hands feeling, coaxing, plying, moving the plane in and out of the shaker, holding it in a precarious balance at the edge of its performance capability.

At their low altitude Sarah could see the ground rushing at them; then they seemed to hover, the wings twisting through the turbulent currents.

"Three hundred feet," said Sarah. "Sink two thousand, fifteen hundred, twelve hundred." She turned her head momentarily toward Dan. An alarm sounded; the CRT lit up with red lights. "Engine failure, number one!" Sarah said, as the left row of engine instruments spun down and they lost thrust. "Ref minus ten, minus twenty—holding."

Hugo registered the engine failure, but not as a cognitive process. He didn't hear the alarm. He heard Sarah's voice, but it entered his concentration as a faint whisper. The failure came at the last seizure of turbulence, just at the moment when it appeared they had flown through the downburst. But now, on the other side of the splash, air was rushing away from them, decaying airspeed. His right foot slammed the rudder to the stops; battling yaw, he dropped the nose instinctively to compensate for increased drag. He lost a hundred feet instantly in a trade to hang on to airspeed.

"One hundred twenty feet."

Within three knots of minimum controllable airspeed, his eyes moved from the instruments to the outside view. There was no time left. Like a numbed swimmer, sinking, he saw the red runway-end identification lights ahead but they were too low; they would never make it.

"Fifty, forty . . ." Sarah called the last remaining feet on the radio altimeter. "Thirty, twenty . . ." At the twenty-foot call Hugo brought the power back and wrenched the yoke to a full aft position. It was a violent movement accompanied by a howl of anger that startled Sarah, until a second voice, louder than Hugo's, filled the cockpit.

"FREEZE!"

Everything stopped. The buildings of New York twinkled on the computer-generated horizon. The airport beacon flashed, one green, one white, from the tower. Cars passed on the Belt Parkway to Sarah's right. The red runway lights lay two thousand feet beyond them. All was a black void where they were.

Hugo was breathing hard, sweating, disoriented by the suddenness of the freeze. The radio altimeter had stopped at a reading of eight feet, a hair from impact.

Dan Danielson leaned forward, his head between Hugo and Sarah over the center console. His eyes watched Hugo, who sat staring outside at the silent, continuing, electronic presentation of life going on indifferently.

"I lied when I said there was no agenda."

Hugo turned to look at Dan. "I gather that," Hugo said.

The chief pilot's eyes had a triumphant seriousness in them, a scrutinizing depth that seemed to ask a question and provide an answer simultaneously. "I froze the simulator just short of impact because I want to direct your attention to a few things." Hugo turned to the instruments. Danielson took a telescopic pointer from his pocket, extended it. "Take a look at the vertical velocity," he said, pointing to the VVI. "Eight hundred feet per minute. That's almost exactly the velocity of impact you experienced with Triple-Five. That's nothing more than a hard landing."

Danielson lay a sheet of paper on the console. "These are the results of flight tests conducted in this simulator under circumstances identical to what you've just experienced, the only variable being the pilot, and that some approaches were begun coupled up. In those cases, the autopilot was disengaged by seven hundred feet anyway, so transition through the windshear was hand-flown in all cases. These are the vertical velocities at impact. Twenty-two hundred, eighteen hundred, nineteen fifty, two thousand; twelve hundred here—that might have been survivable."

Hugo picked up the paper and read through all of the readings. Only one was less than a thousand feet per minute at impact.

"The point is this, Hugo. Your airplane wasn't going to make the runway, period. But on that night, and again just now, you were able to arrest the descent under extraordinary conditions. I don't think any further comment is necessary."

Hugo looked at Sarah. A smile broke on her lips. She reached across the console and took his hand. City lights glowed in the foreground underneath a simulated moon.

JULY 7, 1996

In the months following his return to work, Hugo found a new rhythm to life. On Sundays, he and Sarah took long walks along the riverfront and explored the hidden places of the city. His curiosity came back, and he saw smiles again. Instead of long flights across the Atlantic that played havoc with circadian patterns, he bid to fly San Juan turnarounds. He could fly three thousand miles in a day and be home every night, and he looked forward to returning because now there was reason to be home.

Sarah's presence in his days changed him. He did not feel alone when they were in the apartment, nor feel alone in bed when they were together. In the mornings he did not feel alone, and when he was by himself, he felt her with him. In recalling his previous life, there had been no relief from loneliness.

After months of negotiation and waiting, Hugo and Lydia met for the first time since his hospitalization. A preliminary divorce hearing had been scheduled to file petitions and settle temporary alimony prior to the final decree. Hugo met with yet another attorney, this time a childhood friend named Kevin McIlhenny. Hugo desperately wanted to be finished with it all.

The county courthouse was like a secular cathedral. Frescoes of jurisprudence decorated the high-domed ceiling. Instead of saints, portraits of politicians hung on the walls. Words of eminent men were chiseled into limestone above oversize doorways. Armed guards like brutal altar boys stood by the entrance to chambers. Hugo, reluctant communicant, sat with Kevin in the gallery waiting for the judge. On the other side of the aisle, Lydia spoke in whispers to her attorney, Marvin Goldberg. Her four brothers glowered in plaid suits.

"Kevin," whispered Hugo, goading his attorney, "did you see the deposition?"

"Don't worry," said Kevin, grinning. His large body betokened a genial laziness. His Irish pieface had a big smile stabbed into its crust and Hugo noticed for the first time that he had too many teeth. He's not a killer, thought Hugo glumly, watching Marvin Goldberg fish through his briefcase, pinched, humorless, stern as an evil dentist.

"Kevin, the name Marvin Goldberg strikes fear into my heart. Does your name make men cower at your approach? Do your words fork lightning?"

Kevin laughed. "No," he said.

"That's what worries me."

"Trust me," said Kevin, smiling wickedly. He opened a disorderly briefcase.

"Don't say that, Kevin. Say anything else, but don't say that."

Their relationship still delineated social codes of horseplay evolved in the fourth grade. Hugo rubbed his face to erase chagrin, reflecting that loyalty to friends from grammar school was perhaps unwisely extended to their professions. "What are you going to do if she—"

"—Shhh," said Kevin, pointing to the bench.

The judge emerged like a hatless bishop and the assembly stood. The same dreadful revulsion he felt in church came over Hugo now. They were third on the docket.

He watched with curiosity as other cases proceeded. Venom between other divorcing plaintiffs and defendants was palpable. Hugo discovered himself mostly in sympathy with the women and against their husbands, from whose believable evil each deserved deliverance. A bad sign, he thought. He looked at Lydia, full-figured, radiant Lydia, surrounded by her brothers, the gang of four.

"Price versus Price," called an officer of the court.

Lydia took the stand, but her attorney spoke.

"Your Honor," said Marvin Goldberg, "in view of several documented instances of physical abuse, one of which resulted in hospitalization, Mrs. Price requests exclusive rights to the residence at number 8 Shore Road, visits to said residence by Mr. Price to be limited and contingent on formal notification at least three days in advance. In addition, she requests a temporary alimony of five thousand dollars per month for maintenance and living expenses, and exclusive use of the Cutlass Supreme. The white paper we've submitted will substantiate that claim."

How had he forgotten Lydia's guile?

"Kevin!" said Hugo, suddenly alarmed. "This is outrageous."

"Shh."

Five thousand dollars per month, the house and the newer car, thought Hugo. Analogies that politicians use to image the national debt came into his mind: five thousand dollars in one-dollar bills end to end would stretch to the moon and back. Each month. Kevin, he thought, you twit, you incompetent, you potato-head, you Irish Catholic dolt.

"It's not important."

"What do you mean, 'not important'?"

"She won't get it. The divorce will break down to a fifty-fifty split. If your dirt equals her dirt, it's a wash. Roll with this, whatever happens. It's temporary. Trust me."

"I've seen these figures," said the judge. "Do you have anything to add, Mrs. Price?" asked the judge.

"No, Your Honor," said Lydia, reverently.

Hugo felt like a deaf, dumb, and blind man at an orgy, with inexplicable urges but no recourse, a bystander to his own life.

The judge spoke: "Mrs. Price is gainfully employed with a relatively high salary. There are no dependents. I'll sustain the request for exclusive occupancy of the house, the Cutlass Supreme, and one thousand dollars per month temporary alimony. The court so orders." He rapped his gavel. Lydia left the stand with wicked glee leaking from the corners of her tightly pressed lips.

Hugo discovered himself immune to her. He was free, or nearly, and the terms were palatable. Kevin turned to him. "I told you," he said. "I'll get a court date as soon as possible."

"Why can't we get divorced immediately? I don't want to drag it out."

"It's the law. Justice takes time—and I'm paid by the hour."

In the hall outside the courtroom Hugo watched Lydia and her four brothers on the opposite staircase huddled with Marvin Goldberg. Characteristically dour, he looked uncomfortable. Lydia was pointedly festive, gesticulating for Hugo's benefit, speaking loudly.

"Marvin, join us for lunch," she said, "you were marvelous, wasn't he, Elton?" she said, addressing her older brother. "You were just wonderful. Elton, tell Marvin that wonderful joke you told me this morning. Listen to this, it's marvelous."

Marvelous, thought Hugo. Wonderful.

Elton told a convoluted and thoroughly unfunny Mexican ethnic joke, until Goldberg, squirming, looked at his watch, excused himself hurriedly, and fled down the stairs.

Later, Hugo called Lydia at home.

"No, it's not convenient," said Lydia. "I don't want you coming over unless my brothers are with me and they won't be here until Thursday."

"Where are they?" said Hugo, moving the phone to his other ear.

"They're touring New York. Anyway, you can't come over without at least three days' notice."

"That's not an absolute, it's a legal parameter."

"Well, I'm just sorry. You can't come until Thursday."

"I'm leaving for vacation early Friday. I'd like a little time to get ready. Tuesday would be better for me."

"Thursday at two would be convenient. And what is it that you want?" said Lydia.

"Clothes," he said. "Shaving cream, my stuff, pictures of my mother—for Christ's sake, Lydia, what's the difference?"

"Oh, did I tell you we were robbed?" said Lydia, mistress of the curve.

"Robbed? No, you didn't tell me."

"Your skis and boots were stolen from the basement. I made a police report."

"Nothing of yours is missing, I suppose."

"Nothing. Amazing, don't you think? My theory is that the robber must have been a man about your size."

"Your brother Elton, perhaps?"

Dial tone.

Hugo took a deep breath. It's only stuff, he thought. Keep all of it, Lydia.

Sarah came into the apartment with the mail. "Look what I've got." She handed him a letter with the green Alitalia logo embossed in the corner. He took the envelope and opened it. Two tickets from New York to Naples, and hotel confirmation for Capri. The savor of travel returned, and as his mood changed a smile broke across his face.

AUGUST 18, 1996

T he flight from New York had been crowded and first class was overbooked, so they rode in coach. Sarah had managed to sleep; Hugo hadn't. A woman behind him had sneezed continuously and snored like a stevedore. They made their connection in Rome by seconds, and by the time they landed in Naples, Hugo had reached the point of travel exhaustion when it becomes necessary to hate everyone.

The taxi ride to the pier was a nightmare. For an hour they toured car-clogged Neapolitan barrios. Firecrackers flew out at them from second-story windows. Hugo fingered the cash in his pocket. Sarah removed her rings. She pointed to the notes in *Frommer's Guide*: "[Naples'] city government is reportedly corrupt, many of its businesses dominated by the Cosa Nostra; it has undisputedly the worst air pollution and traffic in Italy, and its hordes of street children make it the juvenile delinquent capital of Europe."

Hugo leaned forward for emphasis, pointed toward the bay, and spoke violently: "Get us to the marina. *Now!*"

"No problem, no problem," said the driver in English. The cab U-turned. After more than an hour, and triple the fare, they arrived at dockside and at last made their departure for Capri.

The hydrofoil gathered speed, rose, and seemed to glide on the surface of transparent blue waters. Strong Italian sun shone on the steep relief of mountains along the Amalfi coast. A tiny village stood on an isolated hill behind the ruin of an ancient fortress. Buses and cars could be seen climbing hairpin roads that disappeared into tunnels. In the opposite direction, Capri was visible, an island oasis removed from the havoc of Naples. The Faraglioni, great stone outcrops that rose up from the sea, loomed in the distance like some great Paleolithic gate.

Distant places have a central role in the search for peace of mind. Sarah felt the wind on her face. Her senses reached out. Yearning, that's what travel is, she thought. Dwarfed by the island cliffs closer in, the hydrofoil slowed and sank to its hull. They maneuvered in the channel to a landing at Marina Grande. The mate jumped down and lowered the gangway. At last, they had arrived.

"Mr. Price, Miss McClure." A man at the wharf in a white uniform called their names. He put their bags on an electric cart and directed them to the funicular. "I meet you at the hotel," he said. The marina dropped away as they made their ascent.

A representative of the Hotel Quisasanna escorted them upstairs to a suite that looked over Moorish domes of the Certosa San Giacomo and across the Sea of Naples. To the right, steep limestone cliffs climbed to dizzy heights above tiny boats below. A slight fragrant breeze carried in from the sea. Faintly, from the hills, the sound of a dog barking could be heard; otherwise, silence spoke the spectacle eloquently.

"Hugo, come and look." Sarah, standing tiptoed, leaned off the portico, her eyes mesmerized by the sunshot cliffs. Their room stood at roughly mid-elevation. Morning sun cast shadows against the craggy limestone, creating quite definite images on the cliff face.

Hugo stood beside her, searching the view.

"I see faces," she said.

"Be careful," he said.

"I see a lumberjack." She turned, pointed. "He has a beard of trees. Do you see him?"

"I see him," said Hugo, suddenly avid. Sarah felt his arm encircle her from behind. She fell back, resting her head on his shoulder. "And look," she said. "To the right of the lumberjack."

"What?"

"The head of a child, round and bald."

"Yes."

"Do you see it?"

"Yup."

She bundled her arms and chuckled.

"But look now," he said. "Superimposed somehow, the face of an old man. Do you see him? His eyes looking in a slightly different direction, come across from the lumberjack."

"Yes!" she said. "I do!"

The image was coherent. Hugo and Sarah continued to study the cliff, the complicated geometry there. They scanned distant mountains of the Amalfi, visible in a blue haze.

"There is a way to comprehend this," Hugo said; he meant a way to articulate the beauty of this extraordinary island, his presence on it, Sarah in his arms, even this sudden poetry of finding faces in the side of solid rock.

There was a knock at the door.

"Come in," said Hugo.

"Compliments from our manager," said the waiter who wheeled in a bucket of ice and a bottle of champagne. When the waiter withdrew, Hugo poured two glasses and brought one to Sarah.

"Look at this, Hugo. Have you ever seen anything quite like it?"

Closer to town in their present view, beneath the cliffs, grand white villas stood pressed into thick clusters of pine and cypress that grew along the ridge. Pendentive arches framed porticoes, giving many of the homes a North African appearance; bougainvillea grew along trellises into interior walls through doors rarely closed in the warm season. Stone terraces opened onto hanging gardens where grapes and limes and figs grew in the constant sun.

Sarah laughed.

Hugo questioned her with his eyes. She shook her head, giddy with all of it. The mountains, Italy, and Hugo all at once: She took a deep breath; it seemed a dream. For so long so much had not been real except as longing. At times, after the accident, during Hugo's depression, she'd felt a kind of panic about life, and it became difficult to be definite about anything. She turned and kissed Hugo then nestled against his shoulder. A scent of earth and flowers and some erotic essence came to her, and she closed her eyes.

For Hugo's part, since his return to work, something unexplainable and good had grown between them. *Love* was a word whose meaning was lost in oversimplification. "I love you," he told her. But what he believed in was the way she fit in his embrace, the scent of her skin, the sweet taste of her sweat, and the nourishment to spirit she brought to him.

The piazza Umberto was crowded with strolling tourists. The din seemed to flow apart from the people, who traveled through the square in search of charming places for food and drink. Hugo had napped and looked rested, handsome in sunglasses, khakis, and a clean white shirt. Sarah wore a black slip dress with pearls that she fingered absently while she watched the passing scene. Bells chimed the quarter hour—or rather, clanged. Late sun shone brightly against the belfry and the dome of St. Stephano in sharp contrast with the shadows. Sarah studied the Moorish dome, its crucifix. A waiter began removing umbrellas from the tables. A darkly handsome man in a blue shirt skipped down the stairs. Impressions of the afternoon attached to all she watched and made the minutes abstractly pleasurable. They had one glass of wine, and then the sun was nearly gone. They left the piazza down a narrow street in the direction of shops and recommended restaurants. It was easy to imagine living happily in Capri, it was a miniature world with comprehensible scale.

"Buona sera, Buona sera." A slight, swift, extravagant young man with self-consciously luxuriant eyes smiled professionally.

"Mr. . . . ?"

"Price. Hugo Price. The hotel phoned reservations for us." Interior walls, a tastefully faded red, were decorated with Hovings-like landscapes and viny plant life. Sarah loved the atmosphere of the place—dark, cozy, timeless. The maître d' scanned the reservations book, serious as a bishop. His finger found the name. At once his expression registered a kind of wistful rapture; he grabbed two menus.

As he turned to lead them on, his aspect darkened suddenly and profoundly. He had noticed a fork on the floor near the steps. Quickly, he collared a passing waiter and barked an Italian epithet indicating the fork. When it was removed, his attention lingered for another moment, suspicious of other, perhaps larger, transgressions against order. His smile returned as rapidly as it had vanished. "This way, please," he said sweetly.

They followed their host down the short flight of steps (he seemed to glide, immune to gravity), past a line of tables against a mirrored wall, up a second set of steps, into a broad fragrant courtyard lit with torches. The cliffs stood at imposing height above them in the distance. Though dusk had darkened the ground, steep rock against the sunset caught the full projection of golden light. Vivid contrasts seemed to capture some essence there. A three-quarter moon hung in the pale sky like an imperfect ancient coin. They were taken to a table near a great birch at the corner of the courtyard. Overhanging leaves cast dappled shadows on low stucco walls; torchlight made the shadows move; grapevines grew on iron grillwork and bunches of grapes.

Voices filled the air with sounds of evening. Hugo studied the fall of light on the mountainside. A vague impression of time moved near the surface of his thoughts. Sarah's face watched from the world of her own mind, all of it suddenly a mystery to him.

"To order, please?" A waiter hovered, pen poised.

"A few more minutes, thank you," Hugo said. Speaking broke a mental logjam, and at the sound of his own voice he returned to the moment, smiling warmly. He took her hand.

"I suppose it's true you can never possess another," he said.

"You can't possess another," she said. "But you can give a person some part of yourself. It's almost the same," she said, then laughed. "Except opposite."

Hugo laughed and squeezed her hand. Sarah watched him. Love, hate, and disappointment form a triangle of emotions, she thought, pressed to another's, it's a six-pointed star that burns brightly for a while. She turned to watch the cliffs with him. They were deep rouge and burnt red at the top, but it was dark where they were. Red faded from the cliff slowly, and lights were visible at the top. The sky darkened and the moon got brighter. A face there too, thought Hugo. Stars were shining now. Sarah felt a rush of pleasure as his full attention fell on her. He reached across the table and stroked her cheek.

In the morning, dressed for hiking, they took a cab to Anacapri, a small town on the higher elevation where Tiberius kept his summer palace in the glory days of ancient Rome. A chairlift opened at ten

o'clock, and they were the first to ride up to the crest of Mount So-
lari. As they drifted upward over hillside vineyards and tiny farms,
sometimes they passed only ten feet above the people working there.
From a lookout at the top they could see the Faraglioni far below on
the other side of the island, and Naples in the watery blue distance.

"Let's walk down," Sarah said.

The path back was steep in places, but there were churches and
ruins to explore along the way, and no other people. They walked
the dirt paths, stopping at views of particular beauty, where rock gardens had been in place for three thousand years. Lizards scuttled in
the dust.

"This is how I imagined the Appian Way," said Hugo.

They spent all morning descending the mountain.

By mid-afternoon they were sitting comfortably once again under an
umbrella at the piazza Umberto. The sun was hot but the air was dry.
The cafes were filled with tourists at rest. Some were dressed casually, in bathing suits or T-shirts; some in carefully chosen clothes.
There were also those dressed almost formally; women in sleek black
dresses that shined in the sun, men with fresh white shirts, silk jack-
ets, and hats. Even time seemed compressed, slowed to a point of endless perfect present. There were many children, running at play, or
pushed in carriages by young mothers who lived in the village. There
was a different rhythm to life. The island stood as though risen whole
from the sea, removed, permanent, and unchangeable.

"Do you mind if I shop for a while?" asked Sarah.

"Do you mind if I don't go?"

"No, dear." She finished a last sip of wine, put the glass down, and
took up her purse. "Your eyes glaze over in stores."

"I'll wait for you here," he said. "I'm going to have another wine
and finish a letter to Robert."

Sarah got up and gave him a kiss, then walked into the flow of passing faces and disappeared into the narrow streets beyond.

Hugo took a leather folder out of the satchel he carried and opened it on the table. He took a blank page from several loose sheets tucked in a flap on the left side of the folder. After arranging the sheet, using the folder for a pad, he sat holding his pen silently until the bell at St. Stephano sounded the hour. Then he began to write in a swift, steeply slanted script.

AUGUST 18, 1996

Our room at the Quissisana looks out at the Sea of Naples over the Moorish arches and domes of an ancient convent. According to local history, Caesar Augustus came here in 29 B.C. Historian Suetonius claims Augustus saw a dried holm-oak suddenly sprout leaves, and took this as a favorable omen.

Sarah and I walked in the Emperor's Garden this morning. Everyone seems mildly intoxicated, and flowers are in blossom everywhere. Exotic natural formations rise up from the sea to trick the eye—and what else?— a million stars shine at night. Last evening, while Sarah slept, I had drinks on the portico facing the village. A steady flow of strollers passed by me. This is a land for lovers. I have been feeling good in the soul these last months.

Yesterday we went early by boat to the Blue Grotto on the northwest side of the island. Lost for years because the tiny entrance is almost invisible, it was rediscovered in the last century by a poet. We transferred *from the motorboat to a punt, and even then had to duck as we slid through a narrow opening, and then you are under a dome in a strange light, and it's like a mind having happy thoughts.*

Everything can seem bleak in one month and then circumstances change and you wake to a new morning, the old hopelessness vanished. It's early afternoon of our third day here. We came to the pool at noon and it's three now. We lunched overlooking the sea. The food is extravagantly good, wine abundant, Sarah reads her book, I doze, and once in a while I leave my chair to soak in the pool for a minute or two. This all sounds uneventful, and so it is, but I feel as if I've crawled out of a black well into a better life than I remembered.

Sarah and I spent most of last evening at a table in the piazza Umberto drinking wine and watching the people. Bells ring the quarter hour over an endless parade, the world on a small scale, with farms and churches and museums and natural wonders in microcosm, all with the feel of dreaming.

We have traveled on foot from one end of the island to the other. This morning we went to the north end. Pine trees grow straight up on steep slopes. I hiked with Sarah down a two-thousand-year-old path that traversed a cliff. The entrance was blocked and a sign warned of falling rocks, but we went over the fence, following others who ignored the warning. We went happily downward, until I noticed that the rock-and-mortar wall along the stone stairway was damaged, giant boulders had crashed down from above, and I thought that there are pointless ways to die and began to wonder that Sarah was oblivious to the danger. I was happy when we went back.

Later . . .

Now I'm sipping wine in the piazza again. The square is crowded with strolling tourists. Unexpected sights: a well-dressed man, drunk or palsied in a three-wheeled electric chair, is smoking two cigars at once. A blind boy and his mother sit across from me; she is explaining the Blue Grotto to him, rather hopelessly, I think. He listens thoughtfully, however. And

I see many mothers and daughters. Most passing faces are intent on destination, except those loitering on the stairs, or those, like me, who sit down for a glass of wine. The piazza is filling with people who park their shopping bags, cameras, suitcases and baby carriages to pause and watch the passing parade. Sarah and I were here an hour ago when a funeral passed through. Priests in black vestments led pallbearers who carried a small child's coffin on their shoulders. Bells rang out. We all stood and were silent as the spectacle appeared and vanished. Capri is like that, a free association of ongoing life and death, no plot or meaning, just an endless flow of faces and figures, a funeral in one moment, a wedding in the next.

I got your message early this afternoon, and thank you. And so I am a free man again? Lydia was uncharacteristically accommodating at the end, despite having to sell the house and split the proceeds, and for that I'm grateful, but she's content now, which makes all the difference. The pieces finally fell together for her when she and Helen found the proper path. Whatever it takes. I'm happy for her, but I'm happier for me.

The cathedral bell is ringing again. Good-bye for now. Sarah sends affectionate greetings.

AUGUST 22, 1996

On their fourth day, Hugo suggested a tour of St. Stephano. "There's a wedding late this morning," Hugo said. "Oh?"

"I thought it would be interesting to see."

The miniature cathedral exerted a central influence on Capri. Its architecture brought to the village a storybook sentiment, and also eccentricity, as Hugo noted one afternoon, observing workmen in the yard renailing the restored figure of Christ to a crucifix.

"Should we dress, then?" Sarah stood on the balcony with her coffee, the brilliant blue sea behind her.

"Yes, why not?"

They walked out of the Quissisana, gathering admiring looks. Sarah had on a pink cotton dress, high heels, her pearls, and her hair pulled to one side. She felt beautiful and special on this morning, which, like every morning since their arrival, was bright and clean and clear and full of the scent of earth and pine. Hugo stopped to buy a flower for her as they went up the cobblestone path to the piazza.

The piazza was already crowded when they sat at a table facing the church under a yellow umbrella. A flock of pigeons flew out from the belfry and passed over them. On the far side a man was hosing down the cobblestones. A waiter approached, holding a tray under his arm.

"Coffee?" Hugo asked her.

"Champagne."

"Champagne," Hugo told the waiter.

The hydrofoil had arrived in the harbor and newcomers walked up from the funicular, and electric luggage carts came through the square on their way to the hotels. After the waiter delivered their glasses, Sarah held hers up. "Let's make a toast," she said. Hugo raised his glass, and Sarah said, "To the imagination and dreams of those who came before us."

"And to our own dreams," he added, and touched her glass.

"And to the wedding couple, may their dreams come true."

The sky was deep blue above and Sarah was noticing its vividness when all at once a thrill ran through her body. A recognition dawned, and it was that she had let everything go, let every sorrow vent from her, every fear and misgiving, and it felt as if she had suddenly dissolved, moved through a barrier of some kind quite unexpectedly, and now at last she was free, and everything would come to her. She felt certain of this. She had merely to enjoy its coming.

After their champagne was finished they got up to go to the ceremony. They went up the short flight of church steps and stood by the entrance for a moment, and turned to the view. The Marina Grande, visible below, bustled with vessels, and the flow of pedestrians crossing the piazza in the bright sun gave a vivid sense of life. When Hugo opened the door of the cathedral and they stepped into the cool vaulted interior, its dark emptiness after the sunshine felt to him indeed like a house of God.

The pews were filled with onlookers to the wedding, already in progress. Faith shined as blazing hope in the eyes of old women who knelt and clutched handkerchiefs. They watched with approval as the bride and groom faced the bishop who, holding his ceremonial miter, was dressed in white ecclesiastical robes with ruby-and-gold filigree that glittered splendidly. His gestures had the grandeur of Moses of the movies. When the formal ceremony was over he nodded to the couple, granting clemencies, issuing benign admonitions, and after blessing their marriage, gave a short benediction that extended the blessing to the congregation. Sarah and Hugo held hands while the bride and groom kissed, then the pipe organ erupted into tortured joyful music with a great fullness of sound. A procession began out of church, and Sarah and Hugo saw the happy faces of the bride and groom, who looked, as most young newlyweds do, entirely incapable of meeting the demands of married life. Their family and friends followed them, and animated talk drifted in from outside as participants clustered on the steps.

"A wedding changes the feel of church," Hugo remarked as they left the pew.

"Wait here a moment," Sarah said.

"Where are you going?"

"I'll be right back."

Sarah went over to a tray of prayer candles near the door while Hugo waited in the vestibule. She took a long thin taper, touched it to the flame, then put it to the wick of the closest candle. The flame danced to invisible currents in the church air. Sarah blew out the taper and went back to him.

"What was that?" he said.

"For good luck."

"Will we need it?"

She laughed, and gave her arm to him, and together they stepped out into the sunshine.

R